JONATHAN CREED

NO BODY AT BEN BHRAGGIE

PAUL PUBLISHING

First published in Great Britain in 2021 by
Paul Publishing Ltd

2 4 6 8 10 9 7 5 3 1

A CIP catalogue record for this book is available from the British Library.
ISBN (Paperback) 978-1-8383331-2-6
ISBN (e-book) 978-1-8383331-3-3

Typeset and Printed in UK by
A4 Design & Print Ltd, 50 Seafield Road, Inverness, Highland, Scotland IV1 1SG

No body at Ben Bhraggie

JONATHAN CREED

Chapter 1

Golspie 1992 Late Summer

She raced through the trees, stumbling on tree roots. She could hear the pursuers back behind her. Breathless, she knew if she stopped that would be the end of her. Onwards up through the dark woods. She had a lamp strapped to her headband, but dare not switch it on. They would see her at once. A new sound came into the night, the sound of a helicopter. Wondering if it was looking for her or another person she raced onwards. Her heart pounded as she crossed the wide track used by the logging lorries. Snatching a rare glance behind her, she could see lights from torches flashing in-between the trees. Grabbing a quick lungful of air, she fingered the pendant around her neck. Then bent down and raced onwards, her foot nearly going into a rabbit hole on the track. Voices were now being heard calling out for her to stop. Ignoring them, she raced onwards up the scree towards the top of the monument. Once there, she would be safe or so she had been told. A door in the base of the statue was access to a safe place to be in the event of a sudden storm or descending fog. As if being chased wasn't enough, there was a roll of thunder followed shortly by a large flash of lightning. Then the rain started, slowly at first, then becoming heavier. The ground that had been nice and firm, now started to have trickles of water running down the pathway. A flash lit up the area. She saw she was now just a few yards from the top. The helicopter swooped low, skimming over her head. She felt her foot slide in the track and instinctively put out her hand to grab something, anything. The stones slide out of her hand and she fell. A shot rang out, but missed her. Now bent almost double, she started back up towards the monument. Ten more yards and she would be safe, she told herself. Torches were now picking her out against the outline of the hill. Even bent down, there was no cover. She knew that she only had a few minutes left. Reaching the brick base, she saw there was no door on that side, so staggered around the base looking for the promised door. After covering three of the side's it only left the one on the steepest side. She peered round nervously. There was no door there either. Swearing, she stretched out her fingers to clutch the brickwork, trying to grab a hold of something, anything, but it was too late. She felt a strong hand grab her wrist and twisted it hard back on itself. Letting out a scream, she released her other hand from the brickwork, it was enough, the person behind her released their hold of her and gave a push with their other hand. She screamed as she fell lengthwise down the side, banging her head badly as she did so. Finally stopping, she fingered the pendant around her neck. With as much strength as she could muster, she tore it off then swallowed it. A flash of lightning lit up the night sky and she heard and then felt a bullet pierce her arm. Half dazed, she looked at her arm where blood was coming out in spurts and gave her last breath.

Two men, coming up behind the gunman, looked down on the body sprawled across the side of the hill.

"One of us will need to go and retrieve the item. We dare not go back without it."

"Have you seen how steep that side is?"

"Yes, but it needs to be done."

"Agreed, but let's return in the morning at dawn. There will be enough light then and we can bring some ropes."

"What if anybody sees her or finds it?"

"I doubt that anybody in their right mind will be out tonight, not even in Golspie. Certainly not up here in a thunderstorm. Come on, it's getting heavier."The rain had certainly increased in the last hour. They gradually made their way back down to the village.

+

The next day, at dawn, saw Maria and Emma, a pair of local runners, set out to carry out their normal early morning run from the centre of Lady Sutherland Road up to the top of Ben Bhraggie. They ran steadily and without using too much breath. Soon they had got into their regular pace. An hour later they had both reached the top and were looking out to sea. The older one glanced down and saw the body sprawled out on the side.

"Here, come and take a look. There is a body down there." She pointed to the spot as the other runner came over and looked down where she pointed.

"They will be soaked. I'll go down and see if they are ok."

"Really? If they were alive, they probably would be moving or waving their hands. No, they are dead. We need to head back to Golspie and report this to the police. Come on." Turning away from the body, they both set off at a faster pace by going down the back of the hill, longer but easier than running through the trees.

+

The three men appeared through the trees and made their way up towards the top. Tired and annoyed that they had had to make a return trip. The fact that it was now later than they had planned didn't improve their tempers either. They had made no sound as they climbed the last few yards. Taking a rope that they had brought with them, they tied it around the base of the monument, then threw it out and down to where the body lay.

Two hours later, a search of the area near the body had not found the pendant. Giving up and taking the body with them, they had vanished back into the trees.

+

A police landrover, it's blue lights flashing, drove up the track around the back of the hill, inside the two runners and two policemen were being driven back to recover the body. The vehicle approached the top and made its way carefully to the monument. Parking alongside it, they all got out. The wind whipping their jackets.

"The body is on the south side, halfway down." Shouted one of the runners.

"Ok, we'll unwind the winch and go down. You stay in the vehicle." He turned back and threw a switch on the dashboard, at once there was a whine as the winch motor started. The other policeman had got out and made his way over to the south side. Holding on to the edge of the base, he peered around and down. Nothing there. Looking to both the right and the left, he saw nothing at all. He stepped back and beckoned at the other policeman. The man stepped out of the landrover and made his way over to his colleague.

"What is it?" He shouted above the noise of the wind.

"Nothing there, take a look." He stepped back to let his colleague see for himself.

"What the ?" He exclaimed as he looked down. He turned back and they both made their way back to the shelter of the Land Rover. Once inside they turned to the two runners.

"Nothing there. If you have been wasting our time.." He left the sentence unfinished.

"Nothing there? There was a body there this morning at dawn. We both saw it."

"Maybe she wasn't dead after all, maybe she was concussed and came around before making her way down by herself." Suggested the other policeman.

"She wasn't moving, not that we could see from the top that is."

"Well, nobody is there now. So, this is what we are going to do. We are going back to the station and suggest you go home and tell nobody about this episode. Agreed?"

"But."

"No buts, if you say nothing then we don't have to do a lot of paperwork about nothing. If you get my drift?" He turned and started the car, remembering to wind the winch back in before setting off down to the village.

+

Once back in the village, the two runners made their way to their respective houses. Both were fuming that the police had not believed them. Yet both knew what they had seen that morning was real enough.

+

The phone rang on the desk. His current flunky picked it up and listened before handing it to 'The Boss', with a smile on his face.

"Yes?"

"We've got the body, but not the pendant."

"Did you look for it?"

"Yes, but no sign of it. It is rather small to see."

"I know that, but it is essential for my safety. Have you disposed of the body yet?"

"Not yet."

"Get to it, put it somewhere where nobody will see it for a couple of weeks, but where animals might feed for free, if you get my drift?"

"Got you." The line went dead. 'The Boss' lent back in his chair and looked across at the man stood by his desk.

"Do the Russians know that the pendant is missing?" He asked the man. Without saying a word, the man shook his head. He knew better than to answer back a rhetorical question. He had witnessed what had happened to his predecessor who had done that. Not very pleasant for anybody to see. The Boss leaned back in his chair before standing and walking over to the window and looking out at the passing boats on the Thames.

"Any other calls or…." 'The Boss' left the sentence hanging. But his flunky knew what he meant. Had the Dutchman been in touch.

"No, I haven't heard from the Dutchman, not this week anyhow." 'The Boss' took out a cigar and cut the end off, before striking a match, lighting it and puffing gently to get it going. He flung the spent match out of the open window.

"Maybe I should take a trip up to East Sutherland in the coming days. See what the lay of the land is. Check on the flat and Inn. Maybe the Dutchman could buy it and set up his own business there." 'The Boss' shook his hand at the flunky as if to say, now get out of here. He left, leaving the Boss to his thoughts.

Chapter 2

Amsterdam same time

The boat bobbed up and down as the tourist boats made their way around the canals of Amsterdam. It seemed busier than ever this year. Goodness knows where they all come from, but that didn't really bother him too much. There was always a market for those who looked hard enough. He and his associates had taken a large financial hit a couple of years ago in Scotland. He had sworn at the time that he would never go back there. Recently though, his associates had been pressing him hard to try again. So far he had managed to resist their attempts, though for how much longer he wasn't so sure. He picked up the phone and dialled the number that connected him to his two strong arm assistants.

"I may need you to go to London. Do you have any problems with that?"

"Not that we know of. Is it a wet job then?"

"No, nothing like that, just a bit of shadow work and threatening behaviour if needed."

"Fine, we'll pack and await your call." He hung up leaving the caller wondering if he had done the right thing in using them again. He looked at the man sitting opposite him.

"Yes?"

"Go and see if our two friends really are where they say they are." His man rose and left the boat.

+

An hour later the phone rang on the boat of 'The Boss'. He reached over and picked it up.

"Hello?"

"Klaas here. Any more thoughts of restarting the business on the Scottish north-east side?"

"Funny you mention that, Here I was, wondering if a trip up there might be a good idea, check out the lay of the land so to speak."

"Look, I don't want to force you to do anything, but myself and my associates are still smarting from the financial hit we took a couple of years ago up there. Now I am a fairly patient man, but they are not so patient, if you get my drift?"

"I've said I'll go and take a look didn't I?"

"Yes, but you will get back to me once you have." The Dutchman hung up and moved over to his window to look out onto the canal.

+

Bill and Jane sat at their two desks looking out the windows of the London International Crime Department. Better known as LICD to those who worked there. While most crime never ceased, it seemed much quieter than usual. Jane screwed up a bit of paper and threw it directly at Bill. Spinning round as it hit him on the head.

"Who threw that?" He said as he looked around the room. Most of the desks were empty. Most of the ones occupied had their heads down working. A pair of moving shoulders gave away the culprit.

"Well Jane?"

"Bored, so bored. Anything new come across your desk today?"

"Nothing yet. You?"

"Not a thing. Missing the excitement of the chase and so on."

"Anything further on 'The Boss'"?

"Heard nothing since the closure of the drug case in Scotland."The internal phone rang on Jane's desk. Grabbing it she picked it up. "Jane Sutherland speaking."

"You both have experience of working in Scotland don't you?"

"Yes Sir, has something come up?"

"Sort of. Come up to my office and I'll fill you both in." Hanging up, Jane moved over to Bill's desk and tapped him on the shoulder.

"He wants to see us, right now." Sighing, Bill rose from his desk and followed her over to their department head's office.

"Close the door." He said as they entered the room. "I've just had a call from downstairs. The words 'The Boss' twice in a short call as well as 'The Dutchman' have thrown them into a bit of a state. There have been three mentions of 'The Boss' in the last two weeks. Do you think it could be the same person as you came across in that drugs case linking Scotland and Oxford a couple of years ago?"

"It might be." Said Bill looking at Jane. "Why?"

"A boat of a similar type to the one that got away has been seen in Oxford."

"There must be hundreds of boats of that style Sir." Said Jane.

"Agree with you. But this one is called BRORA. Unusual name don't you think?" He sat watching the two of them.

"Could be Sir, but we would need more to go on than that, if we were to track him down." Said Bill looking across at Jane.

"Internal division think it is moving up and down the river between Oxford and London. We know there is an unexpected increase of students taking the stuff. We just need to try and keep a lid on the amount of drug selling in Oxford. At least that is what both the Oxford and University police both want." He pushed a file across the desk towards them. "A lot of information in there, some of it good, some not so, take it away and read it through. Come back with a plan tomorrow morning." He waved them out of his office and sat looking at the open door, wondering if he had done the right thing.

+

The phone rang, but nobody picked up. Grunting, the caller replaced the phone and left his flat. It looked as though he would be making a trip sooner rather than later.

+

In sunny Invergordon, Tracy sat in her newly built flat, one of just eight on the High Street in the centre of the town. She had looked at some in Golspie, but they were too small in both size and quality for what she liked. Her Company, founded two years previously, was starting to break-even. She had filed accounts in a proper manner and paid any taxes due in the last year. This made it very unlikely that HMRC would be taking any undue interest in her business. Her biggest expense had been the regularly having to hire the helicopter, but that had already started to pay for itself. Now she wanted to expand but didn't want to get anybody nosing around. Maybe she would go for a walk up Fyrish. Getting up, she called her over to her border terrier and they both left the flat to go to her car. Being a four wheel drive, she would have no difficulty in getting to where she wanted to go.

+

The Boss's boat chugged gently down the Thames towards London. This time, though, it was empty of any drugs or guns. Just a pleasant trip on the Thames. He planned to moor at Marlow, a nice place to stop and eat at *The Meat and Two Veg* restaurant. Newly opened, it was quickly establishing itself as the place to eat.

Chapter 3

Fyrish, Ross-shire, a fortnight later

The two runners had driven from Golspie to run in a different place. Since finding the body at Ben Bhraggie, but it then somehow disappearing again a fortnight ago, they had decided not to run there again. Emma had suggested to Maria that Fyrish may be a good place to go. They got out of the car and did some warming up exercises, before starting to jog slowly across the car park to the open gate leading up to the Folly.

Forty five minutes later, slightly out of breath, they had reached the top. The sun was out and both of them made their way back down to the monument. There appeared to be a person standing against one of the stones.

Emma got to the person first, then gagged and moved back before being sick. Her friend Maria arrived next, but was stopped by Emma from going too close.

"What is it? Maria asked.

"Don't go near it. I think it was a body, but this one is full of maggots and other moving things."

"Another body?" Maria took a step closer. She could make out the remains just as Emma had said. She looked at her friend and then at the body. "We have to tell the police, but this time one of us will stay here. I'll do that, you go and tell the police."

"If you are sure?" Said Emma somewhat relieved that it wouldn't be her staying here.

"Quite sure. Now on you go, fast as you can." Emma turned and started to run down the track back to the car park.

+

At the same time, Tracy pulled her car into the car park and parked near the start of the track. Opening the boot her border terrier jumped down. Not bothering to put her on a lead, she slammed the boot shut and set off up the track locking her car remotely as they did so. Tracy was doing this for two reasons, one, her dog need the walk, two, she wanted to scope the area to see how busy it got. She had got into a habit of taking the dog for a walk here.

+

As Emma ran back down the track, her one thought was to get to the police as quickly as possible. She weaved her way around a lady with her border terrier before reaching the gate at the car park. She ran over to the car and got in and drove off to Invergordon Police Station to report what they had discovered.

Half an hour later the police followed Emma back up to the Folly and met Maria still waiting patiently for them, a little way off from the body.

"You've not touched anything have you?" Asked the policeman.

"Not a thing." Maria moved further away as the police moved in and checked the remains to see if they could find any ID to say who it had been. Nothing was found though and both of the police stepped back and turned to speak to the two runners.

"You'll need to come and make a statement, but we can do that later. For now, you can you go back to the car park. First though, can you let me have your name and addresses and contact numbers. They gave the required information and then ran down the track. The two policemen looked at each other and scratched their heads. The fact that body hadn't died there, the rope around its waist and legs holding it to the stone gave witness to that fact. A call to the station had resulted in a pathologist being asked to attend the scene. Now they just had to wait.

An hour later, the body had been removed from the scene. The two policemen had cordoned off the area and left a junior officer on site to make sure nobody tampered with the scene. Although as one of the officers was heard to say as they walked off, 'this isn't the place the killing took place.'

The following day, the police in Golspie heard that a body, about two weeks old, had been found at Fyrish. It was a female, although it would be difficult to find any identifying marks after two weeks of being left outside. Unfortunately, the two policemen who had gone to the top of Ben Bhraggie were out of the office, one being on holiday and one on training in Oxford.

Chapter 4

LICD London

Bill and Jane sat outside their offices and gazed across the river. It was a dull grey day in London and not much was moving on the Thames. He turned to Jane.

"We never heard any more about the boat 'BRORA' did we?

"No, the file was full of possibilities. Not any real facts that we could act on." She glanced up as a ships horn sounded near to Tower Bridge. She looked towards the bridge and noticed the traffic had stopped and the two halves of the bridge were beginning to raise up to allow the ship to enter upstream. "Bill, see that ship coming in, well now move your eyes along to the one behind it." Bill did as she said, squinting to try and read the name, but it was too far away.

"Can't see a name on it, it is too far away at present. Let's go down to the water's edge and see when it comes closer, what the name is." They both got up and made their way down and across to the river's edge. The large boat was through and moving to tie up on the opposite bank. The smaller one still kept moving upstream in the centre of the river. There was no name on the front that either of them could see. Looking hard at the rear as it moved slowly up the Thames, they could make out the name 'BRORA' painted in red lettering. Jane turned towards Bill.

"Could that be the right boat, if that is correct name." Bill smiled and they both turned and ran back to the office. This was the first piece of the puzzle though they didn't know how much it would end up taking out of the pair of them.

+

On board 'The Boss' was getting ready to receive the cargo from a small warehouse on the south side. He operated the controls with the expert hand that anybody who owns a boat will know about. Alone on the boat, he was pleased with how things were going. He hadn't heard from the Dutchman, for which he was very grateful. As far as he could find out, the area in Scotland was still clean and nobody else had started working there yet. He wondered if his two men up in Tain would have told him though if anybody had done so. He moved the controls to swing the boat alongside to the warehouse. Warehouse, he thought to himself, laughing inside, they had all been converted long ago into expensive pads for the rich to buy up and either live in or just lie empty increasing in value. He had been offered one, but had turned it down on the basis that having only one way in and out it was too claustrophobic for him. The boat bobbed up and down beside the sea wall. A quiet whistle and a parcel was thrown out of a flat window to land squarely on the deck, even as it flew through the air, he was starting to turn the boat away and up towards Oxford. He couldn't afford to be caught with that small packet on board, not in London. The two engines roared and he moved back into near the centre of the river, completely unaware that all this had been seen by Bill and Jane through binoculars. Also, somebody else with a video camera had been capturing the whole thing.

+

The Boss's henchmen were staying in a flat in Tain. They had moved the body to the Folly two weeks ago, it had taken a lot of effort. They had been frightened of being seen moving the body up the track on the back of the landrover. Their luck had held though, so they had tied the rope to hold the body upright. From a distance, it appeared to be leaning against the stones. Both had wondered how long it would stay undiscovered up there. They had done what had been asked of them, now a nice long break was well overdue to them both. 'The Boss' had rented a nice four bedroom flat for them and it had an underground designated car park as well. One night they had changed the number plates, one couldn't be too careful.

+

The Dutchman was sat sleeping in the sun on his boat. He awoke with a start, then realised his phone was ringing. He picked it up.

"Yes?" He said cautiously. Not too many people knew this number. It wasn't his usual phone, the one he kept for business that was.

"You able to supply?"

"Supply what? I deal in lots of things. What is you want and who are you?"

"I need the real thing. About five kilos. I'm prepared to pay cash on the nail."The Dutchman smiled, he hadn't heard that saying for a long time.

"Cash on the nail? Meet me in front of the railway station tomorrow morning." He paused to think of the time frame. "Say about 4.00am."

"How will I know it's you?"

"How many people will be there at that time of day do you think? I'll have a rucksack on the pavement. No funny business or…" He left the sentence unspoken and replaced the receiver. Well, well, he thought to himself, a new player and a cash one at that too. Time for a cigar, he thought and opened the humidifier in front of him.

The next morning, as agreed, he was waiting at the station. A few people were coming and going on bicycles. He took the rucksack off his back and placed it on the ground. A cyclist rode up as soon as he had done so, reached down and picked up the rucksack, leaving another one in its place. This happened so quickly, he didn't have time to react. He looked down to where the cyclist was busy pedalling towards and gave a shrug of his shoulders. Picking up the bag, he made his way back to his boat. Once there, he carefully opened the new rucksack. It was a new one, the price label still showed the price in guilders. Inside lay a bundle of new notes. He flicked through to see if there was just plain paper under the top few, it had been done before. Satisfied it was the real thing, he counted it. It was well over what he had expected to find. His phone rang. He grabbed it and answered it.

"I hope you are pleased with the cash on the nail."

"Very, is this personal or…"

"I'll be in touch." The phone went dead. He replaced it and looked at the money on the table in front of him. Shaking his head, he gathered it up, put it in a bank bag and went out to put it in the banks night safe. Better there than on his boat he thought to himself with a wry grin.

+

Tracy picked up the phone beside her bed. She looked sleepily at the clock. Six in the morning, who rang her at this time of day, she wondered.

"Hello, who is this?"

"Just to say your parcel arrived safely." The person hung up. Smiling now, she got up and moved towards the bathroom to take a long hot shower. It was good to be in business she thought as she stepped inside it and closed the door.

+

'The Boss' phoned Tain, just to be certain of there being nobody else working that area in East Sutherland. The two men, asleep, after a long night out, took some time to answer the phone. When one of them did so, he wished he hadn't.

"Yes?" He said sleepily.

"Where the hell have you been. I want you on standby. Listen to me, if you are not too drunk to do so that is. I want you to go and check the flat in Dornoch and the Inn in Brora along with any empty properties that you hear or see about in that area. Please also keep an ear to the ground, I want to hear if there are any new players up there, got that?" Without waiting for an answer, he slammed the phone down. For goodness sake, did he have to do everything himself, he wondered. In Tain, the man had woken his partner and relayed the message to him. Not surprisingly, both men were dressed and out on the road in half an hour driving towards Brora.

Three quarters of an hour later they were standing outside the Inn in Brora, no longer an Inn, but now a fancy upmarket restaurant - *The Double Headed Eagle*. That was the name painted on the swing board. Judging by the high value cars outside, it was a popular place to eat. An A-Frame board was on the opposite side of the road. The two of them walked over to take a closer look. Breakfast, it appeared, was priced at twenty pounds per head. Gasping, the two men left the board and went back to their car before driving towards Dornoch.

Half an hour later in Dornoch, having parked the car, the two men got out and looked at the noticeboard attached to the flat. 'For Sale by Auction'. The date was shown as being in seven days time. An all-day viewing on the day before the sale was indicated. Taking out his new mobile phone he called 'The Boss'. On the Thames the phone rang a few times, then was picked up.

"Yes."

"The Inn is a fancy new restaurant - *The Double Headed Eagle*. The sign is of two eagles facing away from each other. Breakfast there can set you back twenty pounds or so. The flat in Dornoch is up for sale by auction in a week. Do you want us to stay or come back?"

"I'll look into things down here, go back to where you were based before and await my next phone call." The line went dead as he hung up. Double Headed Eagles, sounded Russian to him. Pushing the throttle downwards, the boat surged forwards and upstream. He was still heading for Oxford…

…Eight hours later, he had tied up the boat in the backwaters of Jericho. It now just sat bobbing occasionally as another small boat passed it. He was downstairs in the main area, busy dividing up the packet that he had received in London. He just passed it to four or five people in Oxford who paid him. It was unlikely that they sold direct, so it was probably cut and adulterated further before finding its way to the student population. Once the four had collected their share, well, then his risks disappeared like snow on a hot day. Then he could turn back towards London. Smiling as he cleared up, he moved towards the desk. A cigar was in order he thought to himself as he smiled.

Chapter 5

Golspie next day

DI Gray sat on the floor. He was spending some time both filing and sorting properly the thirty or so files that lay across the floor of his office. A new, alright, used but empty, four drawer cabinet was beside his desk. An hour longer would see the files in it, nice and neat as his governor liked.

A knock on the door, made him turn his head towards it. A notice was stuck on the outside 'Don't disturb unless very important!' He looked up as DS Cooper peered around the door.

"What is it?"

"Decomposing body found at Fyrish."

"What is that to do with us? I am busy." He waved his hand at the files on the floor around him.

"Wonder if it is the same body that was seen at the top of Ben Bhraggie Sir?"

"Why ask me? Go and ask the people who saw it." Gray paused as he remembered that PC Cameron Gray had been one of the first two on scene after it was discovered. "The file should be on Cameron's desk. If it isn't, ask his sidekick - Hunter." He waved at the door, indicating for Cooper to close it. When he saw that he hadn't, he got to his feet. "What now?"

"Cameron is on holiday. Hunter was training in England, then he was going on holiday straight after. You are the only one with keys to the filing cabinet, where the files should be stored." Cooper looked at his boss standing amongst the files and smiled as Gray carefully placing his feet between the files got to the door.

"Come on then." He followed Gray out of the office with a wry grin on his face. He knew that Gray hated filing. Though it did look as though they were ready for just putting away he thought to himself as they walked down the corridor to the cabinet room.

+

Bill and Jane had taken the photos to the lab to get them enlarged. Studying them under a bright light the name 'BRORA' was clear to see. The computer technology had enhanced the image to such an extent that faintly above the name painted was the top half of painted over letters. Carefully studying it, and the name was easy to read as BAR HOUR, the name of a boat that had eluded them in a previous case. Jane looked at Bill. She said nothing, the look on both of their faces said it all. Then Bill nodded to the other officer.

"Can we have two enlargements of this please?"

"Better make it four or five." Said Jane. Bill looked at her puzzled.

"One for each of us, one for the boss, one for Oxford." She said as she ticked off her fingers one by one.

"Ok, five or six then." Bill smiled at the officer, who turned and left the room to get the copies. "What would I do without you?"

"Just get two copies I think." She grinned. Then as the officer returned with their copies, she added, "Where do we get a fast boat to Oxford Bill?"

"Follow me downstairs." He turned and led the way out of the office, taking the photos off the officer as he passed him. Jane gave him a mouthed 'thank you' before joining Bill as they went down the wrought iron staircase. Reaching the door at the bottom, Bill opened it and ushered Jane through. Bobbing in the water close to the edge was a double engine speedboat. "Will this do, do you think?" Smiling, he stepped on to the boat.

Jane followed, looking around her at the size and shape of it.

"Where did you get this? More importantly, how did you get permission to use it for us?"

"Questions, questions. I'll fill you in as we go up to Oxford." For the first time she was aware that Bill wasn't by himself, but a tall officer in River Police uniform was stood beside him.

"Aren't you going to introduce me Bill?"

"Ok, This is my wife Jane." He paused then "Jane this is Harry of the River Police. Now can we get going?" Harry smiled at them both, then taking the wheel, started to steer the boat out from under the offices where it had been moored.

"You would be better seated and strapped in. This lovely lady goes some when needed. I am told you need to be in Oxford soon, is that right?"

"Correct." Said Jane as she sat down on one of the three seats and strapped herself in.

"There are a number of locks on the way, it will take us about a day if we are lucky and don't have to wait too long at the locks."

"A whole day?" Asked Bill.

"At least. Why is that a problem?"

"It might be, as the person we are trying to catch has a couple of hours head start on us." Said Jane. Harry turned the boat around and drove back under the offices.

"Hey, what are you doing?" asked Bill.

"You would be better going by train or car." He looked at his watch, "Two hours tops, if you left by car now. Stay in Oxford and be there to greet them when they arrive tired and not expecting you." He tied the rope up and they stepped off the boat back on to dry land.

"Come on Jane, let's do as he suggests." Bill lead them quickly back up the stairs to arrange going to Oxford.

+

In Golspie, Gray and Cooper were looking at the file that they had now found. Not that it told them much more than they already knew. It did give the two names of the runners that found the body. Cooper had scribbled the names in his notebook and was ready to go and compare them with the two people who had seen the body at Fyrish. Gray reached out and held Cooper by his arm.

"Not so fast Cooper. See this in the file?" He pointed to where the body had been described as lying when the two runners had seen it.

"What about it?"

"That bit of the hill is just about impossible to get to safely, without ropes that is. If it is the same body as our two runners saw then somebody, well a few probably, would have had to go and retrieve it. With ropes. Not much to tie a rope to up there except." He paused. Cooper realising what he meant finished the sentence.

".around the monument itself. "

"Correct. You go and take a drive up there and see if there are any rope marks or fibres on the monument. I'll go and compare the files to see if there is any similarity between the two. Well go on, don't just stand there." He opened the door for him. He watched as Cooper ran down the corridor towards the main office. Gray smiled at his energy and walked after him after switching off the lights and locking the door.

+

Jane and Bill had quickly put together a few things for Oxford. The hotel had been booked and the Oxford and University Police had been told that they were coming to their patch. It wasn't really necessary, but it did make for good relations between the departments and forces. Jane looked across at Bill, he was engrossed in a file he was reading. Interested, she walked over to see what it was. He looked up as she approached.

"Yes?"

"Which file is it?" He closed it to show her the front of it.

Sutherland Murder/Drug smuggling/Oxford Murder printed in large letters below it read:-

limited circulation to the following departments: followed by a very short list of department heads.

"And your point exactly is?" She asked.

"BAR HOUR or BRORA we know are the same boat. DI Gray knows it got away. Wonder if we ought to let him know it is still around."

"In case you missed it, on the front it is restricted to a very few departments"Tapping the file with her finger as she spoke. " I don't think that DI Gray was among them was he?"Turning the file around in Bill's hand, she quickly read the list. "Thought not. Now come on." She returned to her desk, picked up the current file and lead Bill out of the office.

+

In Amsterdam a boat was pulling out from one of the canals and heading out towards the sea. On board a man sat smoking a cigar with a frown on his face. The boat was an ocean going one, not a sight seen much in Amsterdam, but it did have the advantage of both two outboard and one inboard high powered engines and full tanks of fuel. It would get them as far as Newcastle, but he intended to stop a few miles south of that, where a friendly boat would refuel him in return for a favour he had done some time earlier. Then on to Northern Scotland. He needed to take a fresh look at this new potential area of growth.

+

Tracy got off the train in Brora and walked down to the harbour. The new restaurant was doing a roaring trade, even this early in the day. She glanced at the prices on the boards outside. The prices, displayed in both pound and a few other currencies including the dollar made her winch. She wondered if they were making much, or were the overheads eating into any profits. It was as unlike the previous business that had been sited there as it could be. She had looked at buying it for her own purposes but, when it went for sale by auction, she was way out bided by a foreign telephone bid. Curious as to who might own it she looked up to see if a name was over the door, but it was just painted red. Pushing the door open a bit further she peered in. All the tables were full. She stepped back outside and let the door close after her. Full, this time of year when most of the tourists had left the Highlands for home? Something fishy going on here. She would have to look into this further.

Chapter 6

Oxford

Oxford Canal at night was a quiet place. 'The Boss' had handed over five packets. He was sat at his desk counting the money that the five suckers had paid him. He heard a few footsteps walking up and down the towpath. That didn't really worry him unduly. He had locked the hatchway to the boat. The canal was not the most obvious place that anybody wanting him would look. The phone rang beside him. He picked it up, not really paying much attention.

"Hello?"

"Hello Patrick." Now the Boss really did pay attention.

"Who is this?"

"A friend from over the water you might say." A nasty laugh followed.

"Ok, what do you want?"

"To restart our small enterprise up in Scotland. Why else would I call you at this time of day?"

"I've told you, it's far too soon to restart things. I have had a couple of my lads take a look at things up there. A new restaurant has opened at the old place. *The Double Headed Eagle* it's now called." The caller was heard sucking in his breath.

"Russians?"

"If it is the Russians, then I must stress that I wouldn't want to meet them if that is who is up there right now."

"No, I can understand that. I might take a look at things myself? If you get my drift?"

"Up to you. I am not going up there or planning to be any time soon."

"Ok Patrick. Stay in touch will you?"

"Look, I haven't used that name for years, not since the tunnel job. Just stop using it, will you?"

"Of course, what name do you want me to call you then?"

"Do you need to call me at all?"

"Come, come, we are both businessmen aren't we?"

"Maybe." 'The Boss' growled down the phone.

"I'll be seeing you." The phone went dead. 'The Boss' leaned back in his chair and looked at the phone with distaste. He didn't like the man, never had, never would. Cross now, he swept the bundles of money into a small wooden box and put it away for banking the next day in Oxford.

+

Jane and Bill had checked in to the hotel booked for them. Situated by the railway station it was near to the canal and river. Having parked in the underground car park by the railway station they were now out walking around Oxford taking in the sights.

Oxford River Police had been informed to keep an eye out for a boat with the name of BRORA on the back of it. Now one of the constables, Jeff Richardso, decided to walk along the canal towpath. His colleagues had laughed at this. Now as he shone his torch at the boats that were tied up along the riverbank, he wondered if he was wasting his time. Then the beam of his torch lit up the name 'BRORA'. Trembling with excitement, he took out his notebook and made a note of the location and the number of the berth it was tied to. He could come back tomorrow with assistance. Pleased with himself, he turned to walk back to the Police Station.

Unaware that he had been found, 'The Boss' was sat reading and smoking a cigar in peace and quiet. Tomorrow he would head back to London.

+

The next day Jane and Bill, having risen early and had breakfast, were now in their room wondering what the next move would be. The phone rang beside the bed. Bill reached over and picked it up.

"Is that DI Sutherland?"

"Yes, who is speaking?."

"Oxford River Police. One of ours has spotted the boat you were after. It is at berth sixteen on the canal. Not far from your hotel. I'll get the man to be outside the hotel in ten minutes and he'll show you were it is."

Ten minutes later both Bill and Jane had met Jeff. Now all of them were walking quickly to where the boat was last seen. Jeff had said that parking the car nearby would be a nightmare, much quicker to walk to the spot. He had set off at quite a pace with Bill and Jane struggling to keep up with him. Now he was slowing down as they walked along the towpath. Correctly, bobbing in the water was the boat 'BRORA'. The curtains were closed and there didn't appear to be any sign of life. Bill leant nearer to the boat and tried to peer in through the two curtains, but it was impossible to see in. Standing back up, he turned to Jeff.

"We need to get on to this boat, legally I mean."

"Then we'll need a warrant. This early in the morning we may be able to get one quicker than usual." He hadn't lowered his voice while saying this. Unknown to any of them, 'The Boss' had overheard all that was said. Wisely keeping quiet, he continued to listen in.

"Do you want us to stay here?" asked Jane.

"No, don't think it looks as though they are even up yet. Come on, we'll go and get the warrant to search the boat." Jeff led them back towards Oxford.

+

Once 'The Boss' had heard them going off, he quickly got ready to set off. He wondered if there was time to pay the money into the bank or not. Then decided that there wouldn't be any banks open this early. Minutes later anybody watching would have seen him busy painting the word BRORA over with a thick coat of white paint to match the rest of the boat. Unusually for the time of year, the sun was coming up as he untied the boat and set off downstream. Maybe he could stop again at Marlow for a meal. First though, he planned on stopping in a nearby backwater near Abingdon to paint a new name for the boat. One that wasn't Scottish would be better he thought to himself as the boat chugged along quietly that morning.

+

Tracy, in Invergordon, was trying to make sense of why there had been so many customers in a new restaurant. Particularly at that time of day. Her contacts had not found anything to report about it. Not surprising really, as it was a good drive from her normal place of work. She had been told though the police were still around Fyrish. The remains of a body had been found and taken away. That was as much as she knew.

+

In *The Double Headed Eagle*, the morning breakfasts had finished and staff were clearing up. The manager, Herbert Rose, was pleased with how things were going. He realised though that things could not be this good for ever, and was sat thinking of what new twist would continue to bring the customers in. The bell in his office rang, frowning he rose and shut and bolted the door. It didn't ring that often, located behind the main counter and was only used if the staff were aware of potential trouble. He switched on his computer then clicked on the icon to let him see inside the restaurant for himself. It was connected to at least six cameras dotted around the building, four inside and two outside he noticed a new boat in the harbour. A man was tying up the boat, then stretched and looked up at the restaurant door. Herbert closed down the laptop lid, and went out to greet the newcomer.

+

The Dutchman looked around the place in amazement. He appreciated the work that had gone into designing and fitting out of the restaurant. Shame it wasn't his. It would have made an ideal base for his venture into this part of Scotland. He noticed in the corner a door open and a man appeared. Cameras both in and outside he thought to himself. He moved to an empty table and sat down. A waiter appeared at his side.

"Coffee please. Black and no sugar." The waiter disappeared into the bar area to make it. Herbert swung a chair out and joined the Dutchman at his table.

"So, how can I help you?" He asked, looking at the Dutchman.

"I was just passing, thought I would take a look around. It's a nice place you have here. Been here long?"

"From your accent I guess you are not from around here?"

"No, quite correct, Holland, Amsterdam actually." The waiter had returned with two coffees and placed one by each of the two men. "How long have you been open?"

"Started a few weeks ago. Things seem to be going well."

"It can be very difficult to keep a new business going. Particularly if another business started up nearby. All that effort and time." The Dutchman took a mouthful of the coffee and looked at Herbert.

"There aren't any other locations nearby that anybody else could use, not in the short term anyway."

"Interesting." Another sip of coffee and silence followed.

"So where did you really come from? You can't really be passing through unless you are heading northwards? Especially down here in the harbour. That your boat out there?"

"Ok, cards on the table time, I would like to buy your business, it would suit me perfectly for expansion of my own. I'll make you a good offer. What do you say?"

"That is kind, but I don't own it you see. I manage it, I don't think the owners would not want to sell soon after starting up, but if you leave me your card?" He held out his hand and gazed at the man. The Dutchman reached into his jacket and withdrew a small gold and black card. Without a word, he passed it across and stood up. The manager stood as well and watched as the man left the restaurant in silence. Then he turned and walked slowly back to the office. He had a phone call to make. One that he wasn't really looking forward to either.

Chapter 7

Golspie

Cooper was driving back down from examining the monument in Golspie. As Gray had surmised, there had been traces of blue nylon on the two corners of the base. He had called forensics to take a closer look. Once they had arrived he had left them to it. They knew their job far better than he did. His next port of call was supposed to be the office, but a call came over the car radio.

"Anybody in the vicinity of the old *East Sutherland Hotel*?"

"Can be there in ten minutes. Problem is?"

"Somebody reported trying to break in."

"On my way." Replacing the handset, he changed gear and drove a bit faster as he approached the open gate to the track. Now on the road, he accelerated and turned on the flashing lights and siren as he drove down the twisting and turning road.

Ten minutes later, parked and at the front of the derelict hotel, he was out walking the perimeter. He could see where somebody had tried to remove the ply that covered up the windows. Of any intruder, there was no sign. The door to the staff entrance was padlocked and no sign of forced entry by the boarded up front door either. Sighing, he went back to his car and got a heavy hammer. A few bangs in the right places had the ply back in it's proper place. He'd get somebody to pay a few more visits though. Shame that it had got like this he thought to himself.

Standing on top of the Broch, a man with binoculars had seen all that Cooper had done at the front of the building. He looked at his watch. It had taken just ten minutes from him reporting the 'break in' that he had engineered to them turning up. He now knew how long he had once he had broken in. Smiling, he turned and walked back to his car parked in the car park on the other side of the road.

+

Cooper smoothly pulled into the small layby in front of the police station. He sat and thought for a few minutes. Why would anybody attempt to break into, as far as he knew, an empty hotel? Getting out, he walked in and through to Gray's office. Gray was seated at his desk, the files on the floor all gone and for once his desk was empty except for the telephone and a pad of paper. He looked up as Cooper knocked and then entered the office.

"Anything at the top?"

"Blue nylon. I left forensics up there. On the way down had a request to attend the old *East Sutherland Hotel*. Attempted break in."

"*East Sutherland Hotel*? That place is closed and shut. Why?"

"Exactly, why break in there Sir?"

"Trouble perhaps? Youngsters looking for someplace to have for themselves?" Gray stood up. "Did you get inside?"

"No, a bit of ply was slightly prised off, I nailed it back, took a walk around it. The padlocks are still there in place."

"Who has the keys to that place now do you know?" Asked Gray.

"No idea, the Fire Brigade? If there was a fire they would want to get in quickly."

"Hm, let's arrange a drive past once or twice a day to keep an eye on it. I have had a phone call regarding the body found at Fyrish."

"About what Sir?"

"They have found a small oblong pendant. They are sending a fax of the images of both sides to us once it has been cleaned.

In the meantime, we'll contact the local fire officer and see if we can get keys to take a look around the old hotel." The two men left his office.

+

In a lab near Invergordon, the pendant was being cleaned and dried. On one of the long sides cut outs of the metal at different intervals could be seen. A bit like a key. On the main face was some unrecognisable writing. The reverse face had a sketch of Ben Bhraggie etched into it. Every member of staff had seen it and failed to understand the writing. The map though was clear enough once cleaned up.

+

Cooper, having sourced a key to the padlock, was now unlocking it. He stepped back to let Gray take the lead. Both had come prepared with torches and a few other tools that might be needed. The entrance led to the old kitchen. Pipes stood up forlornly where appliances had been removed. A musty smell lingered over the room. Seeing it was empty, both men moved out into the hall. Flashing their torches around on the ground as they did so. Dust could be seen everywhere. No footprints though, so unless intruders could fly, the two policemen were the first inside for a long time. Gray moved across to the rooms on the opposite side to the kitchen and dining room. They also were empty of all furnishings and even carpets had been removed. Cooper in the meantime had moved towards the two winding stairs that ran each side of the hall, up to the two levels above. Here there was no sign of dust on the stairs. He scratched his head before returning to Gray.

"Anything Cooper?"

"Not a thing Sir, however the stairs aren't as dusty."

"What! They can't be."

"Take a look for yourself." Cooper gestured towards the two staircases. Gray moved over and looked closely. Right enough the dust was a lot less thick. He shone the torch upwards and noticed that it was thicker on the stairs a few steps higher. He bent down and tapped the staircase lightly with the end of the torch. It sounded hollow. Moving forward he repeated this on each step, till arriving at the one with dust. That one made a different sound. Turning around he walked back down to Cooper.

"I think we need to get a team here to look under those steps. It could be a good hiding place that somebody has been using. Now let's carefully move around the rest of the building. Somebody has to have come in here somewhere and either left prints or swept the dust." Both men retraced their steps and moved towards the old bar. But here the dust was just as thick as everywhere else. Now puzzled, they left the hotel, locking the padlock as they did so. Down on the beach, a pair of binoculars had seen them go in and out and lock up. Swearing under his breath the man moved away to return to his car in Golspie.

+

At *The Double Headed Eagle*, things were very quiet. It was too late for breakfast and too early for lunch. In the kitchen the chef was preparing the food for that nights dinner. The manager was helping to prepare veg, more for something to do, than to help. The chef knew when to keep quiet and when to talk. The staff had heard that an offer had been made to buy the business, but that was all.

+

In a sleepy backwater near Abingdon, a new name had been painted on the rear and sides of the boat. Now called simply 'BEN' it was waiting for the paint to dry before moving on downstream. The usual small boat seen hanging off the back, was not in place. It was being tied up at Abingdon and 'The Boss' was banking the money. He reasoned by the time he had returned to the main boat, paint would have dried nicely in the autumn sun.

+

Meanwhile in Oxford, Bill, Jane and Jeff had returned to the site of the boat with the necessary paperwork. All they could see were two empty mooring rings. Bill turned to Jeff.

"One of us should have stayed here."

"He can't have got too far. I'll radio in and get them to keep their eyes open for any boat called BRORA." Suiting the action to the word he did so. Jane had bent down and picked up a piece of paper, she passed it to Bill. Examining it closely, he noticed it was a bank wrapper, the sort that are used on banknote bundles. This one was unstamped.

"Where did you find this?" He said quietly to Jane.

"Halfway between the two mooring rings. Do you think it is connected in some way?"

"Unused bank wrapper. I think we should ask the banks if anybody has banked any pre-counted money today." He turned to Jeff. "We are heading back to Oxford. Nothing much to do here."With a wave of his hand both he and Jane started walking back. Jeff looked at the gap where the boat had been wondering what they would say back at the station, then set off after them.

Later, having visited all the banks in Oxford city centre, it was apparent that no bundles of banknotes had been banked in the early hours that day. Jane and Bill stood at Carfax and moved to a nearby bench to sit and discuss things.

"Well if not in Oxford, where do you think the boat is now?" asked Jane with a frown.

"Southwards, towards London. He obviously overheard us this morning."

"Or he was very lucky and had planned to leave before we got back."

"Either way, we need to find that boat and its owner. We can't go back to London empty handed." Said Bill.

"Come on then, we'll check out and drive along the Thames as near as we can and try and keep an eye out for both." They rose and walked down Queen Street towards their hotel near the station.

+

On a boat a phone rang. The Dutchman picked it up and listened to the caller requesting a new supply. He listened to the price she offered and nodded his head.

"That is a fair price. A lot of stock though. Can you handle that much in one go?"

"I'll deal with that problem my way. Can you supply it in three days time?" He looked at the calendar hanging on the wall. Tight, but he could call a few favours in.

"Yes, four days would be better though. Nearer to the weekend. Which location do you want it delivered to?"

"Nigg. Late afternoon, say about five thirty?"

"Nigg. Ok." The caller hung up and he turned to his henchman seated opposite. "Half a ton to a place called Nigg. Find it and arrange it for me."

"Pure or cut?"

"Top half pure, the rest cut by third. Make sure the good stuff is both on top two layers and the bottom two." He waved his hand to dismiss him and went to get one of his cigars from his humidifier.

+

Tracy punched the air with a loud 'YES' as she did so. He had agreed to her proposal. Now all she needed to arrange was the boat and helicopter. The boat was the first thing to do. Reaching across the desk, she grabbed a Yellow Pages and turned to boats. Within a few minutes she had found one that fitted her use exactly. A call on the phone and after a short discussion, a price was agreed for the long term hire of the boat. She would collect it from Avoch harbour in a couple of days. Another phone call to a nearby sawmill for a ton of cut logs to be delivered to an address in Nigg, ticked two things off her list of things to do.

Two hours later Tracy stopped outside her house in Nigg. It had been a run down property that had required a lot of hard work to make it habitable. Having done all that and a lot of extras that the original builders would never have dreamed of. She now looked out across to the Black Isle. The garden in the back was large to start with, but with some careful talking to elderly neighbours on either side of her had led to her to buying parts of their garden. Now she had a much larger garden for her own use. This suited her purposes down to the ground. Having explained to both neighbours that occasionally her guests arrived by helicopter. On those few occasions it happened, she would always tell them in advance. Paying them to go away for a few days and leaving the place deserted for her deliveries.

Chapter 8

London LICD HQ

Bill and Jane had kept their eyes open on the Thames as they drove back to their offices. No sign of the boat had been made. Bill had thoughtfully pointed out to Jane that he may have gone up the Thames. At the office they went and reported what had happened to their superior, Harvey Spencer. Then returned to their desks to write up a full report on the events in Oxford.

Had they but known it, the boat that they wanted was currently tied up by a proper warehouse on the Thames. Inside the warehouse, a meeting of sorts was underway. 'The Boss', the Dutchman and their respective flunkies.

"I say we should wait for more time. First we need to find a new place. Somewhere where it is easy to get stuff unloaded and not under watchful eyes. In that part of the world it is not so easy." 'The Boss' glared at the Dutchman.

"You been up there recently?" asked the Dutchman.

"No, not recently. Planning to go soon. Why?"

"I took a trip the other day. Lots of potential. That new restaurant in Brora, what is called?" The flunky looked at his boss.

"*The Double Headed Eagle*"

"Exactly." He said, clicking his fingers. "*The Double Headed Eagle*. A nice, an ideal place. Right on the harbour front. I made him an offer, but got turned down, for now at least. Time will tell though. You say we need more time. Look, I personally agree with you, it is the other people on my back. They don't want to wait any longer. Two years is a lot of lost opportunity for them. It is for all of us. They have been hit financially as well as myself,

Looking at you, I ask myself, how have you managed?" He looked at 'The Boss' as if to say, what do you have that we don't.

"Bit of supply here and there, small but needed packets. But that is as maybe. Back to Scotland. Why not try the West side. Glasgow and round there?"

"Because other much larger Italian outfits already have that sewn up tight. The North East side, now that is ripe for developing." He stopped and looked up at the ceiling.

"Ok, how about this then. I'll go and have a scout around up there. If I find anywhere suitable, I'll call you. What sort of price limit, do we set ourselves?" asked 'The Boss'.

"Find the place first. Then we can take a look and discuss the small details like costs etc. Are we done here?" He looked around him and then left the building followed by his two flunkies. 'The Boss' took out a handkerchief and mopped his brow. Didn't like the man. He had a reputation. His own was bad, but by comparison, the Dutchman was a whole lot worse. He rose from the chair he had been sat on and walked towards the door. Scotland had to be the next port of call.

+

Tracy had taken delivery of both logs and other items that had been ordered. With her two neighbours away, she was busy splitting half of the logs lengthwise. The work was not easy, some of the logs had split the wrong way, but she worked on. Tracy could have employed somebody to help her, but that would have been risky. To avoid that and the additional overheads, she preferred to work alone. By six that night she had finished part of the work. The logs that had been split were now in a small pile. Setting up a small outside light and a folding bench with vice, she picked the first half log up to work on. Using the mallet and chisel for the purpose, she hollowed out a small dip in the two halves of the log. A small packet slipped into the gap. This was followed by a trickle of glue around the edges before joining the two halves back together. The final thing to do was to strip a piece of bark away. Essential for identifying which logs not to be burnt. Apart from stopping for some supper she worked tirelessly on into the night. It was about 2am before she had finished the last one and swept up the pieces of shavings and dust. These would be burnt tomorrow on the open fire. The logs would dry overnight, then be mixed in with the remaining ordinary logs before being netted and sold in small quantities to those wanting her product. A trailer sat on the drive, with high mesh sides ready to take the finished products. Red nets, ordinary logs, blue nets 'specials' for her very few select customers.

+

While Tracy had been working hard in the back garden, a small sea-going boat drifted by her house, but she had paid no attention to it. Pity really, as the two men employed by the Dutchman were being paid to pay very close attention to her. A small tracking device had been placed in the lining of the rucksack along with her product. Then it was just a case of following the signal. They now could report back as to both how and to whom she was selling it and where she was based. The only downside was they had arrived just as she was clearing up. All they could now see was a pile of wooden logs and an open trailer. One of the two men went below to phone and report.

+

'The Boss', having returned to his boat, started the engine and swung it out into the middle of the Thames. He planned to park it in a boatyard for refurbishing. James Boatbuilder (Graves End) & Co would suit his purpose as the whole place was undercover. An additional factor was the owner kept asking him, when was he planning to sell his boat. He might decide to do that and get something to replace it. Especially now it appeared the police seemed to be able to identify it. That was the old name of course. With its new name of BEN, it may not be so easy to identify.

+

After two gentle hours of boating down the Thames and getting the best price for his boat. 'The Boss' was now seated on the underground speeding towards London. He planned to fly up to Scotland, but not by a normal plane. A chartered one, complete with pilot, was waiting at London City airport. He planned to return home, change and pick up one or two essentials. Then fly to a small airfield in the Highlands.

Three hours later, the plane was in the air and flying at speed towards Scotland. It would stop on the way to refuel, but that wouldn't be very long. He sat back and closed his eyes to drift off to sleep.

+

In Tain, two men were clearing and tidying the flat. A phone call from London had informed them of new work to do. Truth was, they had got used to the lazy life for a few weeks. One was busy putting rubbish into bin bags, while the other was stripping down and cleaning their guns. Outside the rain hammered on the pavements. It had done so for a week now. The ground was saturated, in places the water ran across the main roads like mini rivers. Council road signs proclaimed 'Flood' or 'Road Closed' on the approach to Tain and Dornoch. They didn't really heed the rain. What they had to do could take place in or outdoors. They worked on into the night.

+

The plane touched down, it's wheels kissing the tarmac of Inverness Airport gently. 'The Boss' looked out of the window of the plane.

"This isn't near Tain."

"No Sir. The local airfield near there is too waterlogged. It's grass not tarmac."

"Anywhere else we can go?"

"Well, we could try the RAF bombing range near Tain, but it is unlikely that they will allow us to land."

"I didn't plan on getting off in Inverness."The pilot sighed and spoke to the air traffic control to inform them he was only refuelling and would need clearance to resume his flight soon afterwards. Then he taxied over to the refuelling area. This was going to take a while he thought to himself. While it was being refuelled, he asked if any areas near Tain or Dornoch were ok for landing on. He was told that an old landing strip near Invergordon was probably the nearest he would get to it. Dornoch had told Inverness their ground was still too waterlogged.

Having refuelled, the plane took off and headed northwards across the Black Isle and skirting Fort George. As the plane approached Dornoch, he dropped down to see if there was anywhere suitable to land. The two golf courses were empty of players. The road winding its way through the course may just be enough. Taking a chance, he dropped down really low but saw that it was covered with a small lake of water. He climbed steeply and for the next few minutes tried to see a suitable place to land. When he couldn't see anywhere, he turned on his headset to connect to the passenger to inform him that Dornoch was, in both senses, a washout.

"Impossible to land in Dornoch. Am trying Tain RAF to see if they will let me land there."

"Let me know once you hear anything." 'The Boss' sat looking out of the window, wishing now he had driven rather than fly.

Twenty minutes later the plane touched down on the dark runaway. Nobody around or answering his call sign, the pilot had taken a chance and landed. As the engine cooled down. He jumped down and went and opened the side door. 'The Boss' stood there and looked out and around at the half bombed properties across the site.

"Where exactly are we?" He asked.

"Tain, well RAF bombing range Tain to be exact."

"Isn't that dangerous? What will the tower say about us landing here?"The pilot, grinning, pointed to the tower about half a mile from them."There it is, go and ask if you want to." In darkness, obviously the base was deserted. He turned to the pilot.

"Can you arrange a car to collect me?"

"Sure. Give me the number." 'The Boss' recalled the telephone number of his two henchmen and once he had done so, the pilot called them to come and collect their Boss from the airfield.

"Not going back tonight then?" He asked as they waited.

"No, not for a few days. I'll see how things pan out."Taking a bundle of notes out from an inside pocket, he handed them to the pilot. "You've earned that."

Twenty minutes later, the car pulled up and 'The Boss' got in. Without saying anything they disappeared into the direction of Tain. The Pilot shrugged his shoulders and climbed back on board to fly back.

In the car, the three said nothing to each other. They could tell the Boss was not in a great mood. Best to say nothing in that case. Once at the flat, he looked around at them and the flat and a slight smile crossed his face.

"Had a clear up then have we?"

"Yes. It was getting a bit of a tip. Everything ok Sir?"

"Not really. I need a bed and a few hours sleep. Did you find out if there were any new players in the area? Discretely of course." He turned and entered one of the four bedrooms. They looked at each other, gulped before leaving the flat to start doing as he asked.

+

In the office of The Double Head Eagle the phone rang and was quickly snatched up.

"Double Headed Eagle. How can I help?" said the Manager.

"Double or quits?" Asked a Russian voice. Informing the manager that he was now speaking to the real owner.

"Quits" His reply was code for its ok to speak.

"I think there may just be a problem developing. Amsterdam and London are showing a serious interest in opening a new venture up there. I have sent some men to, there was a pause, persuade them otherwise. You know that some people can be, another pause, very stubborn. You get my drift?"

"Yes. Do you need me to arrange anything else for you?"

"Yes, I understand another new person, has started to undercut us, so deal with it." The line went dead and the manager sat and rubbed his chin thoughtfully. It was all very well saying deal with it, but he had not the foggiest idea who they were, not yet anyhow. He would need to think of how to approach this. He opened a drawer to his desk, on a small green baize cloth a gun lay. Taking it out, he felt its weight and then returned it back into the drawer. The ammunition for it was stored elsewhere. Though he had been shown how to use it, the thought of actually killing a person up close filled him with horror.

+

Back in Graves End the boat 'Ben' was being radically changed from the original design to a much more cut back look. The white paint had been stripped off and a new undercoat of bright brown was being applied. The man and his team worked on silently. They knew that the sooner it was finished and out of the yard the better for everybody.

+

The Dutchman replaced the phone and looked at his funky, who was sat reading the paper. Standing up, he walked around and grabbed the man by the back of his collar, dragging him out of the chair. He bent close to the man's ear.

"I don't pay you to read papers. Got it?" A strangled sound came from the man. Letting him go, he collapsed on the floor, holding his throat. "Get hold of the usual men in Scotland that we use. Get them to give this newcomer a," he paused, "very warm welcome. Got it?"The man, still unable to speak, nodded furiously at him. Then a look crossed his face. Croaking, he stood up and whispered to him.

"Isn't that the same new customer who paid on the nail?"

"Yes, so be sure that it has nothing to do with me. If she needs to re-order, then that wouldn't bother me, but it will tell me if she has plenty of cash or not. If she hasn't, she will ask for credit, like they all do in time. Now get out of here and get on with it."

The man left and closed the door on his bosses office. Still rubbing his neck, he walked down to where his car was parked. Getting inside, he picked up his car phone and connected to the two heavies in Scotland.

"I've been told to tell you, this is what you are going to do for us..."

Chapter 9

Golspie Police Station

In Golspie a phone rang on DS Coopers'desk.

"DS Cooper. How can I help you?"

"A house near Nigg needs to be looked at." the receiver was replaced and Cooper looked at the phone and replaced the receiver. Was it a wrong number he wondered?" Fishing out the telephone directory, he looked up surveyors, but the number was not anything like the police in Golspie own number. He returned to the paperwork. The copy of the image of the pendant was stuck on the noticeboard, but already other items were being pinned over it.

The phone rang again in Golspie Police Station, Cooper picked up the receiver, only to hear the same message again for the second time. He decided to drive out to Nigg and see what all the fuss was about. Probably a waste of his time, but better to be safe than sorry. Scribbling a quick note for Gray, he picked up his car keys and left the station.

+

Tracy had gone to bed to sleep for the rest of the night. Worn out, she didn't hear the two men arrive with two cans of petrol. Nor did she stir as they quietly poured petrol over the pile of logs. Then removing the cans away from the logs. One of them took a shaving or two off the pile on the side and lit it with a lighter. Once burning nicely, he tossed it into the pile of logs. Both men turned and ran, as the log pile roared up in flames, dancing this way and that in the night sky. Tracy slept on undisturbed.

+

An hour later, a police car pulled up outside the house. Flames were starting to die down, but still lit enough of the night sky to identify the house grounds it was burning in. Cooper jumped from his car and ran over and up the side of the house. Once at the back of it, he could see the remains of a fire flickering in the night. It looked as though a bonfire had been left unattended, but it was a good distance from the house. Was it worth waking up the owner he wondered? He decided to keep watch for half an hour, if it died down, he would leave it and go back to work.

Later Cooper drove back to Golspie. He was puzzled though that the information had come before the fire would have probably got started. Was this a cry for help from the owner of the fire he wondered or something else?

+

Tracy awoke feeling still drowsy and lightheaded. She managed to get up and opened the curtains. A pale drift of smoke came from the back yard towards her window. Looking downwards, she noticed the pile of logs had been removed, then a second look made her realise they had been burnt. Holding her head, she went into the bathroom and drank a glass of water. Feeling slightly better, she grabbed a dressing gown to put on. Tying it as she went down the stairs and out into the garden, the smell was stronger here. She made her way slowly to where she had piled the logs. A large mound of ash lay on the ground. Bending over, she retched before walking back to the house. She sat down in a chair and closed her eyes.

Four hours later, she awoke again and this time was feeling much better. She now realised the smoke had come in through her open bedroom window and had the effect of making her sleep even longer. Armed with a makeshift mask around her nose and mouth, she started to gather the ash together into a smaller, but taller pile. It still smouldered in places as Tracy raked it up. It would probably die down if she left it alone.

+

In Golspie, Cooper was finishing off his paperwork. It had been a long night. He just needed to report to Gray and then he could go home to bed. Despite responding to the Nigg call and finding nothing really, he still had written up a small report of the two calls and his visit.

Gray entered the office and put his jacket around the back of his chair.

"Anything happen overnight?"

"Small fire in Nigg. Here is the report." Cooper tossed it across his desk to Gray. "I'm really tired for some reason. Call me if there is anything urgent. Now I am off to bed." He grabbed his coat and left Gray reading the report.

+

Later that day found Gray in Nigg looking at the burnt remains of a fire. Crouching down, he took an evidence bag from his pocket, turned it inside out and scooped up a handful of the ash. Then reversing the bag, sealed it and placed it in his pocket. He noticed that the house appeared empty, but since appearances can be deceptive, he choose to ring the front doorbell. He waited for a few minutes, but nobody appeared. A car pulled up alongside the house next door and an older couple got out. Taking out his warrant card, he walked over to speak to them.

"DI Gray, do you know the owner of that house?" He pointed to the one next door.

"Not really Officer. She bought some of our back garden off us it was far too large. Now that we are both getting older and finding it difficult to maintain. When she has visitors coming, usually pays for us to go away for a break. Really nice of her it is." He smiled at the Policeman.

"Did she say why she wanted your garden?"

"Oh yes." Said the lady beside her husband. "It was to allow her guests to arrive by helicopter."

"Helicopter eh?" Gray rubbed his chin thoughtfully. "You've been very helpful. Please don't say anything to your neighbour." He smiled and went back to his car and drove off. The two neighbours shrugged their shoulders, picked up their cases and went indoors to unpack.

Tracy had driven to Tain, first stop was the United Bank of Scotland, to check her account. Did she have enough money to buy a second load she wondered as she waited to be served. She also needed to change the means of supply if it could be set on fire that easily. Standing in the queue she noticed a lorry load of stone rocks going by. Maybe that was the means to get the stuff out there. She moved up a place and got served. Ten minutes later, sat in her car, she looked at her balance written on the paper she had been given. There was enough, but it would nearly clean her right out of money. Perhaps half as much. First though, a visit to a quarry to see the price of rocks and who would buy them.

In the office of River Quarry, the owner and Tracy sat discussing the prices of rock and the various sizes.

"The real big stuff, that costs less to buy, but more to transport. Middle size, like the forest firms use for paths and roads through forests is roughly the same for both cost and transport. Unless you have your own transport?" He leaned back in his chair and looked down his glasses at her.

"I have some transport. What sort of means did you have in mind?"

"They use a helicopter to drop 1 ton bags on to site. Costly mind."

"Ok, you have given me a lot to think about."Tracy rose and having shaken his hand, left his office. She did have a lot to think about as she turned out of the quarry and drove off towards Nigg and her current base.

Half an hour later, she pulled up outside her house. Noticing the next door neighbours were back, she quickly walked in and shut the front door after her. The last thing she wanted right now, was to have to stop and talk to them. Putting the kettle on, she saw the pile of ash and was reminded to take it away from the garden. A knock on the door jolted her from her thoughts. Going to the back door, she opened it and saw her other neighbour stood there.

"Wonder if you have plans for that wood ash? If you don't I can use it on the garden for compost and so on." He looked at her hopefully.

"Yes do help yourself, take all of it if you can use it." She smiled at him, it was perfect, she got rid of the ash and it would soon be buried under the veg that he grew.

"Thank you so much." He moved away and returned a few minutes later with a wheelbarrow and shovel. Soon she was hearing the sound of ash being put into the wheelbarrow. Happy, she went through to make a new phone call to call a favour in.

DI Gray had arranged for the sample of dust to be tested. Now as he sat at his desk, he felt slightly tired, unusual for him. Maybe it was more than wood ash he thought as he closed his eyes.

+

At James Boatbuilder (Graves End) & Co. The team had finished the repainting of the outside. Now inside, the carpenters had been working flat out to remodel it. With the cockpit open, rather than the original closed one, and a white streak running down the length of the boat against the red, it appeared to be quite a fast boat. The name BEN had been removed and a new name BRAGGING RIGHTS was now painted on the side and rear of the boat. The owner of the yard came over as they finished and tided up.

"You have done wonderfully. It doesn't look like the one that came in here. A really good transformation. Maybe I'll take it for a spin later down to London and back. See how it handles." He turned and went back to his office to carry on making phone calls to people who just might buy it. He wanted it out of his yard as soon as possible.

+

Gray looked up as Cooper entered the room carrying two cups of coffee. He carefully placed one on Gray's desk and then sat down.

"Any updates?"

" One, I sent some ash residue down to Invergordon, they have sent it onto Inverness. Once I came back I felt really tired."

"Think it is more than wood ash then Sir?"

"Maybe, hence the testing. It's a quiet spot right enough. The neighbours tell me that helicopters come and land at the back of the house."

"Very unusual for that part of the world, don't you think Sir?"

"Very. Tell me Cooper, who usually runs helicopters around here?"

"Around here," Cooper paused to think. "That estate that has just been bought, overlooks the Dornoch Firth, on the left hand side looking from the bridge towards Tain."

"Anybody else come to mind?"

"Forest supplies. Easy to fly them in, rather than overland. You know, bags of stuff hanging off the underside of the helicopter."

"Good thinking Cooper. I think the Estate may be worth a visit sometime, see who they have as visitors."

"Very exclusive though, we might not get in. You need to be invited and I don't think Sir, that we would get invited somehow." He grinned at Gray.

"Probably right, but our Chief might know the right people."

"One problem Sir."

"Which is?"

"Nigg is in the opposite direction to where we are talking about."

"Back to square one. What sort of people do you think are dropping off at Nigg then?"

"Rich visitors or?"

"The 'or' I think. I've arranged a couple of plain clothes to keep an eye on the place, just a regular visit now and then. Meanwhile I want to find out all we can about this new house owner at Nigg".

+

Tracy speed along the main road, before taking the turning to Nigg. Soon be home, she thought to herself. Had she looked in her rear view mirror, she may just have seen a white BMW following her all the way from River Quarry.

Chapter 10

LICD Headquarters

Bill and Jane had been reviewing what information they could get on Drug smuggling and supply in Scotland and Oxford. They had used HOLMES but any links found had just been the case they had both been involved in two years earlier. The phone on Jane's desk rang and she answered it.

"Hello?"

"Korps Nationale Politie. Drug division."

"Hello, DI Jane Sutherland speaking. To what do I owe this honour?" She pressed the record button as she spoke.

"There is a Dutchman, a well-connected businessman we cannot touch. We know he is a supplier of drugs, but cannot prove he is very clever."

"And the connection to us is?"

"His boat is missing and has been spotted going up the North Sea along your side of the coast. We think, only think though, he may be heading to Scotland."

"Scotland is a big country."

"The North East. That is about as much as we know. If you can apprehend this man we would be very grateful. I'll call back in a couple of days' time." He hung up.

"Bill, come over and listen to this." She waited and then replayed the message back to hear it all again.

"Best let Spencer hear it." Bill nodded with his head at their bosses office. "It might allow us to find out more and go back to Scotland."

Jane knocked on the door of his office.

"Come in." Both Jane and Bill entered. "What is it this time?"

"A request from our Dutch counterparts, I've recorded on my desk phone. Perhaps if you have time Sir?" He rose and followed them out to her desk. Once he had heard it, he went back to his office and slammed shut the door. Spencer sat behind his desk and looked at the phone. Sighing, he pulled open the drawer of his desk and took out a notebook. Inside were a series of phone numbers that he really did not need anybody else to know about. Under 'N' for Netherlands, he found the number he wanted and dialled it. A few minutes later the phone was answered.

"Yes?"

"H. Here. Listen up, the KNP are on to us."

"Just how do you know that?"

"Two of my best officers have just taken a call from KNP and I have listened to it. What are we going to do?"

"One, don't do anything out of the ordinary. It would only make you appear suspicious. Leave things with me, It is good to know this sort of information." He paused. "You are phoning from out of the office aren't you?"

"No. Should I be?"

"Of course you should, you fool." He slammed the phone down and went out onto the deck of his boat. In London, Spencer replaced the receiver and thought about what he had just heard.

Jane and Bill returned to their desks. Bill started to look up contacts and planes to Scotland. Jane decided that a quick look on the computer to see if DI Gray was still in Golspie, might be a good place to start. Neither of them had any doubt that they would be asked to return up to Scotland.

+

The Dutchman rubbed his chin, he was concerned that there appeared to be more players entering the area than he had first anticipated. The Inn with the Russian sounding name, who really owned that, he wondered. Then this new player paying cash on the nail. Not even noticing that the second delivery was not 100% pure or concerned that it went up in smoke! Now she rings up and asks for half as much again and cash again. Then there was ''The Boss" ok, he knew Patrick, but that was from a long time ago in Folkestone he recalled. For an area that was supposed to be easy pickings and ripe for a new player, an awful lot of people seemed to be interested.

+

DI Gray's phone rang for the second time in ten minutes. This time he managed to reach it in time.

"Hello, Golspie Police, DI Gray speaking."

"Invergordon. Two things for you to mull over. One we sent the ash on to Inverness. They have got back to us to report that the ash contains a high percentage of cocaine. Two, a pendant has been found inside the body of the woman found at Fyrish."

"We knew a pendant had been found with the body, but you are saying it was in the body? So how did that get there?" He asked.

"Not sure, it was in area of the stomach. We've sent you the images of both sides. Quite interesting in a morbid sort of way." He laughed and hung up on Gray. Gray sat back in his chair. Pendent, where had he heard about that before he wondered to himself. He got up and walked over to the fax machine. Amongst a lot of printed faxes, he found three sheets of paper, two with the images and a close up of the edge of one of the sides. It seemed as though it was shaped like a key. The writing on the other side was undecipherable to him. Maybe, when DC Cooper came in, he might know what it meant. He scribbled a note for Cooper to take a look and went out to his car to get a bag of sweets. Since giving up the fags, he had been eating so many more sweets instead.

An hour later Cooper was peering at the two faxed images. He could work out that the outline of Ben Bhraggie was meant to be one side. The writing, that had him stumped. Giving up, he rose to go outside to take a breath of air. As he walked past the front desk, he accidently knocked a small pile of books off the desk. Bending down, he picked them up and went to put them back on the desk. Then he noticed that one of the books was a Russian – English Dictionary. Spinning round, he forgot about going outside and taking the dictionary with him, rushed to his desk.

Gray looked across at the furious activity of Cooper. Curious now, he got up and walked across to Cooper. Who was busy comparing the side of the pendant and a dictionary on his desk.

"Care to share?" Asked Gray.

"What?" Cooper looked up, distracted for a few minutes. "Oh, sorry Sir. I think it might be Russian. I found this dictionary when I knocked it off the front desk. Here is a sentence, I think, about a door at the Monument. I think this might be the key to fit it." He said excitedly.

"Calm down, first we don't know which monument? We can rule out Ben Bhraggie and Fyrish as there aren't any doors at either place, not as far as I am aware." Gray paused, while thinking of the base of Ben Bhraggie. "You were up there recently, did you see any sort of door?"

"Not at ground level. Some sort of recessed bricked up door frame and window, both are well above ground level though." Gray looked at the image of the pendant and wondered what would have made a person eat it?

"So, if it isn't Fyrish or Ben Bhraggie, what other monuments are there near here?" asked Cooper.

"I'll leave you to find out. In the meantime, I think I might have a word with the higher ups. See if anybody really knows what is going on around here. And Cooper?"

"Yes?"

"Keep an eye on the Old East Sutherland Hotel. There is something strange about that place. Look up the records on the last two years. Who are the current owners etc? You know the drill." With that he left the office.

Chapter 11

Six days later.

The two henchmen followed their Boss down to his car and got in. 'The Boss' didn't like how things were panning out. While he had been based in Tain for a week. He had made several discoveries. Not least that a Russian was behind the new venture in Brora. Double Headed Eagle, what kind of name was that for Scotland? He wondered to himself. His two henchmen had found out that the flat in Dornoch was to be auctioned off this week. A flat, by rights, that should have been his for the last two years. Maybe it would go for a low price. He had been given a bidding number and was now set to go to the auction. "Well get moving, I have to be in Dornoch in twenty minutes and I don't want to be late for the auction." He prodded the driver in the back. The car smoothly pulled away from the flats and soon was on the A9 heading north to Dornoch.

+

Unknown to 'The Boss', at the same time, the Dutchman had booked his own bidding number and arranged for his telephone bids to be allowed. Though he had been required to make a serious deposit of cash with the auctioneers. He had thought that it might make a good place to conduct any new business that might be started in East Sutherland.

+

Bill was reading the newspaper, when he spotted a small advert for an auction in Dornoch of a three bedroom flat. It gave the phone number of the auctioneers and the address of the auction. Getting up, he walked over to Jane and pointed the advert out to her.

"You think that is the same one that was in the last case we helped with up here?" She asked.

"Might be. I'll give them a ring, see if there is any interest."

"Better be quick then. It says it starts in an hour. I'll go and update our boss." Nodding, she went and did so, while Bill found out if there was anybody who might be interested in buying it.

"Yes, thank you so much, I realise that the auction is due to start in a short while, if you can just fax over the list of known bidders as you offered. If you have their addresses too? You do, that is great. Thank you." He hung up and went to the fax machine, after a few minutes it whirled into action and three sheets of paper popped out. Taking them back to Janes desk, he started to look at the list of names and addresses. Jane came up alongside him.

"Take a look at this list, I am trying to see if any name jumps out." They both looked and then Jane spotted the only foreign name. Clicking on her terminal, she soon found what she was looking for.

"Look at this Bill, it's a Dutch name, Klaas Van Miere, could it be the one their police are looking for?"

"Maybe. Why don't you give the Dutch Police a call, I'll go and tell Spencer." He left her to it and walked into Spencer's office.

Ten minutes later, Bill walked out into the main office with a smile on his face. Jane looked up at him.

"What is it Bill?"

"Go home and pack, we are off to Scotland."

"Really?"

"Really. The accommodation will be sorted out while we travel. Flying from Gatwick to Inverness, then being met and driving to Tain. Auction is being told to delay for a day. Now get moving." He followed her out of the office, switching off their two computers as he went.

+

'The Boss' entered the room and looked for a chair, the place was packed, no matter, he thought, I'll stand at the back of the room. Better in a way, I can see who is bidding. The noise level dropped as a man entered the room and strode to the stage area where a table and gavel had been placed. Smartly tapping the desk, to get the bidders attention, the noise died down and everybody looked up expectantly.

"Thank you all for attending today's auction. I have a small announcement to make. We have been asked by the vendor and other parties, to delay the auction for twenty four hours. I know that this is a blow to some of you, who have travelled a long way to be here. We can offer you either a place tomorrow or to allow you to telephone bid. If you can speak to the two members of my staff by the two entrances. Please indicate which option you wish to take up. Thank you very much." He stepped down and a sigh went around the room.

Chapter 12

Dornoch 24 hours later

A hush descended across the room as the auctioneer stepped up again to the table the following day.

"Ladies and Gentlemen, the property on offer by auction today is a flat of one of the highest standards of any flat in Dornoch. It has been available to purchase for nearly two years. While there has been interest, nobody has made a serious offer. To that end, it has been decided to put it up for auction. You will all have had a brochure, if not please indicate and my assistant will bring you one with the bidding pack." He paused as a few hands rose. A young lad touted a few packs around the room. He noticed that some of the people in the room left, once they had viewed the contents of the packs. Although a couple of seats were now vacant, he remained standing

"I have an opening bid of £6,000 any advance?" A gasp had gone around the room and around a quarter of the bidders left the auction. A hand went up. "Thank you at £6,500?" A sound to his left, indicated a telephone bidder. "at £7,000, any advance?"

"£8,000" said 'The Boss'.

"I have a bid of £8,000. They will now go up in thousands. Fair warning. A nod, indicated a new bid from the telephone. "At £10,000 pounds."

"£15,000" said 'The Boss'.

"Against you on the phone. I have a bid of £25,000 on the phone."

An hour later the Boss left the auction having bought the flat for the ridiculous price of £50,000 He had paid over the odds, he knew that. On principle he wanted to get the property. He should have had anyway if things hadn't gone so badly wrong. Better phone the Dutchman he thought wryly to himself. At least he had a base in the Highlands now.

+

In a room in Eastern Europe a phone rang. Nobody answered.

+

Tracy sat in her flat in Invergordon. She looked at her spreadsheet that she had been working on. It would be tight, but still bring in a small profit. Ok, not as much as she had previously thought, but was it worth the risk? Rising, she made her way to the kitchen and made herself a brew. Taking it to the window, she looked across the top of the houses at the mighty oil rigs parked in neatly in order, ready to be serviced. They seemed to put her worries into perspective. Smiling now, she picked up the phone and placed an order for one ton of small rocks to be bagged and ready for collection from the quarry in two weeks' time.

+

The Russian picked up his phone.

"Get me the DHE and quickly."

"Do you know what time it is over there?"

"I don't really care what time it is here, there or anywhere. Just remember who you are working for. Now get me the DHE and call me back when you have him on the line." He slammed down the phone and walked to his window. Gazing out, he could make out the famous outline of the Kremlin. One day, he thought to himself, one day he would be more powerful than the current resident. Turning, he made his way back to his desk and opened one of the two drawers. This one contained two bottles of his favourite Vodka. Opening the bottle, he didn't waste time finding a glass, even though one was in the drawer. He wondered why the Far North of Scotland was so difficult to crack, he took another swig of the bottle and then screwing the top back on, replaced it in the drawer.

+

On a bedside cabinet a phone rang, Herbert Ross reached out his hand and took the receiver off it, then sat up to see who would call at this time of night.

"Double Headed Eagle. We are closed."

"Not this time, you aren't. What took you so long?"

"I am asleep, do you have any idea as to the time it is here?"

"No, nor do I care. What I do care about is have you dealt with your problem yet. The one that I asked you deal with, you do remember that don't you?" Now wide awake, Herbert rubbed the sleep from his eyes. Blast! He had completely forgotten about that request.

"Oh that, yes, completely sorted." He lied to him. Well, he could sort it first thing tomorrow.

"Good. I expect the photos sometime then?"

"Photos?"

"Photos of the body. You know how I work. Want to see the proof. How did you kill her?"

"Quickly. Look I really must be going back to bed. I have a full day tomorrow."

"Ok, but remember send the photos." The Russian hung up and smiled cruelly. Then he pressed the bell for his secretary to come through to him.

"How much background do we have on Herbert? The Restaurant Manager in Brora."

"I'll go and take a look at the file." The secretary turned and left the room. The Russian leaned back in his chair and thought about Oxford and the woman who had died two years ago. She had been a good conduit for his line of work. He looked across the room, the office door was still closed, but the door to the side of it was opening. He frowned, only a select few knew the code to get access. Getting up, he strode across the room and threw open the door. A small red haired man stood holding a book under his left arm.

"Come in. Though what you want at this time of day, I don't know."

"I think we have found a clue to the lost room." The man stopped speaking as the Russian clamped his hand over the man's mouth.

"Don't say another word. Just pass me the book and get out of here." He removed his hand and nodded at the man. Then he closed the door after them and went back to his desk. He looked at the title. '*Pendant Keys and their locks in the USSR Book 1*.' He looked at the back to find the index. Running his finger down the page, he found what he was looking for and smiled cruelly. This could make him rich beyond his dreams if it was handled correctly of course. His Secretary knocked and re-entered the room carrying a couple of pieces of paper.

"We don't have a lot about Herbert, other than he ran his own business in Oxford, till Patrick O'Conner, aka 'The Boss' lent him some money. He had to sell up to repay Patrick. Spent some time looking and running small places in both Oxford and the Highlands. We, you found him in London when you went to the Building Exhibition to talk about the new Dacha you had your mind to build. He was serving the drinks."

"Yes, I recall that now. Thank you. Get somebody to have a word with the rest of my team. I want to know about anybody who has ever mentioned the word 'Amber' in conversation or any other way."

"The budget will be what exactly?"

"No limit on this one."

"Very good Sir." He watched as his secretary turned and left the room. Then he picked up the phone and dialled a UK number in London.

+

In Brora, at the Double Headed Eagle, Herbert didn't go back to sleep. How could he? He hadn't either the knowledge or stomach to kill anybody, let alone take photos afterwards. He had only moved up here from Oxford to stop paying protection money to some gangster in Oxford. His restaurant, 'Charles' had won many plaudits in Oxford. Small and quirky, it was based above a widely known Bookshop in St Aldates. He had sold the Restaurant off to settle what he owed. What was he called?Yes now he recalled, Patrick O'Conner better known as 'The Boss' then he had moved up here after seeing an advert in the monthly magazine 'Catering Jobs Worldwide'. Having never met the owner, he now seemed to be in worse trouble than in Oxford. At least there he hadn't been asked to kill anyone, well not intentionally at least. Now unable to sleep, Herbert made his way downstairs to the deserted kitchen and looked around at the knives on the wall. Stabbing would be the easiest he thought, then put the thought far from his mind. What was he thinking of? He didn't even know who the person was or where they might live, never mind find a way to kill them.

+

In another part of Brora a phone rang and was answered at once.

"I've got a job for you tomorrow. Usual rates."

"What sort of job?"

"Can you go and collect some photos for me? I have asked the Manager of the DHE to send me the photos of the death of the new person on the block who is selling the stuff and how he killed them. I have my suspicions that he is not telling me the truth."

"How do you know that he isn't?"

"Fair question, do you know who the new person is?"

"We have asked around. Word hasn't come back yet. What do

you want done if he hasn't done as you asked?"

"Use your imagination. There is a kitchen there, lots of things get spilt and mopped up afterwards. Kitchens need to be kept spotless don't they? He paused, then continued, "And when you have done that, gather a list of prospective Managers together and fax it over to me." The Russian hung up and smiled at his secretary. Work done, he could do with some downtime at his Dacha.

"Call my car, tell them I am going to the Dacha." He watched as the secretary left the room and closed the door. He wondered what sort of person worked the long hours they did, just for him."

Chapter 13

Golspie Police Station

In Golspie DI Gray stood looking out of the office at the sea. Wondering, not for the first time, what had happened to the East Sutherland Hotel. He realised that having a couple of deaths was not good for business, but still for it to close it so quickly and nobody take it over? He turned and walked through to the front desk.

"Anybody know where DS Cooper is?"

"Last time I saw him, he was heading out to that boarded up hotel."

"Thanks." Gray lifted the flap and went out the side door. Soon he was driving along the A9 towards the Hotel. He hoped that nothing had happened to Cooper. In the boot of the car were a variety of tools suitable for what he wanted.

At the hotel, two cars were parked at either end of the carpark. Gray swung his car alongside Coopers and stroked his chin thoughtfully. Did Cooper know that he might have company or? He got out and took a crowbar from the boot of the car then walked towards the side door which was now open. He peered through the dusty gloom.Then shone his torch on the floor of the room. No dust. No footprints then, well none that would show now. He moved into the hotel, slowly and carefully. He had thought of shouting out Coopers name, but the fact that there was no noise at all now really concerned him.

Upstairs Cooper was unaware of anybody else being in the building with him. One of the Dutchman's henchmen, who had come to give the place a look over, had not expected the local police to turn up. Now, rather than confront Cooper, he kept to the shadows and watched what the policeman did. A creak on the old staircase made him look down. Downstairs he could just make out the outline of another person. Who was that he wondered? Another person like himself or more police?

Cooper also had heard a noise and turned around to see a torch light flashing on the stairs.

"Whose there?"

"Ok Cooper, no need to be dramatic, it's just me, Gray."With a sigh of relief Cooper started to go down the stairway towards Gray.

"Not sure I really like this place, being here alone I mean."

"I can understand that. If the windows were not boarded up, it would be so much lighter." Replied Gray. He shone his torch up onto the ceiling and around the top floor. Broken bits of railing and some graffiti were visible. A rat or something was scurrying around on the top floor.

"Why did you come here Sir?"

"Needed to speak to you, come on we'll make the place secure and go back to the station." Both men retraced their steps back down the staircase.

Hearing those words, the man slowly started to follow them down, he did not want to get trapped in here alone. Getting in the first time hadn't been too difficult. He felt the padlock in his pocket. He cursed silently, the police would see it was missing and start to look around properly. Now he would be caught inside the building so he quickened his pace as he continued downwards. In doing so, he accidently dislodged a small bit of wood that crashed down the stairs the sound reverberating around the empty building. Quickly but not making any noise, he turned back and went up to the floor above him. Down by the side door, both policemen heard a noise and stopped. Turning quickly, they ran back towards the staircase, Gray flashed his torch around the stairwell. Nothing out of place that he could see. He flashed it around the bottom of the stairs, a bit of wood lay there with dust settling around it. He started to walk towards it. Seeing what Gray was about to do, the man gently pushed a longer bit of old wood over the edge. As planned the piece missed the policeman by a wide mark.

"Look sir, the place is really not safe, come back and we'll get out now." Cooper reached forward to take Gray's hand.

"I can manage Cooper, but you are right, it isn't safe here." They turned and left the building. Slamming the door shut Gray looked at Cooper. "Got the padlock?" He said holding out his hand.

"I haven't got it."

"How did you get in then?"

"Now I think about it, there wasn't a padlock on the door."

"Lucky I brought another then. It's in the boot of the car, run across and bring it back." Cooper ran over and brought back a really large brass padlock and key.

"Big enough don't you think Sir?" He asked as he fastened it to the door catch and locked it.

"Should be, but I want somebody out here in a car keeping an eye on this door. If anybody else is shows any interest whatsoever, then I want to know about it. Got it?"

"Absolutely Sir." The two men went back to their cars. Copper noticed for the first time the second car and looked across at Gray with a question ready on his lips. Gray smiled back.

"If anybody is inside, then they are now locked in. That was why I want somebody out here. I wonder just who is interested in this particular boarded up hotel?" Then getting into their cars, proceeded to drive off towards Golspie.

+

Inside the hotel the man had just reached the door as it was locked. He had heard muffled voices, but not what had been said. He tried, fruitlessly, to break the door down by running up to it and throwing his weight behind it a few times, Being well made he soon realised that he was wasting his time and getting hurt into the bargain. With not much but bits of wood in the hotel, he was stuck. His torch was flickering too, not a good sign. Sighing, he turned off the torch and sat down in the empty kitchen. In the silence he could hear the rats scurrying about. Should he put the torch back on and move further in and up the hotel. He rose and closed the door through to the hotel from the kitchen. He flashed his torch around the empty room. No rats, he sighed and sat down on the floor of the empty room. He wondered what Klaas would have to say about it.

Chapter 14

A flat in Dornoch

'The Boss' stroked his head thoughtfully. He knew that Klaas was anxious to establish a base up here. A base was needed for the storing and distribution of the goods. Not too far from the sea. He turned towards his two henchmen who were sat in two chairs the other side of his desk.

"Where can we find a base for things up there?"

"Tain?"

"No harbour. Don't suggest Dornoch, too rich and expensive and no harbour." Said 'The Boss' with a rare smile.

"Golspie? It's got a small harbour and slipway. Bit of a pier and a few houses nearby." Suggested one of the men.

"Look into it. No, go and get the car, we'll all go and have a look together. Bring the tool bag, we might need to force our way in someplace or other." He smiled at the two of them.

A short while later, a car pulled up at the pier in Golspie. The three men got out and walked out to the pier. A few boats bobbed around in the water, turning round he saw a few cottages in red sandstone sitting back from the seafront. Nothing really big enough to be used for the purpose he wanted. He glanced up at the monument on the hill. A useful landmark for anybody in a boat, he thought to himself. Somewhere near to here. He looked across the village at the monument and ran his eye southwards, then northwards and smiling to himself, returned to the car. They pulled out onto the corner of the main road and drove northwards towards Brora. It was as they were near to the Broch, that he tapped his driver on the shoulder.

"Pull in over there, that looks interesting."

"That place? The Old East Sutherland?" Suiting the action to his words, he swung the wheel around and drove across the road and up the drive. He pulled the car alongside the other one in the car park and the three of them got out.

"Wonder where the driver is?" Asked 'The Boss'. He walked up the steps to the main door which was boarded and locked. "Take a look around, see if there is another entrance anywhere were we can get in."

The two men split up and set off in opposite directions around the perimeter of the hotel. It didn't take long to find that there was only one other door which was also heavily padlocked.

"How do we get in then?" Asked one of his henchmen.

"Use one of the tools in the car. Make it quick, I don't want to be here too long." His henchman ran off to the car and soon returned holding a portable angle grinder. It was the work of a couple of minutes to cut through the padlock and push the door open. Inside the dark made it initially difficult to see what was inside. This didn't stop the henchman of the Dutchman from running straight out of the building into the arms of 'The Boss'.

"Whoa, what do we have here?" said the Boss as he held the struggling man. The production of a gun from one of his henchmen, soon stopped the struggling. "Better. Now why don't we go back inside and have a nice cosy chat." Turning to the other two, he added "Bring the tool bag, we may need to use it." Then, twisting the man's arm behind his back, he marched him into the deserted kitchen. His two henchmen came back in carrying a large tool bag. One of them went and opened the door to the rest of the building.

"I'll go and see if there are any chairs about, may as well make ourselves comfortable." The prisoner struggled, but got punched for doing so.

+

The Dutchman slammed his hand into the wall of his boat. He was furious. A flat in Dornoch, that would have been a perfect place, bought from under his nose. Well, he would have to find out who that was and make him or her an offer that they wouldn't refuse. He called out to his flunky outside on the deck.

"Get in here now! I want an update on why we haven't heard from our friend Herge in Sutherland. He was supposed to be looking for somewhere suitable to use as a base. I lost out buying the flat in Dornoch, find out who bought it, and get back to me as soon as possible. Get hold of Herge and ask, no tell him to get a move on finding somewhere if he still wants to stay alive that is."

"Whatever you say." He tossed his cigarette into the oily water and went ashore to make the call.

+

Tied to a rusty metal office chair, the prisoner had given up struggling. He sat there with 'The Boss' and the two henchmen stood looking at him. 'The Boss' stroked his chin. Then leaned in close to the man.

"Easy way, you tell me who you are and who you are working for. I untie you and you live to tell the tale. The difficult way," he paused and waved his hand at the range of tools now laid out on the ground. "a bit more unpleasant for you, but we will learn everything from you. Now which is it to be?" The man sat and said nothing. 'The Boss' nodded to his henchmen, and left them to it. A scream reverberated around the empty building. "Name?" He snapped at the bound man.

"Herge." Screamed the man. "Get me a doctor."

"Well, Herge, who do you work for?"

"He'll kill me if I talk."

"And I'll kill you if you don't."

"Untie me."

"Not a chance, until we know all there is to know." Another finger was broken. He looked again at the man. "Left or right handed?"

"Right." He screamed.

"Better leave the rest of the right hand free to sign his unemployment forms." Laughed the other henchman.

"The man has a point doesn't he?" The screams became louder…

…outside 'The Boss' was busy trying to light up a cigar, he took in the view and thought what an ideal place this would be for a base. Pity he didn't know who owned it. A last loud scream was heard coming from within. A door opened and his two henchmen came outside.

"Still living?"

"Not now. Strong little bugger, only gave us his name and that he was Dutch. What shall we do with the body?"

"Put him in the boot of the car, we'll get rid of it someplace today." His gaze fell on the monument in the distance on the hill. "You can put him up there, nobody will find him there. If they do, all they will find is a skeleton." His two men looked at one another and then at the hill.

"Could we not just leave him here?"

"I might still buy it. Then I still have the problem of getting rid of him."

"In that case the floor of the kitchen needs resurfacing when you fit it out again."

"Have it your own way then, leave him in the building, but put him in a cupboard or somewhere, just in case somebody else looks around." The two men went back in and a few minutes later, left holding the tool bag. One nodded at the door.

"What about the padlock?"

"I'll wait here, you take the car and get a replacement from that ironmongers, Lindsay's, in Golspie and come back with it."

He watched as they drove off before going back inside, a few stains of blood on the floor, but that was all. He scuffed the cement with his shoes to blend it in. Then went and put the chairs back into another of the rooms. Dust showed on the floors where light came in. He flicked a switch, but nothing happened. He went back to the kitchen and left the building. He would try and find out tomorrow who owned it and how much that it would cost to buy.

+

Half an hour later the two men returned and put the new padlock in place before locking it and giving the keys to 'The Boss'. Then the three of them drove off in the direction of Brora, more particularly, The Double Headed Eagle.

Chapter 15

Golspie Police Station

Bill and Jane pulled up outside the Police station. Neither had said anything for the last half an hour. Best laid plans had been totally wasted. First fog at London Airport had delayed the flight for a day. By the time they had gone from Inverness to Golspie, the auction had finished and the hall locked up. They still hoped that their trip had not been in vain. Getting out of the car, they walked into the station. A policeman stood doing some paperwork behind the counter.

"DI's Sutherland to see DI Gray or DS Cooper. They have been informed already that we are coming to see them." Bill looked around the front office while he waited. Three metal seats were spaced apart under the windows.

"I'll go and tell him that you are here then." Leaving the two of them alone, he walked through to the back offices. A few minutes later DI Gray came out and waved them through.

"Good trip?"

"Not really, the flight was delayed. Auction went ahead without us being there."

"Which auction was that?" asked Gray

"The flat in Dornoch. Remember the one that the dead woman was found in." replied Bill

"That flat, well I might be able to help you there. I'll give the auctioneers a ring and see who bought it."

"Appreciate it." Said Jane with a smile as Gray sat down and telephoned a number.

"Mark and Andrews Solicitors. How can we help you."

"Golspie Police, DI Gray speaking. I need to find out the

details of who the final bidder was on the flat in Dornoch that went for auction. Yes I'll hold for a minute." Tapping his pen onto his pad, Gray waited. "A man called Patrick."

"Surname please? O'Conner. Irish then?"

"Didn't sound Irish to me. More refined, but English not his first language. Hope that helps. Goodbye." Gray put the phone down and rubbed his chin.

"So, an educated Irishman buys the flat. A Mr Patrick O'Conner if you please. And just how many of those do you think there are in Ireland?" He looked at Bill and Jane. "So, fill me in as to why you needed to come back up here to this neck of the woods. Or are you not going to tell me until it is all over again, like last time." He looked crossly at the pair of them, then smiled. "Sit down and tell me as much as you can about what is going on up here, then I'll tell you what I have found out. Agreed?" Jane looked across at Bill and they both nodded.

"Agreed. It's very shortened version is, that a man known as 'The Boss' is drug running up and down the Thames to Oxford. His boat was renamed 'Ben' but was known before as 'Brora' and before we think it was called 'Bar Hour' and kept in Brora. The Korps Nationale Politie. Drug division have already tipped us off that a Dutchman, Klaas Von Miere, with a boat, last seen heading towards the north east coast of scotland, is suspected of drug running. Now we don't know if they are connected in any way. But why name your boat Brora or Bar Hour or Ben come to that."

"Did you use HOLMES?" asked Gray with a smile.

"Yes, The only links we found were names that appeared in our last case up here. So here we are again. What is your side of things?" Asked Jane.

"A few things, but taken together," He shrugged his shoulders "they may or may not be connected. A body is reported at the top of Ben Bhraggie. We go and investigate. No body at Ben

Bhraggie. A fortnight later another body is reported, well more a skeleton really, at the top of Fyrish." Bill and Jane looked puzzled. "A monument in Ross-shire. Nice walk if you like that sort of thing. It is recovered and a pendant is found." He pushed the fax with the images across his desk at them. Bill picked it up and studied it. "During this time, we get a call that a fire has been seen near Nigg. Traces of the ash contain cocaine. DS Cooper has found out the pendant is Russian. Oh, the East Sutherland Hotel is empty and boarded up, but I think something is still going on there." He paused and went and put the kettle on.

"What about the Harbour Arms in Brora?" Called Bill across the room.

"Ah, our new restaurant called 'The Double Headed Eagle.' A lot of clients even out of the tourist season. You might want to take a look sometime. Both myself and Cooper are too well known to go inside if you get my drift?" He leaned forward reaching for the tea and sugar. "Now how does that all connect, if it does, I mean? Tea?" They nodded and he came back over with three mugs.

"Sounds as though somebody is wanting to open up in East Sutherland. What do you think Bill?" Said Jane.

"Certainly, it is plausible. Have you translated the Russian on the back of the pendant yet?"

"Not yet."

"We could send it to the Russian section in LICD if that helps at all?" Said Bill, looking at Jane. She nodded her agreement.

"That would be helpful. From the shape of it, Cooper and Invergordon both think it is a key for something."

"Like a code key you mean?" said Bill

"No, more a real key." Replied Gray. "Now do you want to take a look at Ben Bhraggie, or explore the East Sutherland Hotel and all its empty rooms?" He grinned as he took a gulp of tea.

"Neither today. We need to find a place to stay, because we

were late arriving, our hotel has let our rooms. Anywhere you can suggest would be helpful." Jane said.

"The new self-catering flats in the centre of the village. Where a certain lady lived?" Gray said with a smile. "I'll give the agent a ring, shall I?" Both looked at one another and nodded their agreement.

+

The Dutchman watched as his office door slowly opened. The only person not needing to knock was his man outside. He entered and looking straight at him.

"Nobody has seen him. Apparently the last anybody has heard of him was two days ago. He was going to look at an old hotel that is disused. Somewhere between Brora and Golspie."

"Find out who owns it and get them to phone me. In the meantime, get our lazy men in Tain to go and take a look for themselves. Force entry if they have to, but don't leave any traces of them having been there." Thoughtfully he picked up the phone and dialled the number of Patrick.

+

Herbert Ross, Manager of the Double Headed Eagle, had not slept since being told to get rid of somebody. Somebody who he knew nothing about. The restaurant was starting to get busy, it usually started to around four in the afternoon. Herbert saw on the monitor in his office, a car pull up and three men got out. He thought he recognised one of them, but couldn't think where he would have met him. Leaving his office, he went out into the restaurant to greet them and show them to a table. They didn't look like the usual clients. As they sat down, the larger one grabbed him by the wrist.

"Herbert Ross. Well, well, what brings you here to the North of Scotland? Do you need some funds for this place?" He laughed and let go of the wrist. "Get me a bottle of your best wine." As Herbert left, he said quietly. "He borrowed some money off me in Oxford, he ran 'Charles' in St Aldates. Took a bit of persuasion to repay all of it, but he did eventually. Sold the restaurant to do so, at least that was what I was told at the time. I want you to find out all you can about this man. He works for the Russian, the man who owns here. Perhaps we can apply a pincer movement on him, if you get my drift?" They nodded, although neither was really sure what their boss wanted. Better to nod than to ask for an explanation.

In the wine cellar, Herbert was busy down on his knees looking at the best wine. He knew that if he served it, the Russian owner would want to see which customer had paid for it. Since it was very likely that he would end up paying for it. Herbert decided to switch it for the second best one. Pushing the best bottle back in the rack, so it didn't appear from a first glance. He took the red necked bottle out of the cellar and up to a side room to let it come to room temperature.

Three hours and two bottles later, the three men rose, somewhat unsteadily and started to make for the door. Herbert moved to stop them leaving.

"What about the bill? You haven't paid yet."

"You pay it for me. I might remember that sometime."

"But it comes to hundreds of pounds." Herbert shouted in anger. 'The Boss' stopped and turned towards Herbert. Then he grabbed him by the neck and lifted him clean off the floor. When he struggled, 'The Boss' looked him in the eyes.

"Really? I could lend you some money to pay for it, but you would need to pay the interest as well. Or..." He paused and dropped him on the floor. "Some information might be worth the cost of the meal. Meet me at the East Sutherland Hotel in ten minutes. I'll be waiting. Come alone." He swung round and left the man on the floor trembling as he did so.

The three men stood for a minute outside in the fresh air, then got into the car and drove off in the direction of the deserted hotel. Unseen by them, a local policeman watched as the car started off along the road towards the A9, it seemed a bit erratic, so he called in the number plate and found that it was a stolen number plate. He jotted this down in his notebook and then walked on towards the police station, his shift was coming to an end.

Inside the car, much laughter was heard coming from all three men. Had they been more alert, they would have seen a police car turning into the deserted hotel ahead of them.

+

Herbert, helped off the floor by one of his staff, made his way to his car which was parked at the side of the building. Intent on getting to the meeting on time, he didn't notice the policeman walking in the road as he swung onto the road. Didn't notice that he knocked him flying into the river, where, because he couldn't swim and was unconscious he drowned taking his police notebook with him.

+

Gray had said he wanted to check the hotel was still secure. They could drive on to Brora. Jane and Bill had been trying to phone the restaurant to book a table, but having no luck, decided to turn up and see if a table was free. Now they watched Gray's car pull off the road towards the boarded up hotel.

"Bit dark isn't it." Remarked Jane, the night was certainly drawing in.

"More noticeable as we are so far north." Replied Bill as they drove on northwards. The sign to Brora showed up and they slowed down to remember the way there. Swinging right, just before the bridge, Bill neatly parked in the carpark that was in front of the main harbour. Both of them got out and looked across the road at the building. It didn't look busy, so they wandered over to make their way inside.

Inside it was fairly quiet, a couple sat at one table and a group of five youngish men sat round a table at the other end. No staff could be seen, nor could any food be seen in front of the customers. Bill looked around before lowering his voice.

"No staff, no food, something not right here. I'll go and take a look in the kitchen." He started to move forward, but Jane grabbed his arm.

"We'll both go together. Safety in numbers remember." Both made their way towards a swing door with a porthole cut into it. Peering through the glass they could see a kitchen, but no staff. Nothing on either by the looks of things. They turned to return back to where they had entered. The couple sat by themselves did not appear concerned that no food or person had come to ask what they wanted. The other table, by contrast, was looking as though they might decide to leave or complain. Bill took Jane's hand and whispered to her.

"Let's see what develops. Come and sit down between the two tables. With our backs to the wall, we can see the whole restaurant and if anything happens we will know about it."

"Good idea." Suiting the action to the word, they made their way to one of the empty tables. Sure enough, shortly after they had sat down, the five men rose and left muttering about not having any goods. Jane turned to Bill. "Bill, they didn't say not having any food, but not having any goods. I don't think they were here to eat do you?"

"Not sure yet, sounds like something didn't happen that was supposed to. Maybe we should go back and tell Gray." He rose from the table and the other couple rose at the same time. They watched as the couple left the room, the woman saying that she had heard Nigg was now the place to go to.

"Hear that Jane, Nigg, wasn't that mentioned by Gray?"

"Now you come to mention it. Come on, let's go back and bring him up to speed." She turned to leave, then stopped. Bill was looking around the room.

"Now what?"

"Shouldn't somebody lock up or something?"

"Bill we don't have a set of keys. Turn out the lights if you are that bothered and we will tell Gray to send somebody over to guard it. Now come on." They left the place in darkness and crossed the road to their car. Then set off towards Golspie.

Chapter 16

The East Sutherland Hotel (Disused)

DI Gray swung his torch around the outside of the dark hotel. It seemed secure, He made his way to the side door and saw the padlock attached to the bolt. Satisfied, he went back and got into his car. About to put the lights on, he saw another car pull into the carpark. Curious as to why anybody would want to visit here at night, he slipped down in his seat out of view. Loud voices could be heard arguing about a proposed meeting here. He didn't move as they came closer and passed the car without a glance inside. They made their way towards the side door. Risking a glance, he saw they were bent down as though looking at the padlock. Good luck getting in there tonight he thought to himself with a smile. Then he noticed they had vanished. Curious now, he quietly felt, rather than saw, his way around to where the door was now open. He peered around the door, a torch was playing around the room. Three men were stood in a group. Puzzled as to how they had got in, he saw the padlock was still hanging on the door. He fished out the key he had for the padlock and tried it. It didn't turn. Putting the key back in his pocket, realising they must have replaced the police padlock with one of their own. Listening now near the hinges where the gap was he could make out some of what was being spoken.

"…ok, so he was supposed to be here. Where is he then?"

"How am I supposed to know. He'll turn up. There was a car outside. Perhaps he is scared." Laughter came from all three.

"Go and check the car, if it is empty then we know he is on the grounds somewhere." Gray moved back a few paces as two men came out from the hotel. The torch was still being shone around the room, occasionally flashing through the open door. He could hear some crashing and a few curses, then one of them returned.

"Well?"

"Nothing in the car, but another car has just pulled into the carpark."

"Getting like Piccadilly Circus. This is supposed to be an empty disused hotel." A noise of thrashing and muffled cries came close and two other men entered the room. "At last. What took you so long? Anyhow, you are here now. Let's get started." 'The Boss' moved back out of the light to see the Manager and one of his henchmen standing in the doorway. He pulled a chair into the middle of the room, indicating to the Manager to take a seat. Herbert moved to the centre slowly. Once seated, he was quickly tied to the chair. One of his men shone the light on the man, now seated in the middle of the room.

"I held back when I saw the police car outside." Herbert said.

"What did you just say?" Said 'The Boss' with a menacing tone.

"I held back, when I saw the police car outside. Surprised you are still here with them about."

"You two, go outside and check the grounds. My friend and I will have a nice little chat while you're gone." He stood in front of the chair, the light behind him casting a huge shadow on the wall.

Outside, Gray had heard what the man had said the first time and had quickly decided retreat was better than staying. Bending low, he ran quickly across the entrance and was in the car as the two men came out. He locked the doors and started the engine, making sure the lights stayed off. Then he roared out of the overgrown car park and down the drive towards the A9 and Golspie. At the entrance to the hotel, the A9, for once, was empty. Swinging out onto the road, he turned on the flashing lights. Now touching over seventy, he flashed past the 'slow' signs near the entrance to Dunrobin. Breaking heavily as the bend approached. Down through the gears and fast past the exit to Dunrobin Castle. Slowing down as the speed signs came into view. Now for the first time since leaving the hotel, he glanced in his mirror. Nothing behind him. He drove along the road and swung the car to right and parked in the car park behind the police station. Gray switched the engine off and sat there as it cooled down, noises of metal slowly contracting filled his ears. He realised that he had been extremely lucky.

+

Jane, driving for once, had signalled that she was turning left as the hotel loomed up in front of them.

"What are you doing?"

"We need to tell Gray, he said he was going to check things over here. So, he might still be here." Bill smiled to himself in the dark, he couldn't fault her logic. As they swung left and up the overgrown drive, a car flashed past them with no lights on. Looking in her mirror, she saw it turn left to go towards Golspie. Jane started to swing the car to follow, when another car, this one with headlights blazing, followed the first, down the drive.

"One or other of those two cars probably had Gray in it." Said Bill.

"Let's just check the hotel first though." She drove up to the main door and the car headlights picked out the boarded up door. "Nothing doing." Jane started to swing the car around to drive down the other side.

"Slow down a minute. I think I saw a person in the undergrowth, over there." He pointed to the far right of the hotel. Jane could just see a dim light coming from somewhere. Pulling in under a large tree, she switched off the engine and turned off the lights. Then turned to Bill.

"Just before we go charging in there I want to remind you of a few points."

"Later."

"No now. One. It is not our jurisdiction. Two. We are both unarmed. Three. We don't know how many are in the building. Four. We do know that it is a very large building."

"Five. Gray might be in danger." Said Bill sarcastically at her. Then got out of the car. Then with a sigh, Jane got out and having locked the car, followed Bill. Like Gray before him, Bill had taken the long way around the building. Jane followed, her shoes catching in the undergrowth. Eventually both of them arrived the other side of the open door. A torch was being flashed around the room. By peeking around the door, Bill could see a man tied on to a chair with a large man holding the torch in the seated man's face. Bill moved back and indicated for Jane to retreat with him, when they were a good distance from the door he spoke.

"That is not Gray in there. I think we should go to Golspie. Come back with more support." Jane sighed with relief.

"Your best suggestion yet. Now come on." She led the way back around the hotel and was about to go out into the drive, when she stopped dead in her tracks. A car had parked alongside the front door. Two men were outside taking a cigarette break. She pushed Bill back the way they had come.

"Now what?"

"Two men in their car, right by the front door. We either wait or go back round the other way."

"Great, so one way we have two men and a car. The other way we have two men in a room, with an open door, which we have to go past." In the silence an engine started up. Bill looked at Jane, who moved more slowly back towards the front again. Peering round, she motioned to Bill to join her. The car and men had moved across to the other side of the drive. Now their eyes were getting use to the dark, they could see nobody was in the car. Bending low, they ran quickly across to their car and got in and drove off towards Golspie. Had they looked behind them, they would have seen two men come out from the hotel and start to run after them, shouting to stop.

+

Jane swung their car into the car park opposite the police station and looked at Bill.

"Something is going on up there, that much is certain. Let's go and tell Gray."

"I'm in agreement with you on that." Said Bill as he got out of the car. The two of them made their way across the road and into the police station. The same man was on duty, this time without saying anything, he just lifted the flap and they walked through and into the back rooms.

"So, what you are saying is that you saw two men in a car?" said Gray to Jane.

"And the two men in the hotel. Don't forget that." Added Bill.

"Yes. Did you know about this?" Jane asked Gray.

"Not 'til tonight, I didn't."

"So, what are we going to do about it." Jane asked nobody in particular.

"I am going to call up some more bodies and then tomorrow morning, when it is light, carry out a full check of the hotel. Now I suggest you go to your apartment and settle in." He nodded at them, and after looking at one another, they turned and left him to his paperwork.

+

'The Boss' looked up from where Herbert sat as his two men entered the room.

"Well?"

"A car left the car park, turning towards Golspie. We ran after it, but…" He stopped as 'The Boss' put his hand up.

"Later. I have been having a chat with our friend here. Not been that co-operative yet. But that might change. He has told me that he left the place unlocked. Maybe one of you could go and check it out. Look after it for us, I mean him." He looked down at Herbert and smiled.

"Maybe you might be useful to me yet. Just who is the Russian you are working for?"

"He'd kill me if I told you anything." 'The Boss' leaned in close.

"And I'll kill you if you don't tell me everything about the man and his restaurant. Well, I am waiting." Herbert realised that he had no real choice. Swallowing hard, he started to tell 'The Boss' all about the restaurant, thinking that if he spun out the boring bit first, he might yet live.

An hour later, Herbert sat, still tied to the chair, he was a mass of bruises, but nowhere where they would show. He had told them everything he knew, but that was only about the restaurant, he knew very little about the man behind the venture. Now he strained to listen as the two men stood by the door having a conversation in a low voice.

"I think we have had as much information about the place as we are going to learn today." Said 'The Boss'."

"So, what do we do with our friend then?"

"Leave him here for a few hours. We'll come back in the morning and let him drive back."

"What if he talks?"

"You think he will? He has seen what tools we could have used on him. He talked quick enough then. But go and make sure he understands not to blab about us." One man walked over and bending low, quietly told Herbert what would happen if he spoke about any of this to anybody. Especially the Russians.

+

It was later that night, when they were both in bed, that Bill reminded Jane that neither of them had mentioned to Gray about being no staff at . Nor, she reminded him, had they mentioned about hearing Nigg mentioned in conversation. Then turning off the lights they fell into a deep sleep.

Chapter 17

The Double Headed Eagle Restaurant Brora

Very early the following day, the two henchmen belonging to the Dutchman drove to *The Double Headed Eagle*. Finding the place unlocked, they had gone inside and checked the place thoroughly. The only thing of note was some paperwork in Russian. They had found this in one of the desk drawers. Nothing else of any interest had been found. Both men looked at one another.

"He is not going to like this."

"Agreed. Do you have that camera in the car?"

"Think so, why?"

"Take some photos of the paperwork. Shows we have found something."

"I suppose." Grumbling, he left his partner and went to the car. The remaining man walked through and felt with the back of his hand the oven door. Stone cold. He went back to the main room and found his partner taking photos of each of the pages. He looked up as he re-entered the room. "Thought I may as well do a proper job."

"How much longer?" A few more flashes.

"That's it. Done. Just put them back in the drawer where we found them and we can be on our way. I think the manager has done a runner."

"It's looking like it." They turned to leave the restaurant. Blocking the way out were two huge men. Without saying anything, the first one held out his hand for the camera. It was passed without a word. He then opened the back, took out the film and held it up to the light. Then closed the back and handed the camera back.

"Hey! You can't do that." Said one of the two Dutchmen. At a signal from the silent man who had ripped the film from the camera, he bent down and picked up, one handed, the man and walked towards the kitchen.

"I suggest you go now, before my friend comes back for you." Then the second large man followed his partner into the kitchen. Taking a gasp, he looked back towards the kitchen, where the doors were open and he could see a hot fat fryer had been turned on as well as all the gas rings on the range. He turned and left the place, running as he did so towards the car they had come in. He didn't notice that one of the two huge men had come outside and taken a photo of his car number plate. Panicking now, he put the car in gear and drove off through the old village of Brora. Back inside, the three men stood, well, two stood, one was tied to a chair. He looked anxiously as the fryer heated up. The two men stood looking at one another, without saying anything. Then one went and got a long handled double pronged fork. Used for handling meat. He slowly approached the seated man and gently pushed the fork against the man's throat, slightly pricking the skin. Bending down so he could whisper in the man's ear.

"That may hurt you now, but now imagine when it is white hot. You do have a good imagination don't you?" The man nodded as much as he could. "Then you might want to tell me all about what you are doing here, and who work for?" He signalled for the other man to take the fork and put it into the flames…

…Fifteen minutes later, two men left the kitchen and headed for their car. They had found out all they wanted to know. Inside a dead body was still tied to the chair. Thoughtfully though, they had turned everything off before they left.

+

"What do you mean, the place was empty?" Roared the Dutchman down the phone.

"Just that, the place was in darkness and nobody in the building. We both looked the place over thoroughly. Even found some documents that were in a drawer."

"Ok, so what happened to the documents, did you bring them with you?"

"No, but Han did take photos of all the documents, then we left them there."

"Good thinking for once. Let me speak to Han."

"That could be difficult."

"Go on."

"Well, after we had finished and were about to leave, two large men blocked our way out. They took the camera and ripped out the film. Then one of them took Han through to the kitchen. I was told to leave. Last I saw the kitchen range was being fired up and a deep fat fryer being started."

"And you ran off I suppose?"

"Well I wasn't as large as those two. Picked Han up with one hand."

"Go back and see if they have left him alive or dead. Whichever way, make sure that you get him out of there and bring him back here." He slammed the phone down, breathing heavily as he did so. What was going on up there, he had not heard from Noah either. Maybe it was time to take another trip back up there. He sat back down and took a cigar to think about what possibly could be going on.

+

'The Boss' was in Dornoch. Stood looking around his empty flat. He turned to one of his men.

"Get this nicely furnished as soon as possible. Phone the usual people. I want to use this as my Scottish headquarters from tonight onwards." He turned and left them to get on with it.

DI Gray looked across the room at Cooper. Somewhere in the front of the building a phone was ringing, but no sign of it being answered.

"Go and see what that might be about, will you?" He returned to his report that he was writing, partly so that he could keep events in some sort of order. He heard the phone stop ringing and assumed that Cooper had got there in time. Gray looked up as Cooper ran into the room.

"What?"

"A body, floating in the River Brora. A policeman by the look of things."

"Get the car round to the front. I'll phone…"

"No need, Brora have already phoned Invergordon and Inverness."

"You still here? Go get the car." Gray had already got his coat on and was walking to the door.

Fifteen minutes later, both men were at the Harbour in Brora looking at the body of a policeman, who by the look of things had been badly beaten. The time of death, according to the Doctor was between 7pm and 10pm the previous night. No, he hadn't died of his wounds, there was water in his lungs, so died after he entered the water. A nasty blow to the head might have made him concussed and dizzy, he may have fallen in by himself. Gray stood looking at the scene around him, trying to visualise what it would have looked like at night. Not too many streetlights and nobody around most likely to witness what had happened. Few houses along the front though. He turned to Cooper.

"I want you to arrange a house to house to see if anybody knows or saw anything at all." Cooper shrugged his shoulders and then turned and walked towards the two policemen from Brora already doing just that.

Twenty minutes later, while Gray was sill brooding over the death of a policeman, a police car pulled up alongside him. He looked up at the blue flashing lights on the car. A senior policeman got out and walked over to Gray.

"Got a bit of luck. A policeman, probably this one, called in a car that was being driven off at speed. We can contact the owner.

See if they saw anything."

"Yes, that could be a break. Sorry, I am a bit distracted, another case that may be linked or not to this one." Replied Gray.

"Have you been in *The Double Headed Eagle* yet?" He said nodding in its direction.

"No, but have heard it is expensive to eat there. Why do you ask?"

"One of my men has found the door unlocked. Place in darkness, want to come over and take a look with me?" Gray took a last look at the dark water and followed the man across to the restaurant. A policeman was standing guarding the entrance. He stepped aside to let the two men in. Once inside they could smell something that had burnt. Looking around for the lights, Gray found the switch and put them on. The other policeman was already moving towards the kitchen door. Gray realised that the smell of burning seemed to be stronger from that direction. He started to follow in the officers footsteps, but was stopped when the other policeman ran from the kitchen and out of the building. Gray turned and followed him outside. The officer was being sick in the verge.

"Something that bad inside?" he asked him.

"Don't go in there till forensics have finished with the scene of crime. Body, or what is left of it, tied to a chair and tortured. Face is hardly recognizable."

"Fingers might help, if we can lift some prints to look at records."

"Yea, but no fingers or thumbs or hands come to that."

"Oh." Gray turned and walked over to his car where Cooper was sat in the driving seat. "I thought I told you to…"

"You did, but as the Brora police are handling that very well, I just asked to be informed if they found out anything. Now where to?"

"Back to Golspie. I'll tell you about what Brora police have found in the restaurant. If you have a strong stomach for that sort of thing, that is." Cooper nodded and started the engine to drive south.

+

Bill and Jane had risen early. Once they had eaten, both walked along to the police station. After asking about Gray at reception, they were shown into his office. He and Cooper were in deep conversation about something. Both men looked up as they entered the office.

"Morning. Is there something we can do for you or is it a social visit?" asked Gray.

"Something we forgot to mention last time we were here. A couple of things actually."

"Spit it out then."

"We visited *The Double Headed Eagle Restaurant* early last night. A few people in it, but no sign of staff or managers. After a while, the two groups of other people left. One mentioned that it was odd the stuff hadn't turned up. The other group mentioned Nigg was the place to go to."

"Hear that Cooper? Nigg again. I think a return trip is in order." He turned to Bill and Jane. "To bring you up to speed, a body has been found, handless and his face unrecognisable, in the kitchen, tied to a chair. Forensics are looking at the scene as we speak. But not very hopeful of finding anything. Do you want to come to Nigg?" He looked hopefully at them. Bill looked at Jane, she shrugged and nodded her agreement.

"Yes please. Where abouts is it?" asked Bill.

"Follow the main road south, after you cross the new bridge, turn left and at the next roundabout take first proper turning off it. Keep on the road. It'll be signposted from the roundabout." Gray grabbed his jacket and followed Cooper out of the office. After a few minutes, Bill and Jane followed as well.

Three quarters of an hour later, the two cars were parked

outside the small row of houses. Gray had already started to walk up the side of the house. He peered over the garden fence. A circle of black ash marked where the bonfire had been, but there was not much ash left at all. He pushed the small garden gate open and went into the garden. Round the front, Cooper was banging on the door of the house. Since he was getting no answer, he walked around to join where Gray was. Who was now taking a keen interest in some plastic farm bags lying by the back door.

"Smell that Cooper." He opened a bag and passed it to Cooper.

"Drugs?" Guessed Cooper.

"Let's ask our two friends, shall we?" Gray grinned and took the bag out to Bill and Jane. They took one sniff and confirmed it had been used for storing some drugs. "Right then. Let's get a warrant to search the whole place. Inside and out. And if we find as much as a..." he was interrupted by an older man wheeling a squeaking wheelbarrow into the garden. "And who might you be?" Asked Gray.

"Just a neighbour. She lets me take the ashes for my garden. I grow things you see. She doesn't want the ash, no need of it." He pushed the barrow over to the wall and upended it. Leaving it there, he turned to leave them.

"Not so fast. Do you know where she is?"

"She doesn't live here full time. Just pops over now and again. I've got her address in the house somewhere. Do you want me to find it for you?"

"Please, that would be very helpful indeed." Said Cooper with a smile. He watched as the man left them and walked next door. "See that Cooper? A helpful neighbour, one who might lead us to the first link of the chain. Gray looked across at Bill and Jane, wondering, not for the first time, what did they really want up here. The neighbour returned clutching a small bit of torn paper.

"I've written her name and her address and phone number

on the two sides of this paper." He thrust the piece of paper towards Gray, who took it somewhat carefully before putting it in his notebook. Cooper watched all this, while trying to keep from grinning.

"Well thank you very much. It will be most useful." He nodded a dismissal to the old man. Then turned and started to walk back to the car. Bill and Jane moved closer to the pair of them.

"Well, did you get anything useful DI Gray?" asked Bill.

"Think so, an address and phone number of the owner of the house. We'll head back and look into it. See what sort of person we are dealing with here." He ducked down and got into the car. Then leaning out of the open window looked across at Jane. "How well do you know the layout of the former *Royal East Sutherland Hotel*?"

"A bit, why?"

"I want Cooper and a few officers to go and check the place out. I think it is being used by somebody. Probably best to speak to the firm selling it. They will have a board up somewhere or other." He smiled and turned to Cooper. "When you get back, round up some bodies and get the hotel searched from top to bottom. I want to know what is going on up there. Also get a really strong seal for the door. Not just a padlock which can be replaced easily. Now let's get going." He got in the car with Cooper and drove off at speed. Bill looked at Jane and grinning they got into their car and followed them out on to the main road to Tain.

Chapter 18

The East Sutherland Hotel (Disused)

Bill had driven directly to the Hotel. He swept the car around in the half circle and pulled in near to the side door. Jane had suggested stopping at the apartment for some refreshment. She had said that they would be early and they were the first to arrive. Getting out of the car, she could faintly hear some noise coming from the direction of the hotel.

"Do you hear that Bill?"

"Some sort of noise coming from the hotel I think." He moved a bit closer to the side door and the noise became louder. "Someone or something is inside." Moving close to the door he leaned against it and shouted through the crack around the doorframe. "We'll get you out in a minute. Just be patient." It went quiet inside and Bill moved away to speak to Jane. "We wait till Cooper and the other police get here. We don't have a clue as to who or what is inside do we?" She nodded her approval. Moving further back to take in the view of the hotel and the Broch on its mound beside the hotel. Not looking where she was going, she nearly fell after tripping on a wooden sign that lay on the ground. Covered in fast growing weeds, it was difficult to see what was written on it. Bill came up to her as she was about to pull some of the weeds off the sign.

"Don't touch it." He said loudly. Jane withdrew her hand as though it had been red hot.

"It's only weeds."

"Right enough, but you might like to cast your memory back to a certain death that was caused by a weed growing somewhere near the hotel."

"Oh, I'd forgotten about that. Sheepsbladder or something like it. It'll come to me in a minute or two." She sat on the grass. "So, are you going to be a gentleman and help me up?" She asked with a smile. Bill reached out his hand, but before he could do as she asked, Jane had pulled him down to her level. "Be quiet. A car has just come in the drive. It doesn't look like Cooper or the police."They both now crawled back under the shrubs that had been allowed to grow unchecked. A rough gap opened up behind the shrubs and both of them stood up, breathing heavily. Then they slowly crept towards the entrance of the drive, hoping to flag down Cooper.

Jane had been right, it wasn't Cooper or the Police. 'The Boss' had returned to let the Manager out. As he walked up to the door, he spotted the car parked nearby.

"Whose is that?"

"No idea Boss. It was the same one that was here last night. Whoever owns it, probably has long gone by now."

"Maybe. But let's not get too carried away with ourselves. Go and check the drive and then do a circle of the hotel itself. If then, you don't find anybody, I'll know you are right." He bent down to the padlock and undid it. He pushed the door open and was surprised to see the man now still strapped to the chair, but lying on his back, just inside the door. 'The Boss' lent down and picked up the chair, replacing it in the upright position. Then clapped slowly at the man. "Thought you could escape, how long have you been lying there?"

"Just since you opened the door and sent me flying."

"Not intended." He leaned in close to the man's face. "Now, listen and listen good, I hate having to repeat myself. You are to go back to *The Double Headed Eagle* and carry on working there. Any information you find out about the owners, you give it to me or my two men. Understand?"

"Yes. But he will kill me if he finds out."

"Then you had better make sure he doesn't find out."

"Find out what Boss?" asked one of his two men, who had just entered the room and caught the last bit of the conversation.

"Never you mind. This one is going back to the restaurant. You two can take him there. Anybody outside?"

"Not that we could see. The place is huge though, you could hide an army in the shrubs."

"Ok, go ahead and take back. Wait a minute, where is his car?"

"What do you mean Boss?"

"Well, he didn't walk here did he? Go and look for it." The two men left the room muttering to themselves.

Unknown to any of them, the car had been stolen by some youngsters out for a bit of fun. Well, with the keys in the ignition still, it was asking to be stolen.

A few minutes later, they both returned. A look at them satisfied 'The Boss' that they would have found it, had it still been there. He bent down low again.

"How far is it to Brora do you think?"

"About three miles." 'The Boss' bent down and undid the rope holding him to the chair.

"Better get going then, if you have a three mile walk ahead of you." He lifted the man off the chair and pushed him out of the hotel. Herbert started to turn back, but then, changing his mind, decided to start walking. He set off down the side of the hotel, figuring that a walk along the beach might be the quickest and certainly the safest way to get to *The Double Headed Eagle.*

Outside, Jane and Bill had just managed to stop Cooper from sweeping up the drive. He and the other police had pulled in at the layby opposite. Now they were walking slowly up the drive, while keeping under the cover of the shrubs to avoid being seen.

Once at the hotel, Cooper directed half his men to go around the back and half to follow him around the front. Bill and Jane kept back to watch from a safe distance.

Inside the three men were stood talking, when a young policeman peered around the door. 'The Boss' was first to act. Swiftly he pulled a knife and flung it towards the policeman, aiming at the doorframe. The young policeman ducked and backed out. Once he had done so, one of the henchmen ran to the open door to close it, only to have his arm grasped by an out of sight policeman and yanked outside. Realising that they would soon be outnumbered, 'The Boss' grabbed the torch off the floor and ran towards the door leading from the kitchen and out on to the hallway. His henchman, grabbing the chair, ran after him, and once through the door wedged the chair under the handle. Then, breathing heavily, he turned to see where his boss was. He was bent down on the stairs, fiddling with something. Running over, he saw that he had pushed a knot in the wood of the stairs. The bottom three treads moved quietly outwards.

"Get in, I can close it once we are inside." Said the 'The Boss'. Wasting no time, the henchman crouched down and climbed inside." They could hear the police trying to break the door down. 'The Boss' followed him in and grabbing a handle on the inside pulled the stairs in after them. A catch clicked them firmly into place. Both men moved back from the stairs as the sound of running feet could be heard in the dark empty hall.

"Ok. We have the place surrounded. Now spread out and check every room and floor. They must be here somewhere." A sound of doors being opened and closed reverberated around the hotel. Both men kept quiet but made their way slowly away from the stairs. A passageway lead them downwards to a door.

"How long have you known about this?"

"Not that long. That reminds me, where did you put the body eventually?"

"Up in the cupboard on the second floor. Why?"

"Well, if the police are as good as they say, they will find it and probably stay for quite a while." He put his torch on for a few seconds to reveal a large key hanging by a light switch. "Good, I was told this leads to the cellars. But we will wait, in case the police check there first." He put out the torch and the two of them sat down on the ground.

+

In the hotel, somebody had manged to get the electric working again. Lights came on in various rooms and stairs were partially lit. With lights on, the police worked more systematically through the hotel room by room. Bill and Jane, as requested, were there as well. They had both decided, that the best use of their knowledge about the hotel was to go to the top and work downwards to meet the other police coming upwards. It was only a matter of a few minutes before a shriek from Jane brought Bill and Cooper running to her. In front of her a cupboard door was swung open and on the ground, lying face downwards, was the dead body of a man. A man who had been obviously been tortured before he died. Bill ran across to her.

"You ok?"

"Yes, I didn't expect there to be a body inside the cupboard, so when I opened the door and it fell out onto me."

"Quite understandable." Said Cooper, as he radioed in to Golspie that a body had been found. "We need to preserve the scene, so I want everybody to move backwards, away from the body."They all did as he suggested. Then one of the policemen brought out some tape and cordoned off the area.

"I wonder who it is?" said Jane out loud.

"We'll just have to wait and see." Replied Bill and took a last look at the body before going down the stairs to continue searching for the two men.

+

Herbert was more than half-way to Brora. Both weakened by his uncomfortable night and lack of food, he was now stumbling on the stones that formed part of the beach. Aware the tide was coming in fast, he carried on wearily placing one foot in front of the other.

Chapter 19

A flat in Invergordon

Tracy reached for her phone as she sat on the settee in her Invergordon flat.

"Hello?"

"Tracy, it's your neighbour from Nigg."

"Nothing wrong I hope?"

"No, it's just to say that the Police have been here and want to contact you. I have given them your details. I hope that is alright?"

Inwardly cursing to herself, she stood up and walked across to get her car keys.

"That's ok. Did they say what they wanted?"

"Not to me. I did the right thing, I hope?"

"Yes. Don't worry I'll sort things out." She hung up and left the flat to head to Nigg. She began to worry about what they might want or find. Better to have a good clear out before they searched the place, she thought and drove along the high street to the ironmongers to collect a few bits and pieces.

Half an hour later Tracy let herself in to the house and starting at the top, cleared anything that might lead the police back to her new business. She hadn't stored too much of her own stuff here. Using a couple of the rooms. A short while later, there were five black bin bags sitting in the hall. She was busy cleaning the floor with bleach and already had done the bathrooms. Anywhere where she had been, she cleaned.

+

In the former *East Sutherland Hotel,* nothing else had been found. Most of the police had returned to their bases and just Cooper, Bill, Jane and the forensic team remained. Cooper and Bill and

Jane were stood outside the hotel. Now draped with blue and white police tape all around the building. Jane looked across the front drive with its overgrown shrubs and trees.

"Who owns this now it is closed?" she asked.

"The Bank." Replied Cooper, having already found that out.

"Why doesn't anybody buy it then?" asked Bill.

"The history of the two deaths doesn't help sell it. The best thing would be to pull it down and leave it empty. Trouble with that is the cost of getting rid of the rubble. The bank wouldn't pay and I can't see anybody else doing that, can you?"

"Suppose not." Said Jane. "Though it might make a nice house for a large family."

"If we can return to reason we are all here. Where did those two men get to? We have searched the place from top to bottom, even the basement. No sign of them. It's as if they vanished into thin air." Said Cooper.

"Well they can't have disappeared. There must be another way out of the building that we just don't know about yet." Said Bill. "What about taking a look at the original drawings for the hotel. Surely the planning department might still have a set somewhere." Jane said with sudden thought.

Had the police arranged for somebody to stay in the basement, they would have witnessed a door set high up above some shelves, opening and two dusty men climb down from it into the basement. Both men dusted down their trousers with their hands. Then silently walked over to the door leading up to the hotel kitchen. 'The Boss' leant against it, to see if he could hear any voices. Nothing appeared to be the case, as he swung the door open. They walked quickly up the flight of stairs, where a door led into the kitchen. Opening the door carefully, the two men appeared in the kitchen. Nobody saw them leave the kitchen and go up to the side door. 'The Boss' lifted the latch, but it didn't open.

"Hell, they must have locked it."

"So now we are trapped in here."

"No, there must be another way or means of getting out of here." Muttered 'The Boss'. They retraced their steps and in the basement found a length of metal propped up by the fuse box. Taking it back with them, they approached the door again and this time looked at the hinge side of the door. Eight rusty screws held the two bracket hinges in place. Smiling now, the two men attacked the two hinges with renewed strength. A short while later, they pushed the door forward and found them both emerging into the fresh air. Cautiously peered through the bushes and saw that their car was still where they had left it. 'The Boss' felt in his pocket and found the keys. Passing them across, he indicated that he would go around the back of the building and his henchman could meet him on the far side in the car. He turned and started to walk around the back as arranged. The Henchman, gathering up his jacket, walked straight to the car and got in, then turning on the ignition, he did a large U turn and drove to the other side of the drive where the Boss stood in the undergrowth waiting.

Bill looked across as the car engine started and then the car roared across the drive, not a hundred yards from where they stood talking.

"What the hell?" he exclaimed. Then started to run towards the car.

"You'll never catch them." cried Jane as she took out her notebook and pen ready to note the number down as it roared past them and down the drive and out onto the main road. Bill returned to her, panting heavily.

"Did you get the number?"

"Yes. Cooper is calling it in, as we speak. They'll not get far today."

"Let's hope so."

In the car, 'The Boss' looked back through the window, he had seen the woman note the car number plate. Concerned, he tapped his henchman on the elbow.

"We have to get rid of the car, they noted the number plate as we went past them". The driver slowed down as they approached Golspie and swung hard right, turning up the small slope that led through the housing estate above the village. He zigzagged through the small roads and back down and out along Back Road. Now back on the A9, he drove towards Tain and the garage where the car could be hidden out of sight, for the short term, before they worked out how to dispose of it.

The Police radio crackled and Cooper acknowledge it before listening to the message. Putting the radio away, he looked at Bill and Jane.

"They got through Golspie. A roadblock was set up, but not far enough out to stop them." He sighed ruefully. "Gray is not going to like this one little bit."

+

In Brora, on the beach, Herbert struggled up the last few steps and onto the area near the old listening post. Sitting down for a rest. He looked at the deserted building and wondered if it might do as a base for the man behind the restaurant. After a few minutes he rose and walked the few remaining yards to *The Double Headed Eagle*.

Outside *The Double Headed Eagle,* in an unmarked car, sat Gray. He had wanted to return to the restaurant and see what the team had found. Since reporting the body with the hands cut off, the place had been gone over with a fine tooth comb and then left as it had been found. The body had been taken away, but the blood and other marks had, at his instructions, been left in situ. They wanted to know who really ran something that was a lot bigger than just the restaurant. He watched as Herbert walked up to the door and entered the building. Then he got out of his car and sauntered across and into the building. As he suspected, the man was in the kitchen. Peering through the circular window of the door, he saw the man squat down and run his finger in the blood on the floor, before getting up and moving towards the fat fryer where a two pronged kitchen instrument still lay in the fryer. Herbert, picked it up and whirled round as Gray entered the kitchen.

"Who are you? What do you want? You shouldn't be here."

"Who am I?" Gray reached into his jacket and produced his warrant card. "What do I want? The truth for a change. Who do you really work for and the real reason for opening a high class restaurant in East Sutherland? Now I need some answers and fairly quickly too. The people who came here, didn't ask for a meal, they are not nice people to deal with. That is blood on the floor. Now start to tell me what is really going on." The look on Herbert's face, should have told Gray something was amiss, but he failed to recognise the signs.

+

In Tain, the car had been garaged and a new one 'borrowed' to drive 'The Boss' through to Dornoch. Now sat in the flat, he looked again at the man in front of him.

"So, all we know is that one of ours has been caught by the police. The Police have searched the old hotel but not found our escape means. They have the number of the car, but that can be dealt with later. And the manager knows we are on his back for information. Go back to the restaurant and see if he has found out anything. Take the train."

"But Boss, there is no train from Dornoch. I could get a car from the car hire centre in the square. Have you got any false documents though?" Without saying anything, he watched as 'The Boss' went to a briefcase and took out some paperwork. He tossed it over.

"Use that. Then get going. I am going to phone Klaas, our little Dutch friend." He watched as his man ran out of the room and down the stairs. Then he went and picked up the phone and dialled the number, one that he unfortunately, knew off by heart.

+

A voice behind Gray made him turn around. In the doorway stood a large man. He looked at Gray then at Herbert before returning his gaze back to Gray.

"What have you done with him?"

"With whom?" asked Gray. "And who are you?" The man leaned in close to Gray and whispered in his ear.

"You, get out of here." He pushed Gray out of the kitchen towards the main door. Then turned back towards Herbert. "Well, what have you done with him?"

"I don't know what you are talking about. I run the place, but have only just got back. I left in rather a hurry yesterday. A few customers and staff were here then. Now nobody is here."

"My," he paused. "associate and myself were here. He was taken into the kitchen. Now where is the body?"

"Body? What Body?"

"Herge. Now there can't be many places to hid a body in a restaurant can there?" He moved to the oven and opened the door to peer inside, before shutting it again. "Not there." He looked around the kitchen. "Maybe the freezer?" Taking a look, he opened and shut it again. "You need to tidy up. Look at this blood on the floor. It should have been mopped up a long time ago. Untidy wouldn't you say? Maybe we should get some hot water boiling to clean things up? What do you think?" He moved across and put the gas rings on, then waited for a few minutes. "Shall I light a match he asked, as the smell of gas started to fill the area near them." Herbert shook his head in fear. "Pardon, I didn't quite hear that." The man took a box of matches off a nearby shelf.

"No. Don't do that. Turn the gas off. You'll kill us both. Open a window or something." He watched as the man bent down to the oven, then taking his chance, he ran out into the restaurant. Flinging open the main door, he was confronted by Gray again. "He's mad, he has turned the gas on and is talking about lighting a match. Get me out of here now. Please. Grabbing the man by his wrist, Gray half ran and half dragged him across to his car. Once inside he drove off towards the old village. Had they waited a few minutes, they would have seen another man arrive and enter the restaurant.

Inside, the Dutchman was angry that he had let Herbert escape. Venting his anger, he decided to smash up the kitchen. He had only just got started when he became aware that somebody was looking at him.

"And you are?" He asked as he stood in the middle of the kitchen.

"One of The Boss's men. What have you done with the manager?"

"I haven't done anything with him. I was talking to him, trying to make him explain where the body was."

"Body? What body?"

"My work mate. Herge. Two men came and took him and tortured him, before probably killing him. I was told to get out, if I knew what was good for me. What do you know about it?"

"Not a lot. I need to speak to the manger to find out who he is working for."

"But you said you were one of the bosses men?" He looked puzzled.

"Ah, you think I work for the same man as you?" He watched as the other man nodded. "Sorry, I work for THE BOSS." Stressing the words as he spoke. He watched as the other man looked a bit down. Then he asked him. "So, who is your boss?

The Dutchman?"The man nodded and said nothing more. "And the missing manager?"

"He fled when I went to the oven to turn off the gas."

"Right. How convenient. Now this is what we are going to do. Both of us will leave the place and go our separate ways. We will both tell our respective bosses, exactly the same thing, namely there is no body on the premises and the manager has gone away somewhere we don't know about. Agreed?" He watched as the other man nodded and then both of them walked out, turning off the lights and pulling the doors closed behind them.

Chapter 20

Amsterdam

On Klaas's barge, his phone rang.

"Yes?"

"There is no body at the restaurant. No sign of the manager, either. What do you want me to do? The place was empty but unlocked."

"Apparently, there is supposed to be a key stored at the back door. You find it and secure the place. I don't want the police or anybody else for that matter to be getting in there. Then the pair of you come back to the barge." He hung up and drummed his fingers on the desk. Not going too well, he thought to himself.

+

The Boss's phone rang. He grabbed it off the desk.

"Yes?"

"I've been to the restaurant, nobody there, no sign of the manager either. What do you want me to do now Boss?"

"Get back here soon as you can."

+

In Golspie Police Station, Cooper sat at his desk. He was busy writing up his report and filing paperwork. He looked up as Gray came up to his desk.

"What's up?"

"We have the Manager of *The Double Headed Eagle* in the interview room. Perhaps you had better come in with me to interview him?"

"How come?"

"Think we are the least unpleasant of the various options that he has open to him. We may get a break if we can find out who is behind the business and what it is really run for, other than rich expensive food, I mean." Cooper got up and followed Gray out of the room.

+

The Russian drummed his fingers along the table. He hadn't heard anything since asking that two bit manager to get rid of the competition. He hadn't heard back from his two usual men either, now starting to feel uneasy about things, he pressed the button on his large desk. The door opened and his secretary peered around it into the room.

"Did you want something?"

"Yes, did you ever get a report from the two men in the North of Scotland or that two bit manager of the restaurant in Brora?"

"Not that I can recall. I'll go and check for you." The door closed. A few minutes later, his phone rang.

"Yes?"

"Nothing to report at all from either of them." The Russian replaced the receiver and sat back thoughtfully in his chair. Then picked up the receiver and spoke to his secretary again.

"Get me a quick private flight to Inverness and a safe car once there. I need to get to Brora somehow." Then, replacing the receiver, wondered why it was so becoming so much bother to start up in that remote part of the world.

Patrick looked at the men around him.

"Well? Anybody got any good ideas? We seem to have lost track of Herbert, manager of *The Double Headed Eagle.* The Police are looking closely at the hotel. Though I doubt they will find the way out that we used. Once the fuss has died down, I may consider buying it. I need a new base."

"What about the flat in Dornoch?" Asked one of the men. The glare he got from the other man was enough for him to not speak again.

"Too public. No, it needs to be either Helmsdale, Brora or

Golspie. One of the three. Brora was ideal, being between Golspie and Helmsdale. However, this hotel is large enough to run as a business and for me to run the other side as well. I may need to get other finance though, that is the problem." He rubbed his chin and thought of Klaas, would he go into business with him though?"

In Nigg, Tracy had finished cleaning the house, the bags by the front door had been transferred to the car. She could just about sit inside it to drive to the nearest tip. Taking a last look around the house, she stepped outside and locked the front door. As she turned around, a man stood right in front of her. She hadn't heard him come up the path.

"Need some help?" She asked him.

"Not me, you might though." He jerked his hand at her car. "Packing up and leaving?"

"No, just a clear out if it is any of your business, that is. Now if you will just let me pass." She made to push past him, but he put his hand out and held it against her chest.

"You aren't going anywhere just yet. At least, not without my say so. We are taking a quick trip out to sea." He grabbed her wrist and twisting her arm behind her back, marched her down to the boat tied up near the beach. Once on board the boat, he untied the mooring rope and pushed the engine up a few notches as it roared around in a semi-circle and out towards Cromarty. Once halfway across, he cut the engines and the boat just bobbed on the dark water. "See this?" He pointed at the water."Very deep here. Nobody would find you again. A word of friendly advice." He looked at Tracy, who was sat on the floor of the boat terrified. "You are to get out of your new business, against the bigger boys, you don't stand a chance. Do you understand me?" She nodded her head furiously.

"Good. Then I'll suggest to my boss that there is a nice flat for sale in?" He paused and looked at her. "Well?"

"Invergordon" She said, terrified.

"Invergordon. Nice place. You can have this place if you want." He waved his hand towards the Nigg property. She nodded. Anything would be better than being thrown overboard she thought to herself. He bent down and pushed the throttle in and swung the boat around in a large semi-circle before heading back.

Twenty minutes later, he had dropped Tracy off and was heading back out to sea. He had been bluffing, but now knew something that his boss back in Amsterdam didn't, namely a flat in Invergordon. He spun the keys to the flat in one hand as the other expertly steered the craft towards a small pier about six miles north of Invergordon.

In her car, Tracy didn't waste any time, but drove straight to the flat. The set of keys she had given the man, were not the ones for the flat. She knew though that once he found that out, he would soon break in and no way did she want to be present when he found that out. Grabbing a few personal items, she threw them into a small case. Then realised that she couldn't get anything in the car, at least not until the car had been emptied. She wedged her case behind the dustbins, they had already been emptied, so it was unlikely that anybody would go looking there. Then she went back to her car and drove as quickly as she could to the tip.

It had been lucky for her that nobody was in front of her at the refuse centre. Having been to the flat she now had to get back to Nigg. Her next supply of stock was going to be delivered there she had remembered. But first she drove up to the quarry to see if her order was ready.

Patrick phoned Klaas and heard the phone ringing. After a short while it was picked up.

"The Boss here, wonder if you would like to join me in a new venture."

"How much?"

"Forty percent from you, sixty percent from myself."

"Just what is this new venture?" Klaas asked.

"A break from our usual jobs, more of a cleaning job."

"A cleaning job? What makes you think that I would be interested in a cleaning job?"

"Cleaning as in Laundry C L E A N I N G, capital letters." Patrick waited hoping that Klaas would get the meaning now. Honestly, he thought to himself, some people are really slow.

"Ah, you mean like laundering old stuff and making it as new again?"

"Right. Are you in or not then?"

"Fifty per cent each."

"Forty five to Fifty five, I got the idea didn't I?"

"Yes, but you don't have enough money, or you wouldn't be reaching out to ask me." Klaas smiled grimly down the phone.

"Alright, Forty nine to Fifty one?"

"You have heard my terms. Fifty-fifty or not at all. Phone me back if you agree in the next twenty four hours."The Dutchman replaced the phone and took out a cigar and unwrapped it before lighting it and savouring the aroma.

Patrick replaced his phone and sat back. Ok, the terms were not great, but he still needed to get the fifty percent somehow. He scratched the back of his head and then remembered a few contacts from both Folkestone and Oxford who might be persuaded to come on board with the ready money. Smiling now, he leant forward and picked up the phone again.

Having learnt that the rocks were now ready for her. Tracy had arranged for them to be collected. The owner hadn't batted an eyelid, but had reached out and taken the bundle of money she had produced. Somehow she doubted that all of it would find its way onto the financial books. Now driving back to Nigg. Pity that her flat had gone, but she still had some place she could call her own. She parked her car at the back, not wanting to draw too much attention to her neighbours before letting herself in through the back door. She flopped down in a chair in the kitchen and spreading her arms out on the table in front of her, went to sleep.

Chapter 21

Oxford City Centre

In Oxford, a row had developed between the four graduates that supplied the students with the drugs. They had run out three days ago and despite regular phoning, they had failed to make contact with 'The Boss'. The students were getting restless and starting to turn nasty.

The phone rang in the flat in London, but the owner, being in Dornoch failed to hear it or the message that was left.

At Inverness Airport a small private plane chartered in Russia, landed and taxied over to the refuelling part of the airfield. Nobody got out or in of the plane. After an hour, it asked for permission and took off, heading northwards. It's filed flight plan was for going to Shetland. As far as air traffic control were aware, there was no problem with it or any of the cargo it purported to be carrying. If the business in Shetland wanted a new kitchen designed by a Russian business who were they to ask questions?

On board the plane, the Russian leaned forward and touched a button on the arm of the seat to call the steward.

"How long till we get to Dornoch?" he asked her, once she had appeared by his seat.

"About half an hour or so. Do you want transport arranged to meet you?"

"Yes." Nodding to show that was all, she turned and went back to wherever they stayed when the plane was flying. He put his head back and thought of the large amount of money that he had invested in East Sutherland over the last few years. Had it been all a waste, he wondered as he closed his eyes.

He awoke as the plane touched down on the grass of Dornoch airstrip. Nobody was around. He rose and walked to the exit door, a set of steps had been pushed out and his case was already waiting for him at the doorway of the plane. Picking it up, he stepped quickly down off the plane and across to the waiting black car. As soon as he had left, the plane took off and headed for Shetland. A small blip on an air traffic controllers screen, which with a bit of luck, would have gone unnoticed.

The car drove into the centre of Dornoch and as it passed the flat he had tried unsuccessfully to buy. He looked over and saw lights on. Maybe he would call and make an offer for it. Most people had their price he had found over the years. Turning towards the man in the seat beside him he bent forward so that the driver didn't hear him.

"Do we know yet who the new owner is?"

"I've not heard anything. I thought you were dealing with it?"

"I asked the manager of the restaurant, Herbert, to deal with it."

"Do you think he did?"

"He said he had. I asked for the photos, you know, for my collection. Herbert said he would get them sent to me."

"The place was in darkness when we last saw it. Locked up. Police tape across the front door too."The Russian rubbed his chin thoughtfully. He could buy the police in Russia, now Scotland, that was a different kettle of fish entirely. He leant forward and tapped the driver on the shoulder.

"Let's go straight to *The Double Headed Eagle*. I'll see what way the land really lies." He sat back as the car surged forward northwards towards its destination.

Half an hour later, with the car parked on the road outside the restaurant. It's engine slowly cooled down and the sea salt breeze blowing across the harbour, the Russian stood looking at the place. Then he walked around the side and found the small key box. Tapping in the code, he flipped the lid down. Expecting to find a key, he was surprised that nothing had appeared. He returned to the car and looked in at the driver.

"You have anything that can open the side door, without too much noise or fuss?"The driver nodded and got out of the car. He made his way over and after a few minutes, swung the door open and stepped back to allow the Russian inside. Once inside, he felt for the light switch and flicked it on. Neon lights flickered on around the kitchen larder and in the kitchen as well. Grunting with satisfaction, the Russian made his way into the kitchen. On the floor were scattered various kitchen appliances, the oven was still on. On a wall opposite the range, a runny mess of liquid ran down to the floor. Squatting down, he ran his finger across the floor and then looked at it. It was pale red. Blood, he thought to himself and got up and walked through to the manager's office. There, things were tidy and a laptop computer sat on the desk, it's lid down. He flicked it up and a request for a password appeared before him. Sighing, he pushed it back down and looked around the room. It would take ages to sort through this, time he didn't have. Nor did he have the manpower over here to do it for him. Picking up the laptop, he strode through to the main restaurant and over to the main entrance. Blue and white police tape crisscrossed the doorway. He pushed it to one side and reached across to the door and unbolted it, before pulling them inwards and letting the Brora air come to the dusty room. If he had looked around the harbour, he may have seen a couple of men stood with binoculars focused on the doors to the restaurant stood on Golf Road looking down below. The two men smiled at one another and then went to their car to contact 'The Boss'.

Patrick put down the phone and stood looking at the room. Apparently, the Russian owner had been and looked inside his restaurant. Maybe he could deal with the Russian directly, cutting out the need to use the Dutchman at all. He looked at his watch and went down the stairs and out to eat at a local restaurant.

+

In Oxford at the *Horses Head* in Broad Street, the student, desperate for more of his drug of choice. Turned to his supplier.

"Why can't you get more of the stuff? I need it, we all do. No problem supplying it you said, well where is it then?"

"I've told you, I have a problem getting it into Oxford, I'll sort it, really I will."

"You've said that now for three weeks. There are other groups in Oxford who we can use you know."

"I'm aware of that." Stubbing out his cigarette, he looked at the thin face of the student. "You need to take more care of yourself, people will start to put two and two together. Now if you have finished?"

"We aren't finished by a long chalk. Get the stuff by Friday or else." Said the student shaking slightly.

"I'll do my best. Now stay out of my sight, I'll drop you a message when you can contact me. Check your mailbox daily." He rose as if to leave.

"Well, you'd better." The student rose from the table and walked back to his group of friends sat further back and muttered under his breath. "We need to deal with him, I think he is holding out on us. Meet me back here tomorrow evening around six.

Bill and Jane sat at a desk in Golspie Police Station. They had been allowed to sit in on the interview with Herbert, the manager of *The Double Headed Eagle*. He had been slow to talk at first, but now had released a whole lot of fresh information about who was really behind the venture. At the end of the interview, he had asked for police protection. Something that had been agreed. They had been told to return to London as word had it, something was brewing in Oxford.

"Better go and pack up our things." Said Jane.

"Gray will not be happy though." Replied Bill. "I do wonder why we are being called back though. I thought we had to work with the police up here. Something is not quite right." He looked across at Jane. She shrugged her shoulders.

"Are you suggesting we ignore our superiors request then?"

"Not exactly, one of us to return and the other to stay up here and keep an eye on things."

"I assume I'll be returning then?" Said Jane.

"Toss you for it." He brought out a coin and spun it into the air. "Heads or tails?"

"Heads." Bill uncovered his hand revealing a head. "You win. I'll go and pack." He tossed the coin towards her. "You might like to tell Gray when you see him, I found that on the ground outside the restaurant in Brora." Bill left the room and Jane looked down at the coin and picked it up and turned it over, on the reverse was another head. A Russian one.

In a cell in the Golspie Police Station a man was sat saying and doing nothing. Ever since he had been taken by the police from the hotel, he had said nothing. Even when they had charged him with breaking and entering, he had said nothing. 'The Boss' would fix things, of that he was certain. He just needed to wait and bide his time.

Had he known it, 'The Boss' wasn't even thinking about him. An angry phone call from one of his Oxford buyers had made him make up a list of things. He needed to contact the Russian, before returning to Oxford, he needed new supplier for the students. He wondered if anybody had yet found out who the new competitor was in this part of the world. He called one of his men over and told him to find out who or what was supplying East Sutherland at the moment. Then he picked up the phone and redialled a number that showed a missed call.

Sighing, he sometimes missed the easier life of the eighties.

The Dutchman's phone rang. He answered it straight away.

"Yes?"

"You called me. At least the number is showing that on my screen."

"Patrick. I understand you have an interest in the restaurant."

"Funny name for a restaurant owned by a Dutchman?"

"Like you, I need partners for finance and other things. We do try to please all our customers, both East and West if you get my drift?"

"I think so, so what do you want from me?"

"Have you seen Herbert?"

"Who?"

"Herbert Ross. He was the manager of the place. I can't seem to find him. Have you seen him recently?" He stressed the recently. 'The Boss' smiled as he recalled the man in the deserted hotel. He also recalled sending him back to the restaurant. The fact that he had gone missing now rather worried him. "Hello? Are you still there?" asked the Dutchman.

"Yes, still here. No, I have not seen him. I'll tell my staff to keep an eye open for him shall I? I'll phone you on this number if I hear of anything." Without waiting for an answer, he hung up. Now things were getting really busy he thought to himself.

Not for the first time, Cooper sighed as he watched the man through the spyhole of the cell. Not a word out of him. Not like the manager, now he was really spilling the beans. However, when you actually got down to it, there was not really that much new information. Yes, the police and locals had thought it was not owned by the manager, yes they had wondered about the foreign money being used. According to the manager, it was a profitable restaurant. One that had seen a gap in the market and carved a niche for itself. This was the tale he kept retelling again and again. Eventually, tired of hearing the same story,

Gray had suggested he be put up in a local hotel for a couple of nights. Under a new name of course. Cooper had seen that the manager had been booked into a room at the new hotel on the south side of Golspie. Part of a large chain of hotels, they had promised security and total discretion. Happy with that, he had escorted the manager to his room before leaving him for the night. Once back in the police station, he had filled in his reports and waited for Gray to update him. Cooper was still puzzled about the small pendant and pulled the file on it towards him to refresh his memory.

He was still reading about it, with a Russian dictionary propped open on his desk, when Gray tapped him on his shoulder, making Cooper jump.

"I didn't hear you come in Sir."

"Too engrossed, though in what, may I ask?"

"The pendant. I have looked up the Russian dictionary and also read up on this sort of pendant. I thought it may be Russian but the design is very unique. A firm that was based in Dingwall. They closed in the late eighties. Their speciality was a form of key. Unlike most keys that can be copied, they said that theirs was unique. Only one key, one lock. Very secure. So, if the pendant was a key to somewhere, then somebody would be really cross to lose it. They couldn't just go to an ironmongers and ask for a new one." Cooper looked at Gray, who was looking thoughtful.

"Very good Cooper. See if you can find out any more about the original firm, who holds the records for the company. Is there a list of its clients? That sort of thing. Very good indeed." He patted him on the back and walked over to his own desk.

Cooper reached for the phone and dialled the Dingwall Police.

"Hello DS Cooper speaking. I need to find out some background into a business that was based in Dingwall."

"Recent or older?"

"Older, why is that a problem?"

"No, just need to go to the records department. They are in a new building on the outskirts of Dingwall. It used to be a firm that made locks and such like. When they closed the police bought it and moved records into it."

"That's a coincidence, I wanted to find out about the old firm. Any records kept?"

"Come and take a look, but I warn you that nothing is in any real order. You may need a day or so." Cooper hung up and got up from his desk. He picked up the car keys and his jacket from around the back of the chair and left the station.

Two hours later, in a pair of old garages that had been knocked together, he was beginning to grasp the size of his problem. Boxes of all shapes and sizes were stacked on shelves, just dates were penned in on the end of the boxes. As he had been told, there was no particular order to the boxes. Sighing, he took off his coat and reached up for the first one that was undated. He looked inside and found old police notebooks. Curious, he took one out and opened it. Dated 1969. Rapidly closing it, he put the box back and took the next one down.

Eight hours later he found what he had been looking for. The boxes that he had been looking at, now all had what they contained written on the outside. Having gone and grabbed a felt tip pen to mark them with. Now he had three boxes of the firms records. Dated from 1937 when the business had been substantively enlarged to supply locks to the Armed Forces. He stood up and stretched, then went and brought his car close to the storeroom before loading it with the three boxes. He closed the door and went back inside to sign out the boxes and himself. Then he drove off in the direction of Golspie.

An hour later the boxes were all piled by his desk. Cooper had gone home as he would be having an early start next day.

Bill had packed the few remaining items and had arranged for a taxi to take him to Inverness. The hour or so it would take would be much less than going by train. He got in and Jane waved him off, before setting off back towards the police station.

The Russian had found himself a nearby hotel in Brora. Not wanting to be noticed he was pleased to see that they ran a few small cottages in the grounds of the hotel. He asked if they were empty? One was, came back the reply. Paying some money and signing a bit of paper, the keys fell neatly into his hand. He turned and left the hotel to find the cottage allotted to him.

Patrick leaned back in his chair and phoned his London contact, not only was he a good point of contact, he was a computer expert. A side that Patrick had found useful from time to time.

"Any news of new supplies? The customers in Oxford are getting a bit impatient, at least that is what I have been told."

"Somebody new, with cash, is buying up all the good stuff. Supposed to be in North Scotland Boss. Do you want me to look into the Oxford side of things for you?" Said Archie.

"Not at the moment. I'll enquire about the new person. Do you have a name for them?" 'The Boss' waite d as he heard the sound of keys being tapped on a keyboard.

"Tracy, Tracy, no surname. That is all the computer has at the moment. Wait a minute. Based in Invergordon. A flat in a new block. I'll send you the number by post. Too risky giving it over the phone." He hung up and the Boss looked at the phone before replacing his receiver. Tracy, Invergordon, who would have thought of basing themselves there he wondered to himself. Then he called one of his men through.

"I want you to find a person called Tracy, lives in Invergordon apparently in a new block of flats. Go and check them out, when you find her, ask her if she will come with you back to a meeting of, " he paused, "mutual minds. Well go on, don't just stand there." He watched as the man fled the flat and smiled to himself. Invergordon eh? Who would have thought it?

Tracy had been busy. Having taken delivery of the rocks, she had arranged for them to be dropped off halfway up the track to Ben Bhraggie. She had found a couple of disused old farm buildings. One, usefully had been halfway up the track to the top of Ben Bhraggie. A few phone calls had resulted in her getting a small contract to supply both wood lengths and small rocks and boulders for a new pathway to the Ben from the track halfway up. Her original plan was to build a legit business flying rocks and tree trunks for a few years. Then to develop her new illegal business alongside it. However, if things changed, well she could adapt as well. She had already arranged to sell the Nigg property and a surveyor was booked to attend today in the early evening. She watched as the helicopter flew overhead and dropped the bag of rocks neatly on the 'X' she had painted recently on the ground.

Chapter 22

London: Two weeks later

Bill sighed as another bundle of paperwork dropped on to his desk. The young officer grinned and walked away. Bill reached out his hand and took the top file off the pile. Placing it on his desk, he opened it without really bothering to look at the cover. The photo inside changed his mind at once. He flicked the cover back over and took in what he should have read the first time. In bold capital letters it said:

FOR YOUR INFORMATION.
ONLY PEOPLE LISTED BELOW TO HAVE ACCESS TO THIS FILE.
ONE HOUR TIMED USE STARTS ONCE SEAL BROKEN
DO NOT COPY IN ANY FORMAT.
WHEN FINISHED PLEASE USE THE DESTROY DOCUMENT BAG ATTACHED.

Inside the photo was of a body of a woman laying on a hillside. The next photo showed a partly decomposed body on another hillside. The following photos were of a pendant, a man's body and a car number plate along with two pictures of a boat. One called 'Bragging Rights' and another called 'Brora'. Bill switched his gaze from one photo to the other, it appeared to him to be the same boat, ok some bits had changed but enough remained to see the similarities between the two photos. A file of a few pages accompanied the pictures. Bending down to reach his coffee on the floor beside him, he took a sip and then set about reading what he could of the notes.

An hour later, he looked at his watch and looked at the file again. He had seen enough to remember what the gist was. He tore off the destroy document bag and put the pages and photos into it, then sealed it and left it beside the desk. Some cleaner would take it away and dispose of it he thought to himself. He needed to speak to Jane, but he needed to go to Oxford as well. Perhaps it was better that he stayed put for a day or so. What he had learned was going to change a lot of peoples perceptions.

Jane was bored. The case seemed to have come to a halt. The body in the cupboard of the boarded up hotel was found to be a man connected to the Dutch crime scene. Yet nobody could figure out what such a person would be doing in East Sutherland. *The Double Headed Eagle* had remained closed with no notice as to why. Cooper seemed engrossed these days in some pendant or other that had some Russian words on it. That was as much as she had managed to gleam from the other officers. She drummed her heels off the floor and looked up as DI Gray approached her desk.

"Wonder if you fancy a ride to Dornoch. A flat you may know about has been recently bought at auction. Today, we get the name of the buyer from the Scottish Land Register. Care to take a guess?" He watched as she looked at him.

"No idea sir. Yes, I would like to come to Dornoch if that is ok with you?"

"Come on then. Grab your coat." He led the way out to the cars at the back of the station. They sped out of Golspie and down the A9 towards the Mound and on to Dornoch. Gray turned off the main road once he had driven over the Mound, before the hairpin bends started to wind up the road in front of him. The narrow road stretched in front.

"Where are we?"

"This is the old railway track, it has been turned into a small road, it connects to Dornoch via the villages of Embo and Great Ferry. We are heading for Dornoch, but may return to Great

Ferry in due course." He concentrated as the passing places zipped along on both sides of the road. Eventually he pulled up at a small area that had been closed off with wire mesh. From the buildings that were inside the area, Jane could see it was an old railway station and other buildings. She nodded her head at the area.

"The old railway?" she guessed.

"Absolutely. They closed it down. Left the buildings and bits and pieces lying around. Sealed off the whole place. Not too secure, say compared with a certain hotel we know of. " He smiled at her.

"So why here Sir?"

"A piece of Russian newspaper was floating around the site. The date, according to Cooper, was two weeks ago. Now we have not heard or seen any sign of any Russians. Apparently, just over two weeks ago, a light plane, bound for Shetland, landed to refuel in Inverness before taking off again heading North."

"And the connection?" Jane asked wearily. Wondering where he was going with this.

"Plane flew along its flight path before vanishing for a few minutes and then reappeared again shortly afterwards. Landed in Shetland. From the time it left Inverness to when it dipped down, Air Traffic think it landed here in Dornoch, or very close to here. Long enough for somebody to get off or on it." He started the engine up and drove on through Dornoch heading towards the airfield. A few minutes later, Jane and Gray were both stood outside the metal hanger looking down the grass landing strip. Gray started to walk down the length of it, on one side. Jane, sighing, started to do the same on the other side.

"What exactly are we looking for Sir?"

"Anything that might be Russian or not Scottish at least." He smiled across at her, but she failed to notice it, as she was too intent on looking at a small plastic box lying in the ground.

"Over here Sir, I may have found something." He ran over and looked down at the box. The side had a label partly torn, in read on the remining bit: '........erry, Dornoch, United Kingdom.' A piece of green customs form was also attached. It read: ..or human use. Inside she could see the box was over half full of something.

"I'll get some gloves from the car." He ran over and then drove the car over to her. Carefully pulling on two gloves, he reached down and lifted it into the boot of the car. "We'll go to the flat, then drive to Invergordon, the centre is there for dealing with this. Whatever that is." He jabbed his finger towards the boot. "Hop in." Jane got in and looked around them. Apart from a possible golf enthusiast, the place was deserted. Perfect location for quick drop or pick up. Gray drove off, leaving the place to its peace and quiet, apart from a noisy 'fore' from a nearby player of the game golf.

The Russian, still in Brora, was on the phone to Russia. He had discovered that a small parcel of high quality pure opium had somehow not been transferred to him when he left the plane. While an easy mistake to make, it was a very costly one, especially if it got into the wrong hands. Any lab worth its salt, would soon realise what it had and inform somebody or other. He had pulled a few favours in and had everybody looking for the box, but now, two weeks later, still not a sign of it. Also, he had heard someone had started a helicopter flying rocks and tree trunks up onto the local hills. Why he wondered would anybody do that when humans could do the job just as well? Then he remembered that he was in the UK not Russia.

Tracy was happy, her Nigg property was on the market, true it had not yet sold, but in time it would. She had found a new property, it needed a bit doing to it, but it was situated on the main road leading into Golpsie. Ok, it needed a lot doing to it, the roof was missing for a start, but it was local to her work.

The contract for shipping the stones and tree trunks in had been a lifesaver. She watched as a new load was put down on the now well marked path with bags of rocks and small piles of tree trunks at regular intervals. The men who would construct the pathway would start working in two weeks time. Then maybe, she could start to run her second business. Tracy waved to the pilot, who dipped the helicopter nose in acknowledgment and peeled off towards Dornoch.

Bill left his desk that evening with the intention to drive to Oxford. He was walking down to the carpark, under the offices when a couple of men moved out from behind one of the pillars. They moved in close. Not close enough for him to do anything but listen.

"You called Bill?"

"Yes. And you are?"

"You don't need to know that. We have a message to deliver to you."

"Go ahead then." He folded his arms as if bored.

"You had a file today, a special one. We need a copy of it. A simple request. Think you can do that for us?"

"Not a chance. The file I think you are talking about has special attachments, it cannot be photocopied, it is marked as to who has had a copy. Sorry, but cannot help you I am afraid." He made to move away. One of the two stuck out his hand and stopped him.

"No is not an option. Two days, we will return and need to have that copy in our hands by then."

"It's impossible I tell you. I didn't even order the file, it came to me, and no name of who had ordered it for me on the cover."

"You do like your wife don't you?"

"Yes." He replied softly. "Why, what has she got to do with anything?"

"Do as we say, and nothing will be done to harm her.

Otherwise…" he laughed nastily and both men moved back into the shadows. Bill stood for a few minutes and then walked towards his car. The front and back tyres had been let down. Sighing, he unlocked the boot of the car. Inside was a note typed in capital letters.

DON'T THINK OF TALKING TO ANYBODY.

He took out the note, screwed it up and threw it onto the passenger seat. Then took out the foot pump and started to reinflate the tyres.

In Invergordon, the plastic box was now being closely examined. Jane and Gray were now heading back up the road to Great Ferry. This time Gray had driven into Dornoch and out down towards the track that led to the village. He turned sharp right at the bottom of the hill and after about a hundred yards pulled up alongside a derelict house, next to a couple of other houses and a petrol station and, surprisingly, a shop that was open. A woman came out and offered to fill the car up while they shopped. Nodding his agreement, they both went into the shop and made a few purchases. Having paid for them and the fuel, they drove on a bit further and parked at the edge of the water, a series of tree stumps stood on either side of the water. Gray nodded at them.

"The remains of the pier on this side. It used to ferry cars and people across the water to the other side. Little Ferry. Since the road has been improved, the ferry has closed. A few villagers remain on both sides, but for how long?" Sensing it was a rhetorical question, Jane remained silent. "Anyhow, the reason we are here is that somebody has been seen hanging around here at night. Somebody who drinks vodka."

"How do we know that Sir?"

"Shop has sold ten bottles over the last two weeks. It previously sold one bottle in five years. Had to order some more in. Now who buys vodka on that scale, unless they are either having a party or Russian."

"Do they live around here?"

"That we don't know, yet. But we may tonight. I want to return with you and Cooper and we will stake the village out. There is only the one road, so anybody can only come out the same way they went in."

"Ok, but why tonight?"

"It's because the shopkeeper informs me that the buyer comes every three days, tonight is three days since he last bought some." He popped a grape into his mouth and walked along the road, through the village and back to the car. "See it's not that large an area. We'll catch the person and bring them in for questioning."

"For what reason Sir?"

"Drunk in a public place to start with." He smiled and started the engine. "Well get back in, unless you want to stay here?" Jane shook her head and got in, the car roared off towards Golspie.

In his small cottage, the Russian was looking at the row of empty vodka bottles lying in a heap at the base of the fireplace. He had bought a bottle at the hotel, but the look he had received had made him get one of his men to try and bring some in from Dornoch. Frustrated, he had phoned a contact in London to see if they could find out where Patrick was holed up. It had been three weeks since he had been approached about taking out 'The Boss', to make way for a clear run of carving up the far north between him and his associates. He had learned from London, the police had been compiling a file about a series of events that had been taking place in and around East Sutherland and Ross-shire. He had asked that a copy be obtained and sent to him. Far too much interest he thought to himself. He reached for the bottle, but found it empty. He flung it angrily at the fireplace, hoping it would smash, but it just glanced off the wooden frame and joined its brothers in the heap at the bottom.

Bill had driven home to their flat. Now changed and packed, he had phoned to arrange for a hire car to be delivered to his home address. His own car would be stored at the hire car's offices while he was away. The front doorbell rang. He walked down the corridor and peered through the spyhole, you couldn't be too careful, it was the car hire man. He opened the door and signed the paperwork. Then handing his own car keys over, he picked up his suitcase and rucksack and left the flat. He was going to Oxford. Word had it that there was some unrest with the students, not that that was unusual. It just might have a connection with the drug smuggling. Hence his drive there. He had posted a note about being threatened to Harvey, his Line Manager, to keep him in the loop.

Patrick had decided that not being able to contact the Russian, he may as well go to London and collect some product to take to Oxford. One problem was that he couldn't go by boat anymore and would need to arrange a new safe place to hand over stock. No matter, he would sort that problem out when it arose. In the meantime, he had settled back and was being driven to Oxford. Twelve hours they had estimated it would take. Quicker if he took a turn at driving, so with two drivers up front, he could relax for now.

Chapter 23

Invergordon

The Lab in Invergordon started work early. In reality, it never closed, but the main staff only worked from eight in the morning to seven at night. A small skeleton staff were on call during the night. Now as the main staff arrived, the first thing that greeted them was a plastic box with a note from Golspie requesting it be given priority. With murmurs of ill grace, two of the staff set to analysing the box. Ten minutes later they started to examine the contents. Half an hour later they phoned Golspie.

Cooper was sat looking at a file from one of the three boxes he had recovered. While most of the work was traditional locks and keys, a Russian who had managed to get a boat out of Russia before the Germans had arrived, had brought with him some tools and some Amber. A difficult material to work with, he had in his own time fashioned three slightly different pendants, one lock that needed all three to open the boxes. The sequence of the keys were different for each box. So box one might be say, A B C but box two might as easily be C A B or B C A. The file mentioned a box being sent to Russia eight weeks later. He stared at the pendant, it had been constantly on his brain for three weeks now. To start with he didn't hear the phone on his desk ring. Then he grabbed it off the handset.

"DS Cooper. Hang on, slow down. You have analysed the box, and the contents as Gray asked. And? Five kilos of Opium. Yes, I got that. One hundred percent pure. Unrefined. Russian label on bottom of inside of box. Ok, I have all that. Just out of interest, likely value? What did you say? Half a million dollars.

Yes, I will see he gets the message." Cooper replaced the handset. Then got up and went to the window. That sort of information would put a totally different slant on things. Too much money for one person, it was a business amount, but very rare to find opium, rather than cocaine. He watched as DI Gray pulled up in the car and Jane got out of the passenger side.

DI Gray had seen Cooper at the window. Jane went on ahead and he followed her into the police station.

"Any news?" he asked the front desk officer.

"Nothing happening at the moment." Gray walked on into the back office and across to his desk. Cooper was already stood waiting.

"What gives Cooper?" He asked as he sat down.

"Invergordon have been on the phone. Plastic box, pure opium. Five kilos. Half a million dollars' worth. Care to fill me in Sir?"

"Easily done. Jane and I looked at Dornoch Airfield, she found a plastic box, we got it to Invergordon, they analysed it. Result phoned through. We are all going to Great Ferry tonight, A stake out to catch a man who likes his vodka. Be there about seven o'clock." He smiled at Cooper.

"Ok. Why vodka?"

"A Russian who likes a lot of vodka, enough to buy it every three days. In Scotland? Worth seeing who would buy that sort of quantity these days. By the way, anything come from you looking at the pendant for weeks on end?"

"Nothing came up from LICD. Jane asked for us. All they confirmed was the writing is Russian, but of an older version than the current version. There may be more than one pendant.

I wonder if another visit to the Ben might be in order."

"Ok, but don't be too long up there." He nodded towards Jane. " Take Jane with you, she might be able to help in some way."

"Thanks Sir." Cooper walked over to her desk. Shortly they both left the room and set off to drive up to the Ben. Gray sat back in his chair mulling things over.

Half an hour later, Cooper and Jane were walking up through the woods and had reached the halfway point. A pile of tree trunks and two bags of rocks were on the side of the track. Poking out from under them, was white paint. Jane pointed at them.

"What the?"

"Probably going to do some path restoration. It gets a bit muddy in places. The rocks act as hardcore."

"And the tree trunks?"

"Sides for the path. Come on, we haven't got all day." Cooper walked on with Jane following more slowly. As they neared the top, she could see a woman with a border terrier stood by the path. The dog was pulling on its lead. Overhead, a helicopter was heard coming in towards them. Cooper waved his hand to Jane to stop walking and watch. The helicopter came in with a large bag under it. The woman indicated where to have it dropped and after a few minutes the bag was on the ground and the helicopter flying off. Jane caught up with Cooper.

"That looks a lot easier to get up here than walking."

"True. But think how fit you will be." He grinned and walked on to meet the woman in front. "And you are?" he asked as he pulled his warrant card out to show her.

"Tracy. Have a contract to provide logs and rocks for a new pathway the estate are making."

"Which estate is that then?" He asked.

"The Ben Bhraggie Estate." Tracy replied. Cooper said nothing, then looked at Jane who had arrived beside him.

"Good work if you can get it. How long is the contract for then?"

"Open-ended. If they like this one, then there are a lot more for me to supply. Now I must get on." She turned and pulled on the lead, as the dog had shown interest in the pile of logs on the side. Taking a last look, the dog followed her down the track. Cooper stood rubbing his chin in a thoughtful manner. "The Ben Bhraggie Estate." He said out loud.

"What about it, it's just an estate isn't it?"

"Look it up when we get back. Now what I want to find is some door that we can get into."

"Up at the monument?" She pointed to the large statue on the hill.

"No, there are no doors at ground level. I want something that will take this pendant, which I think is a key of some sort. A firm in Dingwall, now closed, used to make them. They are supposed to be unique. Copies cannot be cut and they can be used as both a pendant and as a key. A body of a woman was reported to us as being on the ground in front of the statue, but when we came up here,"

"No Body at Ben Bhraggie." Said Jane with a smile.

"Exactly. So, either the witnesses were wrong, or it was moved."

They split up and searched the ground that went up to the statue on three sides. The side in the front was steep, too steep in Janes mind to risk climbing down and looking. And yet, if the body had been there, how had it been moved?

"Cooper?"

"Yes?"

"How would anybody manage to get to the body to recover it, the ground is very steep in the front."

"They tied rope around the statue base and lowered themselves down. Blue plastic rope threads were found on the base."

"You would need a lot of that sort of rope to go around the base and down to anything on the slope though. "Jane went over to the base and paced its length. " It's huge Cooper, who would be that equipped to bring rope of that length up here. It would be heavy. You would need a vehicle of some kind."

"A four by four at least." Replied Cooper, who had walked over to where she stood. He looked across at pile of stones near the top of the path. "Wonder why they are here?" He moved towards them. Jane walked after him.

"For the new path I expect."

"Take a look around you. No pathway needed after this point. And if you look down, it is very steep and a gully for draining water forms most of the path. You wouldn't create a path on a drainage ditch. Besides, those are not the same colour as the bags that we saw being dropped off." He bent down and took a closer look.

"I think they were just brought up here for some purpose and then forgotten about." Said Jane as she watched him stand up and look up and down the hill.

"You are probably right. Come on, we'll go down the long way round, the track is wider and easier to walk side by side."

An hour later, both of them were almost back in Golspie. Jane turned to Cooper.

"Where is the library these days?"

"Back of the school, in the playing field, a large detached building in the corner. Why?"

"I want to check up on The Ben Bhraggie Estate. If that is ok?"

"Be my guest." He smiled and walked towards the car and left Jane walking along to the Library. Once in the police station though, he walked over to Gray.

"Ben Bhraggie Estate. What do you know about it Sir?" Gray leaned back in his chair and looked up at the ceiling.

"Ben Bhraggie Estate. Now there is a name I haven't heard that for a while. They set up in the eighties. Intending to buy land around these parts of the woods, trouble was the other landowners wouldn't sell. They don't own any land as far as I am aware. Why the interest?"

"We met a woman called Tracy, with a dog, she claimed to have a new contract to supply logs and rocks for paths on Ben Bhraggie for the Ben Bhraggie Estate. Interesting eh?" Cooper smiled at his boss.

"Very. Go and have a chat with the other large estate landowners, start with the Strathben Estate in Golspie. See if they have sold any land to this group. Take a look as usual at Companies House in Scotland to see if they have filed accounts. Who owns what?" He waved his hand at Cooper. "You know what needs to be done."

In Brora the Russian was on the phone. He had heard that a plastic container had been found in Dornoch. Now he wanted to get his hands on it. He thought it might be what had gone missing.

Tracy was on the phone to the Dutchman, she wanted to try out her second attempt at distribution.

"Yes, I need about half a kilo. Good quality."

"But you wanted a lot more last time. Why change now?"

"Different way of distribution. A sample test to begin with. Maybe more in the longer term. But if you can't get the stuff.."

"Oh, I can get what you need, it was just the size of the order that surprised me. Price has gone up slightly. Some of the stock went astray, or that is what we are being told anyhow." He took a puff at his cigar. "Same place to hand over as last time?"

"No. Top of Ben Bhraggie. You will find a large bag of stones there, put it inside the bag, cover it with the stones and leave it. The landmark is a statue on the top of the hill. Overlooks Golspie Village, you can't miss it." She hung up.

'The Boss' had arrived in London. First thing was to check in at the flat. He saw as soon as he entered, there was a message flashing on his phone. He moved over and pressed the play button.

"Where the hell are you? You haven't been to Oxford for three weeks. The students are getting restless. If you can't supply us, we will have to go somewhere else. I, we do need the stock now. That is this Thursday. I'll meet you at the usual spot on the canal. Ring me back when you get this message."

He tapped the pen on the paper in a thoughtful manner. No boat, so he couldn't use the canal as his base. Didn't want to stay anywhere where records were kept. 'The Boss' looked at his machine again. It was still flashing. Another message then. He pressed the play button again.

"Agh!!" A voice was heard screaming. A new voice came on the tape. "Listen up, we have your suppler. A new supply by the end of Thursday or he dies. Your warehouse, now move. We aren't messing about you know." The line went dead. No more messages then. Quickly he moved over to his safe, inside were his five packets of special reserve stock, just what he needed right now. Weighing them, one in each hand, he took just three and put then put the other two back in the safe before spinning the wheel to lock it. Then he went down to the garage below the flats and unlocked his car. He would drive direct to Oxford he had decided. It would take him about an hour and a half to get to his old warehouse at Eynsham.

In the warehouse, a man sat tied to a chair, he was twenty feet up on racking. His little finger was half cut with a crude bandage around it. Beside the chair was an electric jigsaw. Blindfolded, he could only hear or imagine where he was. If 'The Boss' turned up with the drugs, then he would be ok. He was scared though, very scared.

Down below and far enough away for him not to hear anything, a group of four men gathered playing cards. They knew exactly what was needed to keep Oxford's students happy. Until three weeks ago, they had never met. Then by a simple slip of information, they had realised 'The Boss' was dealing with them all, and at different prices. So, they had found the weakest ofThe Boss's contacts and tricked him into meeting them here. Four against one, easy. He had cried out when they had half cut his little finger though. Now all they needed to do was wait, they carried on playing cards.

Bill drove the car fast, cutting through the lanes of traffic on the outskirts of Wheatly as he approached the signs for Oxford. Straight through Headington and down into Oxford would be the quickest he thought as he drove around the roundabout. Headington came and went quickly as he drove on. He had stopped at High Wycombe and phoned ahead. Oxford and University Police were waiting in St Aldates for his arrival. Twenty minutes later, he drove into the carpark at the rear of the police station and went inside.

Jane had found out that the Ben Bhraggie Estate had been dormant for some years, but two years previously had been brought back to life again in Oxford. So far as she could see nothing had been sold or bought. Yet, it showed on the balance sheet a capital item of some thirty thousand pounds. No depreciation either. Which meant a building or land or somebody with money buying up a negative equity property to help somebody out? Cooper or Gray could pull a few strings, then she stopped. Of course! She would simply phone Bill and he could check the Company Register in London. Stopping off outside the apartment that they were using, she went in and dialled his office number. It went to message to tell her that he was out of the office and to leave a message unless urgent, in which case to phone another number. She recognised that as their bosses direct line. No point in bothering him. He would be out in London somewhere, she thought to herself with a rueful smile.

+

"Look, I've been threatened by two people in a secure car

park in London. A file I have seen, a secure file, links a criminal we have been chasing in the LICD for over two years. We need to find him and his boat. He had a boat called 'BRORA', changed it to 'BEN' and has now changed its appearance to one called 'BRAGGING RIGHTS'." Said Bill to the group of officers in front of him.

" And the connection to Oxford is exactly?"

" He used the boat to ship drugs up from London."

"A long route to use, surely a car would be faster?"

"Yes, but nobody would look for a boat travelling over two days between London and Oxford. Well would you?" Bill gazed in frustration at the group of men in front of him.

"No, you are right. We do know about the boat called BRORA, one of our officers called it in, but by the time we and you went to find it, it had vanished into thin air." He waved his hands in the air as if to illustrate the point. Seeing the look on Ben's face, he decided to carry on. "Our colleagues in the River Police in London," He stressed London, " Have seen a boat called Bragging Rights a couple of times going up and down to Gravesend from Oxford. Do you have any information on the Gravesend side of things?" He looked at Ben hopefully.

"Nothing at all. Where does it go in Oxford?"

"It doesn't stop there, it goes onto Eynsham."

"Unusual don't you think?" Asked Bill.

"Very, but the area would be a lot quieter there than the Oxford Canal, wouldn't you say?"

"So why aren't we in Eynsham then?" Bill got up from the desk. Prepared to go at once.

"We have received some information that a certain underworld person is going to be there, so we would like to catch him as well. Goes by a couple of names. Patrick O'Conner, aka 'The Boss' was heavily involved in a plot to blow up the Euro tunnel some years ago. Now we think he has links to drug supplies and a commercial rental business. We have been looking for him for a number of years. Nearly caught him a few years ago, but he escaped. Have you heard of him?"They watched Bill as they waited for an answer.

"Short answer, yes, but can't say any more at present. We crossed paths in a case a few years ago. As you say, we missed him by a few minutes apparently." One of the group of policemen tossed a folder onto the table in front of Bill.

"Ok, listen up then. A dormant company, suddenly goes live. Our friend, well we think it is him, starts to run it and report accounts. Take a look at the last two years accounts." Bill picked up the file and opened it, inside a stapled couple of sheets showed no trading but an asset worth thirty thousand pounds suddenly showed on the books. No means of showing where the money came from though. "We are trying to find out from the accountants who filed them, where the asset is. The problem is the accountants are based in Ireland. They have offices in Oxford and Edinburgh, but the paperwork, they say, is kept in Ireland."

"And the connection with Eynsham?" Asked Bill thoughtfully.

"We think it may be one of the new warehouses that are opening up on a government backed estate."

"How many estates are there out there?"

"Just the one. But it has twenty different firms and thirty different buildings some of which are empty." He shrugged his shoulders as if to say that is as much as we can do to help you. "It's just too many bodies on the ground with the sparse budget we have. You can go and take a look if you want. The address of the estate is in the file. Keep us in the loop."The group broke up and left Bill by himself. He looked around the empty room and sat down and reread the file in front of him. Helpfully he found a pad and pen inside the folder as well. He started to make some notes…

A tap on the door of the warehouse made the four men look up from the table. One got up and walked towards the small door besides the larger roller door. The knocking was more instant.

"Who's there?"

"Don't play games with me. Open up. You wanted to see me. Well, I am here now." The other three men had also approached the door and nodded to open the door. 'The Boss' burst through and stood looking at the four men in front of him. "So, you got together. What was the scream I heard?"

"One of your suppliers, didn't want to do as we asked. He is up there." He jerked his hand in the direction of the racking. "So, have you brought the stuff as we asked?"

"Yes. But first I want to see him brought down and standing in front of me."

"Fair enough." One walked over to a forklift and started it up, exhaust smoke bellowing from its rear, and manoeuvring skilfully took another of the four up in a makeshift basket. The rest kept a careful watch on 'The Boss' as the forklift returned, stopping a few feet in front of them. He could see in the basket was the man who was tied to a chair. A very bloody bandage was wrapped around his little finger. His face was very pale.

"What have you done to him?"

"Half cut his little finger. Just enough, you can see he is not dead. Where is the stuff?"

"Do you think I am going to hand it over without payment? What kind of fool do you take me for? I have a sample here in the briefcase. Try it and see if you are satisfied. Price is the same as before." 'The Boss' watched as he flicked the case open and the four men moved together to look inside the case. One leaned in and took out the small clear packet. He glanced at the others, who nodded and they moved away to cut open the packet leaving 'The Boss' and his man alone. Quickly 'The Boss' moved over to the basket and removed the blindfold. Then he glanced down the warehouse where the men were laughing. From his coat pocket, he took a sharp knife and cut through the bindings holding the man to the chair. Taking the man's arm, he guided him out of the warehouse, keeping an eye on the four men down the aisle. Once outside, he took a padlock from his coat pocket and locked the warehouse.

"That should keep them at bay for a while." He got into the car. The man looked in at 'The Boss'.

"What about me? I need to go to hospital."

"The proper services will all be here in a few minutes. If you know what is good for you, you will wait and say nothing about me." 'The Boss' wound his window up and drove away. At the first telephone box he saw, he pulled in and phoned 999 to report a burglary and somebody injured in a warehouse in Eynsham before replacing the phone. The material that he had passed to them would be quick acting. Pity it meant writing off the warehouse, but it was better that than them talking about him. He drove off in the direction of Oxford. A few people to speak to and he would have to sort out some new contacts that he could trust.

Bill was on his way to Eynsham. Using notes he had made, it appeared there could only be one of eight units. He was going to bang on each of the doors until somebody responded. At least, that was his plan. Unknown to him, an unmarked police car was following at a distance. As he approached the signs on the outskirts of Eynsham, two police cars and an ambulance suddenly overtook him, heading in the same direction. Bill put his foot down and followed them, they were heading the same way as him. The road only lead to the one Industrial Estate. He may as well get there at the same time. All the vehicles swept into the yard in front of the warehouse. Smoke was coming from under the roller door. A few minutes later the fire engine arrived and set about gaining entry. Ten minutes later, all the smoke had gone, but four men lay dead on the floor of the warehouse. Smoke inhalation, was thought to be the primary cause at first glance.

Standing in the shadows of one of the other buildings, Bill looked on thoughtfully, then made his way back to the car. He had arrived too late. He got in and drove back to Oxford to see if he could get any information from the Police about what had really happened here.

Bill was sat at the same desk, when a group of policemen entered the room, at first they appeared not to notice him. They were celebrating the fact that four known criminals had died. Then the noise died down as they realised somebody else was present.

"What the?" asked one of them, looking at Bill.

"Bill, DI Sutherland. From LICD. Taking a look at a file left for me here." He picked up the file off the desk and offered it to the man. "Been busy?"

"Out at Eynsham. Four dead from smoke in a warehouse. We've just identified that they are all known criminals, ones who supply drugs to the students. A successful conclusion to an accidental fire." He smirked as he said this. "DS Green. What do LICD have to do with Oxford then?"

"Drugs being run up and down the Thames. London to Oxford. You have found four men who supplied the students." Green laughed and looked at the other policemen.

"He catches on quick doesn't he?" Then looked at Bill. "What of it?"

"Just wonder who supplied them?" Green shrugged his shoulders.

"Don't know, does it matter?" He stepped back as Bill stepped up close.

"It matters, because all you have done is allowed the people behind this operation to find four new people, people that you or I will not know anything about, and they will start peddling drugs again. Only this time we don't know who they are." Poking Green in the chest, he went on. "So instead of sweating the four men you did know and finding out who their boss is, a lot more students will get sucked into the drug scene. How many students in Oxford?"

"Don't really know."

"Take a guess." Said Bill angrily.

"Don't be too hard on him." Said one of the other men coming over to them both. "It's just that the four men had been causing a lot of break-ins for stuff to sell, so the students can buy the drugs. I guess we were not thinking the whole thing through enough. In answer to your question around twenty three thousand, give or take a few." Bill sighed and moved away.

"Sorry, it has been a hell of a week. Three weeks ago, in Scotland, and now here. It seemed as though they may be connected, I was hoping to speak to the main man who might be behind all this." He waved his hand at the desk in despair.

'The Boss' had driven fast but kept just below the speed limit. He had skirted around Oxford on the by-pass and was now on the road heading towards London. Cross that the warehouse was no longer a possible unit for his purposes. Maybe the Company would have to be shut down before anybody else took too close an interest in it, he mused to himself as he drove along the road.

Chapter 24

Great Ferry near Embo

Night in Great Ferry came quickly in the late Autumn. Gray, Cooper and Jane were sat watching the shop, waiting for the customer who bought vodka in quantity to show up.

"Maybe they'll not come tonight?" Suggested Jane. They had been sat for about an hour and nobody had showed up yet.

"No, they'll turn up." Said Gray confidently. A car pulled up alongside the shop. "That might be them." They watched as a man got out from the passenger side then a second man appeared from the driving seat.

"Hello, that's different to what you have told us Sir." Remarked Cooper.

"Let's just wait and see, shall we?" Gray replied anxiously. A man had got out and was walking towards the shop.

The shop bell rang as the man opened the door quietly. From the back of the shop a lady appeared brushing down her hands as she walked up to the counter.

"How can I help you Sir?" She smiled at him. New person, she thought to herself.

"I need a case of Russian Vodka. My associate has been buying the odd bottle or two, so think that a case might mean less trips."

"I'll go and check to see if I have a case at the back. Shall not be long." She turned to go and look and felt a hand on her shoulder.

"We'll both go together then, shall we?" He gripped her shoulder hard and followed her down a small ramp towards a room at the back of the shop. There were racks of shelving, groaning with stock of all kinds, near to the back door were four shelves with drink of all kinds. He nodded at the lady. "This door open?" pointing at the rear door.

"Yes, I bring my stock in that way. Easier than through the shop."

"Good. Unlock it." She hesitated for a moment, then unlocked the door. He tapped her on the shoulder. "We are going to go back to the shop. No funny business." She sighed and lead the way back, his hand still on her shoulder. At the till, she stopped and turned towards him.

"A case of vodka, would be…" She stopped as he produced a gun and pointed it in her direction.

"…a donation to East – West relationships perhaps?" He smiled cruelly at her. She nodded, frightened now. He left the shop and she quickly moved towards the door of the shop intending to leave it. Silly idea, she thought, where would I go to?

Outside the three had seen the man enter the shop and then his car had started and reversed around the side of the building. Gray looked at Cooper and Jane.

"One of you go around the back, I don't think he is buying the usual amount tonight. The car has reversed up the side, ten to one that there is a rear door. I don't like the way this is going." He picked up the car radio and called for assistance from Dornoch and Tain.

"I'll go round the back." Offered Cooper.

"Then I'll slip around the other side as a pincer movement." Said Gray. He turned to Jane. "Can you drive the car across the front to block the other car in please?"

"No problem." They all got out and Gray passed her the car keys.

"We need to try and stop them, Do be careful though, in case they are armed." said Cooper. Then the two men slipped into the darkness. Jane turned the engine on and drove across to block off the other car.

At the rear of the shop the two Russians were busy moving not just vodka but most of the boxes of drink from the shelves to the boot of the car. With both of them working, they hadn't noticed the two policemen walking their way around the building towards them.

"Right, that's the last of the drink. Let's go."The two Russians got in the car and then realised that it was blocked in.

"What the?"Then realised that there were two policemen, one on each side of the car doors. Quickly they locked themselves in and started the engine. Cooper banged the car window and showed his badge.

"Police, turn off the engine and step outside, Now." He shouted, but they ignored him and reversed hard back into the undergrowth that surrounded the shop. Then spinning the wheel hard, it drove forward across the rough undergrowth.

"Stop them Cooper." Shouted Gray with frustration. As the car rear lights disappeared. Cooper had already run to the police car and got in the front.

"Drive to the other side of the road, sideways on. They can only go..."

"Yes in a circle, I know that." Jane drove forward as the Russian's car came fast towards them. Jane and Cooper got out and slammed the doors closed before diving to ground behind the car.

Instinctively both had put their hands over their ears. They didn't see the cars miss each other as one drove around the front of the police car, scrapping the front of the car as it did so.

Aware that there had been no crash, both Jane and Cooper got up to see Gray stood there.

"They got away then." He muttered under his breath.

"Sorry Sir. We tried, they must have a good driver to avoid having an accident at that speed though." Remarked Cooper thoughtfully. The three turned back towards the shop, a lady had appeared outside the main entrance.

"Get the police, I have been robbed. All my drink stock has been stolen. Get the police."

"Calm down, we are the police. We saw what happened, but DS Cooper will take a statement from you."

"If you are the police, why didn't you stop them then? All my stock they have taken. All of it." She said indignantly at them.

"We tried, but they had a good driver." Said Cooper with a sad smile. "Now, let's go inside and I'll take a note of all that you can remember about them." Gray nodded his approval and he watched as Cooper and the owner went back into the shop. Jane looked at the shopkeeper and then at Gray.

"Nasty business. A robbery like that. Nobody out here to help her, if we hadn't been here that is. Clever though, be a regular customer, build up trust then Wham! Hit them with a robbery. Though why all the stock I wonder?"

"I've been thinking the same thing. Could be for a larger group of people. A gang perhaps? Ah well, we will have to wait and see." He walked around the car, noting the damage to the front of the car as he did so. Smiling, he called in the new information that the police would now be looking for a car with damage on the driver's side, probably scratches and bumps running the whole length of the car.

Chapter 25

A flat overlooking Docklands in London

'The Boss' sat back in his chair in London. He had been up all night working on figures and places. Trying to make a decision about best place to run the business from. A Road map of England and Scotland was spread out on the table in front of him. Wales had been roughly torn off. His market was from Oxford to Scotland. He had realised that other players would not take kindly to him taking too big a slice of their areas. That had been three hours ago, stretching, he got up and looked out across the Thames. The sun was starting to rise and its first golden rays were flashing across the water. Leaving the room, he went and freshened up. Maybe he should look at this from a buyers perspective he wondered to himself. Pouring a drink of pure orange, he put some ice into it and walked out onto the small balcony to enjoy both the drink and the sunrise.

In Oxford, the police had been informed that the men had not died of asphyxiation as had been first thought. They had come into contact with a new type of poison. It appeared as though it came through their hands touching something. The fingertips had turned a bright orange. An opened packet had been found near the bodies. This had now been sent up to the HMG's Technical Poison Laboratory in Scotland.

Jane had spent the night trying to work out who would want to rob a shop in the middle of nowhere. Obviously the Russians had to be prime suspects, but where to find them? *The Double Headed Eagle* remained closed. Gray was trying to get a warrant to search the place from top to bottom, but it wasn't going too well. She decided to get up and go for a run along the front, before going to the office. Perhaps Gray or Cooper may have come up with something.

The three Russians sat in easy chairs in the cottage. A growing collection of empty bottles were piling up in front of them and beside each of the three chairs. The Russian leader was still awake, just, but his two men were fast asleep. Not impressed, he thought to himself, and rose to leave the flat and take a breath of air. Outside the sun was starting to rise. The cool air blew across his face. Maybe it was time to cut and run. It would cost a lot and a huge loss of face, but it was better than being locked up in a UK prison. Inside the cottage, he could hear the phone ringing. He strode through and picked it up. His two men never even stirred.

The Dutchman waited impatiently for the Russian to answer his call.

"Come on, pick up, damn you." He muttered under his breath as he waited. Eventually a Russian voice spoke.

"What sort of time do you call this, who is it anyhow?"

"Klaas, your Dutch friend. We need to talk, there are too many players in that part of Scotland. If I pull out, will you agree to a suitable arrangement coming this way?"

"How suitable?"

"I need to crack the London markets, at the moment it is a closed shop to me. My information is that you might have a contact there, maybe they could be persuaded to work for me?"

"Maybe. There is a man who smuggles stock from London to Oxford and then it gets distributed to the Students. Called Patrick."

"Irish then?"

"From a long time ago. He now prefers to be known as 'The Boss'. He does seem to control a large area. Just his name tends to put a lot of fear into anybody who hears it mentioned." Said the Russian.

"Patrick. Any last name?"

"Not that I have found out yet. Do you know of any other new players that might be in the area?"

"Well apart from Patrick, there is some young woman. Only just been dealing with her as a matter of fact. She wanted a small, very small amount of stock. Trial run she said."

"Might be worth pursuing. What about the restaurant, do you want to take all of it over if I pull out?" The Dutchman thought for a few seconds, then laughed, "I am thinking of pulling out of the area myself. What would I do with it? Especially one that the police are probably keeping an eye on."

"Run it as a purely clean venture. Totally separate to anything else. Watch the police tie up their resources keeping an eye on it. Change the name though. I was too vain. Look, I'll see if I can find anything else about Patrick. You find out about the new woman." The phone went dead and the Dutchman smiled and sat back and took a cigar out of his humidifier. Things were starting to get better he thought to himself as the sun rose higher in the morning sky.

Cooper had arrived early at the office that morning. Overnight he had remembered where there was another monument to a Duke of Sutherland. Now having found it on a local map, he scribbled a note to Gray and left it for him on his desk. In his eagerness to leave the building, he almost knocked Jane over.

"What's the rush?" She asked.

"The pendant. I may have worked out where it goes." He looked at her. She remained standing and looking puzzled.

"The first body, it had a pendant in it." He dangled the faxed picture in front of her. "I don't think it was Ben Bhraggie that it was meant for, but another monument entirely."

"And so?"

"If there is a doorway of some sort there, then the pendant might open it for us." He beamed at her excitedly.

"And the actual pendant is where exactly?" Jane said as she crossed her arms in front of her. Cooper stopped smiling.

"In a lab in Invergordon. I suppose that without it, we can't gain entrance?"

"Probably not. But we could go and get it." She smiled at him and they walked around to the back to get one of the cars.

Inside LICD Bill sat at his desk. Frustrated as to how things were turning out, he looked across the room at the office where his boss was seen talking on the phone. Sighing, he pulled a box folder towards himself and opened the lid. A note lay on the top of the paperwork.

YOU HAVE TWO HOURS OR YOUR WIFE GETS HURT. NOW GET THE FILE COPIED AND LEAVE IT IN YOUR CAR. 7.45am

He glanced at his watch. It was now 9.00am Only three quarters of an hour left. He didn't even know where to start looking for the file, never mind photocopying it. Bill pulled the phone on his desk towards him and dialled a Golspie number. Better to check than to worry unnecessarily, he mused. He could hear the phone ringing, but nobody bothered to answer. Now very concerned, he got up and walked towards the closed door of his boss's office. Frustrated, he walked up and down outside, while waiting for his boss to finish the call.

Tracy heard a phone ringing, sleepily, she reached out her hand and then remembered she wasn't at Nigg. She was staying in a hotel on the outskirts of Golspie. Swinging her legs out of the bed, she walked over to the phone on the desk by the window. As she picked it up, she pushed the curtain back to see the sunshine pouring in.

"Hello?"

"Is that Tracy? It's your Estate Agents. Look we have

somebody who wants to view the house. We are a bit tied up at the moment, can you meet them and show them around it?"

"Yes, ok. What time and when exactly?"

"You can, that's great. Ten thirty today. Can you get there in time?"

"Make it eleven and I can."

"Eleven it is. Thanks", He hung up and Tracy looked around the room, then went and had a shower to freshen up and go and meet this perspective purchaser.

The Dutchman thought for a few minutes and then phoned his man on the ground in Scotland. He remembered asking the man to get rid of the newcomer, now he wanted to make sure that he had done as he asked.

"So, did you get rid of her?"

"Sort of." The smile on the face of the man vanished as he realised that he would now have to produce some evidence of her death.

"Sort of? What sort of answer is that? Did you or didn't you?"

"I didn't kill her, I frightened her off. Don't think she is going to stay around here much longer."

"Why do you think that? She still has somewhere to stay. Or did you destroy her house?"

"No. But that does give me an idea. I'll phone you back tonight." He hung up and decided to go and take a look at the flat in Invergordon. A quiet sort of place, if he recalled correctly. Smiling he left his room and walked out to the car.

Twenty minutes later, he had discovered the keys didn't fit the lock. Not of the flat she had said it would anyway. Now feeling foolish, he ran down the stairs and back to his car. Doing a fast turn, he set off in the direction of Nigg.

The Russian put his phone down. The conversation had been rewarding for both parties. Now he just had to see if London did what he asked.

Bill looked up as the door opened and his boss walked out.

"Sorry to keep you. Had a phone call that wouldn't wait. Come in, I need to talk to you about an update I have received." He led the way back into the office, closing the door behind him. "I understand you have been up to Oxford and seem to have stirred up things a bit. At least that is what Oxford Police are telling me. Care to explain? And while you are at it, why hasn't Jane been in touch?" He drummed his fingers on the desk and looked expectantly at Bill.

"I don't know about Jane, tried to reach her today, but couldn't get an answer. Look Sir, I have been threatened if I don't produce a copy of the file I received yesterday."

"And what file is that?"

"It had a for yours eyes only and it was timed. Who left it on my desk, that I don't know. I assumed it was yourself Sir."

"Not me. I would suggest you forget about the file and concentrate on finding out what is going on between London and Scotland. Go and explore the canals of Birmingham. The stuff was going from London to Oxford by boat, Birmingham has a good waterway connection, see if there is any link there. But keep out of Oxford, understand?" Without saying any more, he nodded at the door and bent down to carry on working. Bill looked, then turned and left the office, slamming the door behind him. Once Bill had left, his boss picked up the phone, sighed and dialled a long number. He had had to do that, or his family would have been targeted.

Jane and Cooper had arrived in Invergordon and witnessed a car speedily turning round and roaring off up the main street. She had noted the type and number and Cooper was now calling it in.

"Yes, a red car, BMW. No, I don't know model, Registration number is DHE91BR. Yes DHE91BR. I'll wait." He put his hand over the mic and turned to Jane. "A special number plate apparently. What is that? You are kidding me. Ok." Sighing he turned to her. "It's a Russian diplomat's car. We cannot touch it apparently." They turned the car and carried on towards the lab. Off a side street and up a flight of stairs to a portacabin sitting on top of two similar ones beneath it. The metal steps clanged as they both ran up them.

An hour later, paperwork signed and the pendant was in their hands. They were heading back to Golspie.

Tracy had arrived at the house and was busy opening windows. She wondered if she should light a fire to make the place seem cosy. The doorbell rang, she walked towards the front door, putting on light switches as she did so. Throwing open the door, the man pushed her back into the hall.

"We have some talking to do."

"About the house?" Tracy asked. Meaning Nigg.

"Exactly. Now sit down." He pointed at the kitchen chair. She did as he asked. "The key doesn't fit the lock." She looked at him again and now realised it was the man in the boat. The one she had given the wrong key to, Damn!

"I must have made a mistake. Let me get my bag and..."

"...and nothing." He produced a gun and levelled it at her head.

"Do you have a key that fits the flat? Think carefully now."

"Yes it is in my bag." Keeping the gun pointed at her, he moved towards her bag and reached down and picked it up off the floor. Just at that moment the doorbell rang. He looked towards the door. It was enough, Tracy moved out of her chair, grabbed a heavy metal table lamp and brought it down on the mans head. He crashed down onto the floor. The doorbell kept ringing. Tracy stepped over the prone man and went to answer it.

"Good morning, we are here to see the house." A young couple smiled at her. "We want to get away from the city and all the violence. Up here that sort of thing doesn't happen does it?" She opened the door wide and they walked through the hall and into the room. The man lay still, a pool of red blood coming from his head. Taking a quick look, they turned and left. "I don't think this is for us, really it isn't. Thank you for your time, nice to have met you." The front door slammed shut and Tracy returned to the body on the floor. Bending down she felt for a pulse. Nothing! Sighing, she picked up the phone and dialled 999.

Having read the note that Cooper had left for him, Gray had phoned Companies House to see if they had any more information about Ben Bhraggie Estates. He tapped his finger on the desk and made some notes as he went along.

"I am the second person to ask for that Company file today you say? It's only just gone ten o'clock. People from Europe can access an hour earlier than we can. I see. Ok, so, who exactly is behind the Company, the directors I mean?"

"Two names appear to start with, then one resigns. Leaving only the Secretary on the papers."

"What's her name?" He put the phone to one ear, propping it by his hunched shoulder.

"Him actually. A Mr J O'Conner. We did some digging, too Irish, the computer flagged it actually. He is a Mr Patrick O'Conner. Has had dual nationality from birth. We think he may have had some trouble in Ireland with the IRA, but nothing on file in UK. So, he was allowed to be on the register of Companies House."

"And the other person?"

"Some foreign sounding name, Count, wait a minute." Papers were shuffled in the background. "Count D R C ULLA .Yes D R C Ulla."

Gray pencilled it on the pad and laughed down the phone.

"A false name if anybody bothered to check. Thanks for that

info." He hung up and pushed his chair back against the wall. Why would a Russian help an Irishman and then step back from control? Then he remembered he hadn't asked the question about the balance sheet. Sighing, he dialled the number and asked to speak to the man again.

"Sorry to bother you again, the balance sheet, did it show what the capital had been spent on by any chance?"

"Yes, a warehouse. Wait a minute, there is another piece of paper. Ah, and a half stake in a boat. Doesn't say what the boat was called though. Anything else I can do to help?"

"Thanks, no nothing else." Gray replaced the receiver and went outside to think things through.

Chapter 26

London LICD Headquarters

The Russian had heard his phone ring, but was too drunk to answer it.

Bill's Boss, Harvey in London at LICD, replaced his phone thoughtfully. No answer. That could be for a number of reasons. Now alarmed, he picked up his coat and briefcase and left his office. He needed to see that his wife was alright. As he walked out into the main office, Bill looked up from his own desk.

"Going out Sir?"

"Never you mind about me, what have you got on Birmingham?"

"Nothing yet, but Oxford did..."

"Oxford? Didn't I tell you to leave Oxford alone? Got it?" He snapped at him.

"Yes Sir. Leave Oxford alone."

"Concentrate on Birmingham." Then picking his case off the floor where he had put it, he left the office. He didn't want Bill going anywhere near Oxford. That was what he had been told to do, get his DI out of the Oxford Area. Well, he had told him now, hadn't he?"

He got to his car in the underground car park and was about to get into it, when two men appeared from behind other cars.

"Going somewhere important?" Asked the first.

"We wouldn't like you to go off without a small chat with us. Would we now?" He nodded at the other man who reached forward and took his briefcase. Putting it on the roof of the car, he snapped the locks and the lid opened. A file lay inside clearly marked.

FOR YOUR INFORMATION.
ONLY PEOPLE LISTED BELOW HAVE ACCESS TO THIS FILE.
ONE HOUR TIMED USE STARTS ONCE SEAL IS BROKEN
DO NOT COPY IN ANY FORMAT.
WHEN FINISHED PLEASE PUT THE FILE IN THE ATTACHED BAG AND SEAL AS SHOWN

"How very naughty of you. It says to destroy it. We can do that for you." He picked up the paperclipped file and passed it over the roof of the car to his colleague. "Look after that. It is important."

"Let me have that back, I need to..." He stopped as the man pulled a gun out of his pocket.

"You don't need to do anything more."Then felt a syringe jab his neck and feeling suddenly very sleepy, he fell into the car as the other man had opened the rear door. Once inside, and now unconscious, the two men shut and locked the car door. Then they both walked slowly away to their own cars, one took out a petrol can. Returning to the dead man's car, he splashed it around the petrol filling cap, which he had already prised open. Then put the can on the floor beside the car and walked away. The other man, stood and light a match, carelessly throwing it in the direction of the petrol. With a woosh, the car and the ones beside it were engulfed in flames.The two men had already got in their own cars and were driving out of the car park at speed. As they left, an alarm could be heard ringing from the car park. It was followed by a series of explosions.

In the office above the car park, there was panic as alarms went off. All practice drills about walking out of the building were forgotten about in seconds as people fled to the exits in droves. One or two sat at their desks and watched as the remaining members of staff left the offices. In the distance fire engines could be heard approaching..

Bill had walked down the stairway and gone and outside. Now along with the other staff they were just waiting for the all-clear. Firemen could be seen dousing the flames in the car park, blackened cars were also seen. He wondered who or what had been responsible for this happening. He moved across to a small group of staff, who were discussing it.

"...apparently a car was being refuelled when the engine was on."

"No! How stupid is that. I mean they always tell you to turn off your engine when you go to a petrol station."

"Yes, but this was from a small petrol can."

"Still, you can't be too careful can you."

"You worried about your car in there?"

"Not today, I came in by underground. Car is being serviced." Bill moved away, an accident if they were to be believed. He wondered if his boss had got away before anything had happened. Then he felt a tap on his shoulder. Spinning round, he was confronted by the head of LICD.

"Come over here DI Sutherland. When did you last see your superior?"

"About an hour ago, he was going out, he didn't say where exactly though."

"Did he seem anxious at all?"

"Well, come to think of it, a bit anxious. A bit abrupt. He told me to concentrate on Birmingham as a new hub for drug dealing. The canals in particular. Why?"

"We can't seem to get hold of his wife. Do you know where they live?"

"High Wycombe way, I think. Not sure of the exact address mind."

"Ok, here is the address." He passed Bill a piece of paper torn from his diary. "We think he may have been blackmailed over something. See if you can find anything out from his wife. Be discrete though, it is possible he may be dead. It seems the fire started in the bay where he would have parked. Hence the reason why I asked when you last saw him." He turned and left Bill holding the paper with the address on it. Bill looked at it, not too far from High Wycombe though. He looked towards the car park. Some people were starting to drift back towards the building. He made his way across to a fire engine parked near the exit to the carpark. Two firemen were coiling up hoses, they looked up as he approached.

"Can we do anything to help you Sir?"

"I wondered when I could get to my car. It's in there." He pointed at the, now smoking, car park under the building.

"Not for a while. The police have to examine the scene first, also some cars are still hot from the fire. Best find another way to get home and back here tomorrow Sir." They turned back to coiling up the hoses. Bob looked across and then decided to join the other staff going back to the offices. He could collect the paperwork and go home, get Jane's car and drive to High Wycombe. Pleased with his thoughts, he walked towards his office.

On his desk sat a piece of paper.

"TIME IS UP. What a shame..." He picked the paper up and screwed it into a ball and tossed it into the bin. Then leant over and, picking up the phone to dial the number of Golspie Police Station.

In Golspie DI Gray got up and walked over to Jane's desk and picked up the phone.

"Golspie Police DI Gray Speaking. How can I help you?"

"DI Gray? It's Bill Sutherland Here. Can I speak to Jane please?"

"Sorry, she is out with DS Cooper. Can I take a message for you?"

"When did you last see her?"

"Last night, we were staking out a business for a potential..."

"Has she been in touch with you since?"

"No. What is this about?"

"I have been threatened, I want to make sure she is safe."

"Look, I'll get in touch with Cooper and get her to give you a ring back. What is your best number for her to call?"

"Tell her to phone me at home in an hour."

"Ok. Will do so." Gray hung up and stroked his chin thoughtfully.

Tracy had been sat in her Nigg house for an hour, the police had been and questioned her. At last, satisfied with her explanation, they had taken lots of photos. Now that forensics had finished, the body had been allowed to be removed. As the last of the police left, she looked down at the chalk outline on the floor. Sighing, she rose and went and turned the tap on. Might as well clean up now as later. She thought to herself as the water flowed into the bucket.

The Dutchman looked at his watch. His man should have got back to him by now. He picked up the phone and dialled his other contact.

"Hello, I need you to go and check out Nigg. I haven't heard from our mutual friend for a while. Unless you have heard from him?"

"Not a word Sir. I'll go and check out Nigg as you want." He hung up and sat back to think about the Russian's offer to him to buy The Double Headed Eagle. Maybe it would be a way of getting out of Amsterdam he wondered to himself. Then taking a cigar out of the humidifier, he cut off the end and after lighting it, sat back and took a contented puff.

Jane and Cooper had swung into the small car park by the station. Sited opposite the main drive to the Castle, it could only hold one car. Both of them got out and looked across the railway line. They could see a small monument on the other side, but it was far too small to be what they were looking for.

Jane nudged Cooper's arm excitedly.

"Look further up and to the right." She pointed with her hand. Cooper followed where she pointed and saw the top of an overgrown monument of some kind or other.

"I see where you mean. Come on." He started to move towards the tracks, stopping dead, as a goods train thundered right in front of him. He glanced at his watch and smiled ruefully.

"Forgot that the freight train ran about this time of day." He moved forward and pushed the gate open for Jane to follow him. Once inside the tracked area, he closed it again and then after crossing the railway, did the same again on the other side. Before them lay a tarmac road. Some weeds were pushing up the centre of it. Muddy tracks off tractor tyres could be seen on both sides. The two of them made their way slowly up the steep incline. At the top, the road curved to the left and an earth track, flattened with years of use, lay to the right. They moved to the right and carried on walking for about a mile. A gate on the left hand side formed a barrier to the field. Jane approached it.

"It's not locked, just need to push it." She pushed against the gate, but it didn't move.

"Try lifting it and pushing it." Suggested Cooper.

"Why don't you come and try yourself if you know how to do it?" replied Jane. She watched with some satisfaction as Cooper tried to do what he had suggested and failed. "Well?"

"Climb over the top then." Suiting the action to the words, he put his foot on the first bar only to find it snapped under his weight. Jane took a close look at the gate.

"It's very rusty on the bottom two bars. The third one looks in better condition." She said as she placed her foot on it and climbed over. Cooper followed her. Once on the other side, they could see a bit more of the monument. "How far do you think it is from here?"

"Half a mile or so." Replied Cooper. Then he set off towards the monument, Jane following behind.

Not much later, they arrived, and discovered a monument, but covered in very thick ivy. It had overgrown it everywhere, as they discovered walking around the base of it. A few bits of old discoloured litter had been caught in the ivy. Jane bent down and picked up a crisp packet. She looked at the faded front. Then put it back. Cooper looked across at her.

"Litter picking is not what we came here to do."

"Agreed, but that crisp manufacturer went out of business in the late seventies. If that is the most recent bit of litter, then nobody has been up here recently."

"Well not and left litter anyhow." Cooper bent forward and pulled at the ivy, it came away in his hand. Behind the leaves, he could see thick twisted ivy stems. "We haven't got the right tools to clear all this away. Where to start anyhow?" He said out loud.

Jane had walked to the North side of the monument, the ivy didn't seem to be so thick around there. Bending forward, she grasped a handful of ivy and gave a good pull, it came away easily, but like Cooper, the thick stems were underneath the leaves.

"You're right, we need to return with proper equipment. I am not so sure that this is the right monument. I mean there doesn't appear to be anywhere for a key to fit. Not at first glance anyhow. Think about the problem that we had getting to it. No, if somebody would want quick and easy access to it, then they would have kept the ivy clear of that part anyhow." She took another look and walked around to where Cooper stood scratching his head in frustration.

"I was so sure that this was the monument for the pendant. We have been to the Ben and nothing there is at all like a door or a place to put a key. Now the same applies here as well. Where else is there a monument? Think Cooper, think." He banged the top of his head, hoping that would somehow aid the process. Jane looked at the monument and then up at the one atop of the hill. By moving around to one side, she discovered they both fell into a straight line. Running her eye up to the monument, she saw a dark building about halfway between the two monuments. Excitedly she turned to Cooper.

"What's that building up there, between here and the monument on the Ben?" She pointed in the direction and Cooper went over and looked, following her line of direction. He could make out the dark building that she had spotted.

"Don't know, but we'll go back and get some tools and find out. Come on." He led the way back towards the car, almost running at times as the road wound down towards the car park and the railway.

'The Boss' had awoken and phoned his man in Scotland. He had remembered that the police had got hold of the pendant, he did need that if he was to get in.

"Look Boss, if I knew where the pendant was, I would go and get it. Probably the police are looking at it and trying to figure out what it is for as well as understand its meaning. Hell, I don't even understand it, other than it is supposed to be written in Russian."

"Go to the place where it is supposed to unlock the doors. See if there is any sign of anybody having been there. It is very valuable."

"Ok, I'll go straight after breakfast."

"Mind you do." He hung up and went to eat his own breakfast. No sooner had he started than the phone rang. Sighing, he rose and walked over to his desk and picked it up.

"Yes?"

"We have to do something about the boat. LICD have got

information on who owns it. I want out and I want out now. You understand?" A slurred Russian voice said.

"Calm down. The boat has been repainted and changed appearances, further to that, I sold it. Anybody trying to find the owners that way will be disappointed." He took a bite off a bit of toast.

"Ok, that takes care of the boat, what about the warehouse?"

"The police found a fire raging, four people dead apparently. Don't know what people were doing in there anyhow, not at night time, that is." He took another bite.

"My contact in Oxford, tells me that somebody from LICD has been sniffing around. I learn that some kind of poison was used, one with links to Russia, this is not good, not good at all. Also, a Detective has been sniffing around the warehouse and has got a lead. Don't worry though, I have got my contact in London to point him in another direction completely. Birmingham of all places." A nasty laugh came down the phone at 'The Boss'. "So, since the fixed assets are gone, perhaps you can refund my share of the initial investment, Hm?"

"Where do you think I can get that sort of money quickly? I have lost my share as well. That is the risk in business we take."

"Wrong! I was a sleeping backer, you took the risk, I took half the rewards. However, I am an agreeable man, I have a restaurant I want to dispose of, you buy me out of that successful business, and I'll forget about the boat and warehouse. What do you say?"

"Well how much are you talking about?"

"Ten thousand gets you my restaurant. It's a fair price. Get back to me tomorrow with your answer for my share of the boat and warehouse." The phone line went dead. 'The Boss' walked over to the dining table and sat down, Suddenly he didn't feel as hungry anymore for some reason. He thought to himself, the restaurant would be a good site, but and it was a big one, why did the Russian want to get out now? Did he know something else that Patrick didn't? He wondered to himself.

The Russian leaned back in his chair and beamed at his two drunken henchmen lying on the floor. A cascade of empty bottles reached from the fireplace to the chairs around them. He belched, got up and went outside. When he returned, one of the two men was awake and rubbing his forehead.

"What time is it?" He asked quietly.

"Half past nine, time you were up and out." Said the Russian.

"Don't shout. Please don't shout."

"I wasn't." He laughed and went and sat down and reached for the phone. One more call before breakfast. He thought to himself and dialled a number in the Netherlands. It was answered almost immediately.

"Hello my friend. Have you thought about my offer to sell you the restaurant yet?"

"Of course, I have thought about it, what is your price?"

"Twenty thousand pounds."

"Make it fifteen and it's a deal."

"Done. I'll get the paperwork delivered to you in the next two days. A pleasure doing business with you." He hung up and rubbed his hands together. Then looking down at both of his men, said. "So, who is for a full fry up?" Then laughed as the two men rose together and ran outside.

Gray reached for the fax machine as it whirled behind him. A piece of paper with a car registration and address was coming through. The accompanying note informed him it was the one that had got away at Great Ferry. Happy at an address to go to, he picked up a piece of paper and his coat and went out to his car.

The sight of a police car driving up Golf Road made one of the two men take a second look, then ran into the cottage.

"The police are here. What are we going to do?" He asked.

"Tidy the place up and let them in. We have nothing to fear from them." He stood and picked up a few bottles in each hand and took them out the back to the box by the bins. By the time he returned, the other two men were already hard at work doing the same, only they had brought a couple of boxes into the room and were filling them up with alarming speed. A knock on the door made them all look up. The Russian moved to answer it and his two men quickly picked up the two boxes and went out to put them with the ones already there.

"How can I help you Officer?"

"DI Gray. Can I come in please?"

"Of course, do come in. I'd offer you a drink, but am afraid I am out of the drink at present." He gave a laugh. Two empty seats sat on each side of the fireplace. Now empty of bottles, it looked cold and harsh.

"I'll get straight to the point, last night a robbery took place. A lot of drink was taken." Gray paused.

"But Inspector, what would that have to do with me?"

"Who owns the car outside?"

"It's hired. Why?"

"There is a nasty scratch all down one side. I think the paint might be a match for the front of the police car we were using to stake out the place. Shall we go and take a look."

"Sure, why not?" He rose and followed Gray outside. Without a word, Gray pointed to the long scratches. Then he produced a piece of paper from his pocket.

"Funny thing paint. The car manufacturers are careful to keep the type of paint to themselves. For example, a BMW will not reveal the paint they use, to Vauxhall. However, if asked by us, they do let us know what the paint is and usually send a sample. Time being urgent, today they faxed the details." He held the paper against the paintwork of the car. "A match, don't you think?" The Russian said nothing and nodded. Inside he was furious with his men, but his demeaner didn't show it.

"Let's go inside Inspector, I am sure it can be sorted out amicably."

He led the way back indoors and sat down. Gray remained standing.

"Did you drive the car last night Sir?"

"No, I had had too many drinks. It was parked there last night and still there this morning."

"Does anybody else drive it for you?"

"No. The hire documents would have been too complicated. I am only here for a day or so. Then I return to Russia." He smiled.

"So, if we say there is a match against the paint and you were not driving it last night, how do you explain the scratches?"

"Yobs. Vandals, kids out for joyriding. Inspector, I don't keep it locked. The keys are probably still in the ignition. Go and see for yourself. Anybody could have driven it to Great Ferry and back." He smiled at the Inspector.

"As you say Sir. Now don't leave the country and if I can take your passport for now?" Gray held out his hand. With a sigh the Russian rose and went to a briefcase on the sideboard. He opened it and took out his passport and passed it to Gray, who looked inside and then put it in his pocket. "I'll leave you now Sir. If you do find out who caused the damage, do let me know and I'll probably let you have your passport back." He left the cottage and smiled to himself. A mistake there my friend. A big mistake. Then he walked back to his car and drove off to Golspie, but not before driving past *The Double Headed Eagle*.

Chapter 27

Golspie Police Station

Cooper and Jane pushed the door open and went in. Cooper looked across to the desk where Gray usually sat. It was empty. Jane went and put the kettle on.

"Bit empty isn't it?" She remarked.

"Wonder where everybody is?" He looked around before sitting down at his desk. "Can you make one for me please?" Then he opened his computer to find out where he would obtain the tools they needed.

Bill was driving in Jane's car to High Wycombe. He had been back to their home and grabbed a suitcase. He planned to drive north after seeing if the Boss's wife knew where her husband was. He thought it was a bit of a wild goose chase, but he had his orders. He pushed the radio on. A new radio station had been announced, the first time for a national radio station for a long while. He turned off the A40 on to a side road that led to his destination.

Half an hour later, he had been around the large property. No sign of anybody being in. At the back, a small window had been broken and a bit of tape covered the crack. It looked old, not recent, so Bill moved his attention to the triple garage that stood apart from the house. He tried each of the three doors in turn, the last one opened towards him.

"Anybody there?" He pulled the door open a bit more. Daylight shone into the empty garage. Well not really empty. Sat, tied to a kitchen chair, was the body of a woman. On the floor lay a syringe. He noticed the fingers had gone bright orange. Closing the door carefully, he moved back to the car and called it in. While he waited, he took another look around the premises and spotted a ladder lying in the grass. Looking up, he saw that on the first floor a bedroom window was wide open.

+

The Russian looked across at his two men, still nursing their sore heads from the drinking the night before.

"How could you be so stupid as to use the car outside? Don't answer that. The last thing we need right now is a nosey local copper keeping an eye on us. I give you enough money to buy the stuff, you didn't need to steal it. Buying now and then, the shopkeeper is happy, I am happy, and no nosey policemen. We now need to move out of here and fast. Get hold of the Dutchman, tell him we are moving out and if he can get the money to me today, then we will leave the keys in the key safe at the restaurant. Now move."

"Sure Boss, but please don't shout."

"I am not shouting. This is talking." He turned and left them in the cottage to see what the real damage to the car was. In the daylight, he could see the long scratch and dents that ran down one side of the car.

Cursing silently, he looked inside, as he had told the policeman, the keys were still in the ignition. Sighing, he went back into the cottage.

An hour later the three Russians had left the cottage and locked up. The boot of the car held the few items that they had brought with them.

"Right, all the items in the hall, they need to be got rid of. See if there is somewhere you can get rid of it. Rubbish tip, that sort of thing."

"Sure Boss, just don't shout."

"I'll wait for you by the railway station. Just do it right this time."

"Ok Boss."The two men went out to the hall and picked up the bits and pieces as well as the boxes of empty bottles. Once the car was loaded they drove off out of the grounds of the cottage. A sign on the main road pointed to a household refuse centre. Shrugging their shoulders at one another, the driver swung the car in that direction. Soon they were busy transferring the boxes of bits and pieces to the four open skips. Alongside the skips were two large containers, half filled with empty bottles. They swiftly added the empty bottles into it and drove off. The manager of the site had observed them doing this and noted the car number as it seemed a lot of bottles for one person to get rid of. If he had the number, maybe he could find out if it belonged to a restaurant or Inn, they were supposed to get a licence to dump their rubbish here. He would check it out.

Happy with what they had got rid of, they drove over to the railway station and took their luggage out of the car boot. The Russian looked at them.

"Did you get rid of all of it?"

"Yes, there was a place to dump everything, even the bottles. What do you want us to do with the car?"

"I want you to leave it somewhere with the key in it. Then each of you to make your own way back to Russia where I'll speak to you there about your next assignment. Here is some money, don't open it now nor spend it foolishly. It is for travelling and not leaving any paper trail. Understand?" Both men nodded.

They would return to Russia separately, although, given the mood he was in, that might not be a good idea.

Gray entered the police station and looked across at Cooper and Jane.

"Your husband phoned earlier, he was a bit anxious. Give him a ring and let him know you are Ok."

"That's not like him. Did he say why he phoned?"

"Only that he had been threatened. Wanted to make sure you

were ok."

"I'll phone his office now." Jane moved over to an empty desk and sat down and dialled the number of their office. "LICD? Can you put me through to DI Sutherland please?"There was a pause. "It's a bit busy due to a fire in the car park? Ok, can you take a message and see he gets it please? Just say Jane phoned and she is ok." She replaced the phone and looked across to Gray who was still standing. "There has been a fire apparently in the staff car park. The fire brigade are still damping it all down. Still, nobody hurt, that's the main thing."

Cooper looked up from his desk.

"We can get the tools at Dornoch. Come on." He rose from his desk and stopped as Gray put out a restraining hand on his shoulder.

"Stop right there. What tools? For what purpose? Tell me before you go haring off to Dornoch."

"Well Jane and I went to see if the pendant fitted in another monument, north of the railway at Dunrobin."

"Go on."

"Well, it was very overgrown with ivy, then Jane…"

"DI Sutherland." Corrected Gray with a smile.

… "Then DI Sutherland, spotted a building between the two monuments. About halfway. We came back to get some tools and see if we could get access to it. It might be unlocked, or it might be." Cooper paused as he looked at Gray. "What sir?"

"Do this by the book. We need to get permission first. That is probably on Estate land. Find out who the land belongs to, get their permission to enter the building and then we will all go." Gray waved his hand, as if to say, that is the end of it. Cooper looked across at Jane, sighed and sat back down at the computer.

Meantime at the same building one of Patrick's henchmen was sat in his car looking at the pair of well made metal doors. A very heavy ornate padlock was holding the two doors together.

That was not what was keeping him from gaining entrance though. The ground around the building was very overgrown. He had walked right around it. At the back, a panel had been removed and placed to one side. He had seen the marks on ground, the grooves ran exactly the length of the panel, he had measured them. A glance inside had revealed that whatever had been inside before, wasn't there now. He leant forward and took a camera from the passenger side door. Then he went and took a few photos to prove what he had seen. Returning to the car, he drove off down the track towards the main road. He didn't look forward to telling 'The Boss' what he had found out.

Tracy was pleased with herself. She had been allowed to leave Nigg, the police would be there for some time yet. She was in the clear for now. Two days ago, having returned to her room in Golspie, she had collected her border terrier, Jack, for a long walk. While out for the walk, she had found a building, all locked up, but a quick look at the back had resulted in finding a loose panel. It hadn't taken much effort to remove it. Inside were large wooden boxes, each one with a padlock holding a clasp firmly in place. A few local phone calls had resulted in her getting a removal firm to move, whatever it was, from there to a unit in Golspie. A unit that was now full of boxes and firmly locked, with only her having the two keys. Smiling she made her way along the seashore.

On the barge, the phone rang.

"Hello?"

"My boss said to tell you that he wants the money today. If you can do this, he will leave the keys in the usual place at the restaurant. Do you think you can do this?"

The Dutchman swore under his breath. While possible, it would take some organization.

"Yes, it isn't much notice though. I thought I had a couple of..."

"Yes, yes, do it. I don't need explanations." The phone went dead on him. He looked at his desk, smiled and opened his phone pad to ask an old Irish contact about some money he was owed from years ago.

In London, Patrick paced up and down his flat. He had heard back from Golspie, the place had been broken into. He was sure he would find that the Russian was at the bottom of it. Flinging some clothes into a suitcase, he decided to set off for Dornoch. There he would be, at least, on the spot. The newspaper he had been reading, was spread out on the table, the headline read; "Suspect arson at London International Crime Department headquarters say experts."

In the LICD, a phone rang on Bill's desk, but not being there, it went unanswered. The fire brigade had found the main car, with the remains of a body inside. It had been taken for forensic examination. Meanwhile the team in High Wycombe had confirmed that the woman in the garage was the late wife of Bill's boss. So far, nothing of note had been found in the house.

Eight hours later, Bill was driving still northwards. Having explained how he came to be at the site, and given his details to the officers, he was allowed to leave the scene. He pulled into a privately run service area in the Lake District, deciding to see if they had a bed for the night. Once in his room, he phoned Golspie.

"Hello, is Jane Sutherland there? It's her husband Bill. Yes I'll hold." He heard steps, then somebody running back to the phone.

"Bill, is that really you? I have been trying to get hold of you. All I have been told is there has been a fire at the car park. Are you alright, is anybody dead, what is going on?"

"Hold on. One thing at a time. Yes there has been a fire, I am ok, no there doesn't appear to be anybody dead, at least not when I left, there wasn't. I had to go to the Harvey's home. His wife had been murdered. Nobody can get hold of him. Look, I am driving up to Golspie. I am staying at a nice hotel tonight. I'll make an early start, expect to see me late afternoon."

"Why are you driving up?"

"I'll explain when I get there. I am fine, now don't worry." He hung up and went down to have a meal before retiring to bed.

Jane replaced the phone and went back to Cooper. He had managed to get permission to access the building. He looked up as she re-entered the room.

"I found out who the building belongs to."

"Who?"

"The original Ben Bhraggie Estate. The shareholders still own the building, not the land though. It was to store tools in. Happy to meet us there tomorrow morning and unlock for us to go inside. Apparently it had a very ornate padlock that can only be opened by using a special type of key. It has a design of the Ben on it. It will be interesting to see if it looks like ours." Gray looked up as Cooper finished speaking.

"You two go there first thing, I have to speak with the Russian Embassy in London.

+

In a small cottage in rural Russia, a very old woman sat fingering the Pendant around her. It had been a long time, she was now the only surviving person to know the real story behind the Pendent. Holding it against the light, she saw the outline of the hill with the statue on the top. This one was just the one for the store room. To get access to the three crates It needed all three padlocks, which would unlock the real secret inside them. So many people who thought they knew, now all dead. She leaned back in her chair and closed her eyes.

Chapter 28

Golspie Police Station

The banging on the door of the cell in Golspie attracted the attention of the officer in charge. After a few minutes of discussion, he agreed to go and get DI Gray. He entered the office and looked at Gray, who was seated behind his desk.

"Sorry to butt in, but the man downstairs wants to know how long we intend to hold him for? While he wants our protection, he thinks that being in a cell is a bit much." Gray looked across alarmed.

"I'd completely forgot about him. Ross, that was the name, bring him up here. We'll go to room one. I'll join him shortly." He bent over his desk paperwork again as the officer left the room.

Five minutes later, Gray went into the interview room and sat down opposite Mr Ross.

"First let me say how sorry I am to have forgotten about this meeting. Now can you tell me, for the tape, your full name and job tile please."

"My name is Herbert Ross. I was the restaurant manager of *The Double Headed Eagle.* My employers are a consortium of Russians. The restaurant is a cover for being a base to distribute drugs and other things across the north of Scotland. Can you find me a safe house to live in?"

"I expect so. Do go on..."

Three hours later, Gray left the room clutching a handful of sheets of notes he had made. He passed them over to a secretary.

"Please get these typed up as well as the transcript of this tape." He passed the notes and the cassette tape across to her. Then went straight to his desk. He had a very important call to make to the Russian Embassy, but first a call to his bosses to update them.

Cooper and Jane had driven to the building, where outside two older people stood waiting. They looked up as the police car approached and stopped in front of them. Jane got out and stretched out her hand in greeting.

"Thank you for coming. Can we go inside, now that we are all here?"

"Yes, but don't be too disappointed. As I said, it was for storing tools and such like. We had plans for replanting the land with Scottish native trees, rather than loads of identical Christmas trees." He reached inside his pocket and removed the key.

Unseen by any of the group, The Boss's henchman was watching through a pair of binoculars at the whole exchange. He gasped out loud when he saw the pendant. Assuming, wrongly, it was the one that had been at Ben Bhraggie. He knew the Boss would not like the way things were going. He carried on looking through the binoculars, while occasionally glancing at the rifle lying close beside him.

"It looks like a pendant, but acts as a key." So saying, he put it to the large hole on the ornate padlock and turned the padlock instead of the key. It unlocked and he took both off the doors and stepped to one side. "There you are. You can go and look inside. We will wait in our car over there." He pointed to a 2CV on the track. "Ideal for getting around these off road areas." They turned and walked back to the car. Leaving Jane and Cooper to enter the building.

Jane pushed the door open, it scrapped on the concrete floor as it did so. Cooper looked surprised as they moved inside.

"It's empty." He exclaimed.

"Well done Sherlock. Even I can see that. Take care not to step on the floor." She pointed to where the dust lay and more importantly, where it didn't. They both could see the outlines of pallets that had been there before. She bent down and looked closely at the door hinges. "Did you notice anything when we came in?"

"Only that the door didn't squeak as it opened."

"Good for you. Look the hinge has been well oiled. See there are drip marks on the concrete where too much oil has been put on the hinge. I think it was done in the dark, the person couldn't see what they were doing." She stepped back outside and went to the side of the building. Cooper followed and went on ahead to the rear.

"Over here." He shouted. Jane followed where he had gone around the back.

"Oh!" She exclaimed as she saw the flattened weeds and the panel resting against the back wall. Neat enough to not notice if you were quick, but very easy to remove if you knew where to look.

"This must have been how they got in and out." Said Cooper.

"I'd agree, but I don't think the two in the 2CV would have anything to do with it. Let's find out if anybody has seen anything going on in the last few days. Lorries coming up here, or forklifts. A lot of energy would be needed to move all those pallets."

"We don't know what was in them, or if they were empty and light to move. In which case a single person probably could have done it on their own." Argued Cooper. Jane nodded thoughtfully.

"You are right of course, but it must have been heavy, the concrete has scuff marks on the corners of each pallet. She went back around the front, Cooper followed. Pulling the door open again, she bent down and ran her finger along the marks. "Hello, they are deeper than the surface. This means they must have been put there just after the floor had been laid. Come on, we need to research when this was built." Jane started to move back to their car, but something caught Cooper's eyes. Above the door was a stone plaque with a number. 1941 carved into it,

"Jane wait a minute will you?" She stopped and turned. Cooper was pointing at something over the door. Sighing, she made her way back to him. "Look at that." He pointed to the number over the door.

"Would that be the date the building was made do you think?" she asked.

"No, more likely the date it was finished or topped off. Still, that is a long time ago. Now what are you doing?" He asked as she ran back to the doors and went inside. He followed her back in. She was scrapping a sample of the concrete into an evidence bag.

"See if we can get a date as to when this floor was laid…"

"…We will know when the pallets were put there." Finished Cooper. Going back outside they were surprised to see that the 2CV had gone.

"Wonder why they didn't stay?" said Jane out loud to herself.

"Well, they do have both key and the padlock. Maybe they knew more than they were letting on. Come on, we will put tape around the building, not that that will stop anybody, but it may deter them from entering, " Cooper replied. The two of them soon made a secure job of taping the building and then drove off towards Golspie.

The man put down the binoculars and picked up the rifle. He glanced at his watch. 'The Boss' should be in Dornoch by now. Time to report to him that he had seen.

Tired from driving and helping himself to a large glass of

whisky, he sat looked at his henchman.

"Two old people and they have the pendant?"

"They used it to unlock the building. It was empty though, I told you that before."

"Why keep a building like that locked with such a rare lock and key?"

"Maybe there is something under the floor. It was concrete, I went and peered through the back panel. It had been left leaning against the wall. Date on the front was 1941."

"How much concrete would have been around then?The war was on, pill boxes and the like being built all over the place. Spare concrete for a floor, no chance. " 'The Boss' rubbed his chin thoughtfully. "How secure is it?"

"Not very. Why?"

"Let's do nothing, for now at least. We will see what the police find, and if they don't dig up the floor, we can have a go ourselves. In the meantime, have the police finished with the hotel?" He looked at his two men. "Well, have they or not?"

"We'll find out and get back to you."They backed away and left the flat. Once they had left, they breathed a sigh of relief. Inside he had reached for his glass and found it oddly empty. He stood up and walked over to refresh his glass then went and dialled a Russian phone number.

The Dutchman was speaking to the Russian.

"The money has gone through. Are the keys where you said they would be?"

"Yes. It's been a pleasure doing business."The phone was replaced and the Dutchman gave a small 'yes.' Before phoning his new contact in Scotland.

"I have the building we need. What I want from you is to go and completely destroy it. I am starting with a new building and a new legal business. Now get on with it." He hung up and sighed contentedly.This way any trace of his name being linked to the Russians will have gone up in smoke. Smiling, he pulled a cigar towards him and struck a match to light it. Nothing better, he thought to himself.

The Russian's phone rang, and his secretary picked it up, then placing his hand over the mouthpiece said quietly.

"It's 'The Boss'. Wants to discuss the restaurant in Brora. He has the money you want for it."

"Tell him that it has been sold to a higher bidder." He watched as his secretary retreated from the office.

Gray had been on the phone to the Russian Embassy for an hour, having being put from one person to another, finally having found the right department, he had to wait to speak.

"Good afternoon. DI Gray of Scottish Highland Police. I have seen a car that may have been involved in a crime. First indications are that it has diplomatic plates. Can you check them for me please?"

"Certainly, always glad to help the police. What is the number?"

"The car number plate is DHE91BR There was an oval with a large black capital D beside it. When DS Cooper enquired he was told that it was a Diplomatic plate. Can you confirm that for me please? Yes, of course I'll wait." He smiled down at the phone.

"I am afraid Mr Gray that is not one of ours. It may be a false one. Good day." The phone line went dead. Gray sat and looked at the phone and then smiled. Rounding up a couple of his men, they drove over to Brora to arrest the Russian and his men.

Fifteen minutes later, Gray was banging on the door of the cottage. He had tried to peer through the windows, but it was getting dark and he couldn't see clearly enough. He nodded to the two officers.

"Break in." There was the sound of the door giving way. Then a light was put on in the cottage. Gray went inside. The place was totally empty. Gray was furious and moved back outside.

"I want a watch kept on this place for next two days. Get a joiner to fix the door. New lock as well." He turned and went back to the car where the other policeman already was sat inside. Gray turned to him.

"Get me back to Golspie with all speed."

"Yes sir." Putting the car in gear, he roared off down Golf Road towards Golspie.

Gray ran over to his desk and pulled the phone towards him. He flicked through the list of numbers on his notepad. Then, finding the right one, he dialled and waited impatiently for the person to answer.

"Heathrow Airport. How can we help?"

"DI Gray. Scottish Police. I think that three Russians may be trying to leave the country. I'll send you details of them. I would appreciate your help in this matter. Thank you." Replacing the phone, he swivelled in his chair and opened a filling cabinet. Inside a file, he removed two typed pages and feed them through the fax machine. Now things were motoring, he thought to himself.

He wouldn't have been so happy, had he known the Russians were already on their way home. A couple of joyriders had found the car and taken it for a ride along Brora beach. Once it ran out of fuel they had left it for the tide to wash over it. A lady walking her border terrier might have seen it, had she been looking that way.

Gray flicked through the reports on his desk. The old hotel had not really produced any answers as to who the person was that had been put in the cupboard. Only that he had died after being tortured and he appeared to be Dutch. At least the clothes were all purchased in Holland. The suggestion was it should be sealed back up and put on the market again. Sighing, he scribbled his signature to agree and tossed it into the 'out tray' on his desk. Paperwork was what slowed policing down in his mind. The next one was to allow Herbert Ross to use the police safe house next door, until a better solution could be found. Signing his name again, he repeated flinging the file into the out tray. Really, at this rate he might get some real police work done. He reached for the next file. About to sign it, he stopped and re-read it. Accidental death of a man in Nigg, the address seemed familiar to him. Gray sat back and thought for a minute. A house in Nigg, something had bothered Cooper about that, what was it? Ah yes, he, Cooper, had felt tired having attended a small fire there. Interesting. He set the file aside, then got up and took it over to Cooper's desk, where he scribbled a note and affixed it to the top. 'Same place where fire was, attend and see if there is a connection.' He returned to his desk and carried on catching up with his paperwork.

Tracy, having caught the bus back from Brora, had walked to the unit. Now looking around to see if anybody saw her, she unlocked the padlock and then went inside, closing the door after her. She climbed the stairs to the offices above the unit and switched on the light. Divided into three, she now sat in the first one. Furnished from some business that had long gone bust, the desk stretched in front of her. She ran her hands over it, smooth and ideal for what she wanted to use it for. Sighing, she retuned downstairs to the boxes that lay on the floor of the unit. Each one was piled four high. Being prepared, she produced a sharp knife and cut through the tape and wax seal that tied the top box four ways. Inside was newspaper screwed up. Tracy pulled it out of the box and put her hand down to feel around inside. She screamed as a trap snapped on her fingers. Withdrawing her hand, she gazed at a mouse trap attached to her fingers. Quickly she released her hand. It was throbbing already. What kind of person puts a mousetrap in a box? Then taking hold of both sides, she carefully lifted it off the pile and placed it on the floor. Now she could see into it. Pulling more newspaper out, something yellow flashed in the light. She bent down, now far too intent on what she had seen to notice that a man stood at the doorway to the unit. Nor that he had taken a gun out of his pocket, screwed a silencer to it, and then taken aim and shot her. Her last thought was why? As she collapsed onto the floor. Sighing, he unscrewed the silencer, using his gloved hand and replaced it into his pocket. Then he went up to the open box, replaced the mouse trap and producing a bit of string, retied it as before. Then he moved a few of the boxes that had been beneath it to the floor. He put the open box on the bottom and replaced the other boxes back on top of it. With a bit of luck nobody would notice that one had been opened already. Now he moved to the roll door at the front, and pulled the running chain to raise it. Once up, he made his way to the car, and one by one, took the two bodies of the old couple out of the back seats of the car, before taking them into the unit. He carefully sat them down near the boxes. Then closing down the roller door, he left the unit and put a strange looking padlock on the back door, before producing a pendant and locking it. It would be safe enough there for a while. Whistling, he looked up and down the row of eight units that ran at right angles to the four older units. Nobody about. He walked over to the 2CV and drove off. Easy when you followed the clues, he thought to himself.

Chapter 29

East Sutherland two weeks later

'The Boss' stood looking at the hotel. He had managed to buy it, persuading a person who owed him money that now was the time to pay up. He had also used some of his own money as well. Now it was his. He had arranged for a tame surveyor to look the place over with a view to what he had planned for it. It was as well not to take any chances. He would do it really proper, he thought to himself. He had learnt that the Russians had returned to Russia. The Dutchman had bought *The Double Headed Eagle,* well good luck there, he thought to himself with a chuckle. A name change didn't mean a lot in this part of Scotland. Inside the surveyor was busy with his young partner taking measurements and drawing on a pad of paper. He had given him the outline of what he wanted, now it was just up to him to draw something that he liked and approved of.

DI Gray and Cooper had been trying to get hold of Tracy, they had tried her address in Golspie that she had given them. The owner had said that she hadn't seen her for over two weeks. Thinking she had moved away, her disappearance was put on the back burner. The couple and the 2CV were soon forgotten about.

Cooper looked across at Jane and smiled. She smiled back, but was concerned that the investigation seemed to be slowing down. She and Bill were back staying in the apartment in Golspie. If they hadn't had to work, they could have almost treated it as a holiday. Jane shook herself and wandered over to Cooper.

"Did you ever get the report on the likely stuff stored at the building between..."

"I know where you mean. Nothing found there. Concrete is

around fifty plus years old. To break it up, no budget for it, at least that is what he said." He nodded at Gray sat at his desk. The door to the office opened and Bill beckoned towards Jane.

"Can I have a word?" She moved across to him.

"What is it?"

"Heard from LICD. They have recovered and identified a body in the car where the blaze started."

"Who was it?"

"Harvey."

"What! He is dead?"

"Along with his wife. LICD are asking for an independent enquiry into what has been going on. Both died the same way, syringe of poison. Fingertips turn orange after death. Likely source is Russia. Though that is only for our knowledge."

"Oh." Jane paused and thought about what he had said.

"LICD want us to stay up here for the moment. They think it is safer. Remember, I was threatened too. Now I know that nothing happened to you, but they want us to take the risk seriously. So, we are to stay put for at least another three weeks. You ok with that?"

"Have to be. Still, we are together at least that is a positive." She bent forward and kissed him lightly. "Well, better get back to work then." Jane went back to her desk and watched as Bill walked over to Gray and bent down to talk. Shortly, both of them left the room. Cooper glanced up and then returned to the reports on his desk.

Along the road in Brora, a demolition crew were putting the finishing touches to their handiwork. Sticks of explosive stuck out from various parts of the buildings. A notice had been put in the papers and the proper authorities had been informed. The night was drawing in and it was getting too dark to see properly. Concerned about safety, the Council official had said it was to go ahead first thing in the morning. Two workmen set to putting up metal fences and clipping the fence panels together. The road had been closed for a week, so one more night was not going to make that much difference. They finished working, threw their tools in the back of the pick-up and drove off towards the A9. From across the river, a man with a rifle and binoculars watched all of this unfold. Smiling, he walked along the road to his car. This was working out perfectly he thought to himself.

A quarter of an hour later, in the shadow of the industrial units, he pulled up in the 2CV and went to the rear of the unit. Satisfied that the padlock was still untouched, he removed the pendant from around his neck and unlocked the fancy padlock. Twenty minutes later he had done what he needed. As he left the unit he looked across at the streetlight and taking careful aim shot out the lamp. Then he drove off and the place returned to its now dark silence.

He pulled up outside the restaurant. The metal fence was easy to move to one side. Once the opening was wide enough, he opened the back of the car and took out the body. Heaving it over his shoulder, he kicked the door of the car closed and headed into the dark empty building. Nobody saw him or what he was up to.

Half an hour later, he was having a nice meal in the nearby hotel, where he was staying.

"Five, four, three, two, one. Fire in the hold." An enormous bang, rang through the harbour and bricks and cement dust were brought together in a tidy pile. Once the dust had cleared, the manager of the demolition team looked over at the site. He turned to the rest of the team.

"Well done. We can go home, another job well done." He shook hands with the local policeman, who had been required to attend, just in case, but he could now go as well. They all moved off to their various vehicles. Further up the road a JCB and three lorries were patiently waiting for them to go. A day or so, and the site would be totally clear. On the opposite side of the river, a man sighed with relief and looked out across the road. Perhaps a game of golf, now his work was done?

The fence was quickly taken down and the JCB moved down the wooden ramp off the trailer and across the road onto the site. With the building now flattened, it was easy to scoop the rubble into two piles. Once he had done so, the driver of the JCB moved up onto the larger of the two piles. He set about transferring the remaining pile into the lorries as they moved up to take their place alongside him.

It was late afternoon before he moved off the pile and onto the compacted earth. As he took his first scoop of the new pile and tilted the scoop back to shake the contents down, he spotted a what looked to be a dangling hand from the load. Switching off the engine, he climbed down from the cab and took a closer look. It was a hand, attached to an arm by all appearances. Swearing loudly. He made his way to the nearest lorry.

"That's torn it. No more work now for a while."

"Why? What's the problem?"

"Dangling arm." He pointed towards the scoop and in the fading light, the lorry driver could see the outline of the hand and arm against the fading sun.

"Best call the police then." He watched as the JCB driver walked across the road and got in a car and drove off. Quickly the lorry driver got out and walked across to the site. He wasn't concerned about the hand, but would be more concerned if they found anything else on the ground. But he couldn't see any other bits of body. Satisfied he went back to his lorry. The police arrived shortly and taped off the whole area. He and the other driver drove off back to the quarry on the outskirts of Tain.

"Brora are taking charge. There are some fingerprints on file, we may be lucky and get a partial match, but with decay, that may be a problem. A team are looking at the arm tonight. Then in the morning we will get a copy of the report that Brora receive."

"It could be one of two women missing, the old couple and that lady from Nigg?" Suggested Jane. She looked at Gray, but he had gone pale and was clutching his chest. Bill ran forward to try and hold him, but he collapsed in front of them. Bill shouted to get an ambulance.

Two days later in Inverness Royal Hospital, Gray was still in bed, but sat up. He looked at his two visitors. Bill and Jane.

"Thank you, you saved my life. At least, that is what the Doctors are saying to me. It was your quick actions.." His voice trailed off and he looked down at the sheets.

"You would have done the same. Now get some rest."

"What have you discovered? Fill me in."

"Not a chance. You get fit first. Then we will fill you in. Cooper has been told to take over for the present."

"But you have a senior rank to him."

"Yes, but we are visitors, so it is better that he takes over. Anyhow, he knows the full case." Jane smiled and they left the bedside.

Cooper had sat at his desk. He looked across as Jane and Bill entered the office.

"How is he?"

"He'll live. Wanted to know the full case." Jane said.

"Told him we would tell him, once he was fit again." Bill added.

"By which time, you may have solved it." Said Jane with a grin.

"Unlikely. But nice of you to say so." Replied Cooper. He turned back to his desk.

""Um, Cooper,why are you at your desk? Shouldn't you be sat at Gray's?"

"Didn't seem right somehow. Anyway, I know where everything is at my own desk. I'd have to keep going between the two desks to find anything." He smiled at them. "Too much like hard work." Looking at the pair of them, he passed the note that Gray had left him. "Take a look at that will you?" Bill took the note from him and read it to Jane. Same place where fire was, attend and see if there is a connection." Jane took a file that Cooper offered her and opened it. Quickly reading the few items in it, she nodded, then passed it over to Bill.

"Fancy a trip to Nigg?" She asked him.

"Why not, if that is ok with you Cooper?" He nodded at them and returned to the paperwork.

An hour later, Jane pulled up outside the house. Overlooking the sea front, she could see what had made the person build it here. Bill got out and stretched.

"Nice place to live." He remarked.

"Yes. Let's go and take a look around the back." She moved towards the lane that ran between two of the properties. "Let's see where this goes to?" Bill followed a bit more slowly. At the back they both could see the wooden gate that led through to the garden. A burnt circular circle, was near to the gate. Jane pushed the gate open and they both walked in to the garden. Bending down, Bill picked up some of the cinders, they were cold. A man in the next garden, looked across at them both.

"Just what do you think you are doing?"The owner is not here right now. Are you wanting to buy it? I have her phone number if you are interested that is."

"We are police." Said Jane, producing her badge and holding it up. Can we come over? We'd like a word if that is ok?" Without waiting for an answer, she moved across the garden, carefully avoiding the cinder patch. "I'm DI Jane Sutherland. He is DI W Sutherland."

"Quite a coincidence. Married are you?" He looked from one to the other. "Thought so. How can I help you?"

"We are wondering if you saw anybody around here in the last month or so?"

"Lots of people, anybody in particular that you have in mind?" He smiled at Jane.

"Ok, anybody that you didn't normally see around here." Asked Bill.

"Well, there was a couple of men, came in by boat and watched that house, where you are standing. They did go around the back of the house. Didn't see what they did after that, I was in the front room bird watching." He looked from one to another and waited.

"When was that exactly?"

"Must be about six to seven weeks ago, the day before her pile of logs got burnt. That's right, the day before her logs and kindling got burnt. She had been outside all day making the bags of logs and such like into a nice heap. Next day, it was just ash. I took it away and used it in the garden. Compost you know." He stepped back and looked up and down his garden. "She lets me have any ash that might be lying around for my garden. Funny though, the last lot doesn't seem to have done the plants any good." Jane looked at Bill and raised her eyebrows.

"Compared to what exactly?" Bill asked.

"Well, take the line of leeks over there." He pointed to a neat row. "They all had her usual ash from the bonfires. Healthy as anything. Now look at the winter veg." He pointed to a long length of dead and drooping small plants. "They are in the soil which has the last lot of ash. All dead. I don't understand it." He tutted and turned away.

"Just one final question please?" Jane asked. He turned back.

"Well alright. What is it?"

"Can we have a sample of one of the dead plants, soil as well."

"We might be able to find out why they died." Added Bill with a smile.

"Ok, that would be helpful. Come and help yourself, but don't stand on any of the good plants." He waved at them and went back indoors.

Jane turned to Bill her face smiling.

"Could be ash from drugs. There was that case in Oxford, a few years ago mind, but the plants had all died. The the roots getting damaged from the drug ash."

"I'll go and see if there is a bag of some sort in the car." Bill walked over and returned a few minutes later with a large plastic carrier bag. "This will have to do for now." He climbed over the wall and picking up a spade moved to the row of dead plants.

Emma and Maria had decided to go back to running up Ben Bhraggie, ever since they had discovered the body, they had been unwilling to return. Then finding another body in Fyrish hadn't done their confidence about running in hills any good. Now they ran up the winding route through the trees and on to the top. Neither spoke while they ran. Maria was the first to get to the top. She leaned against the base of the monument and got her breath. Emma wasn't much further behind and soon reached the same place.

"Don't think I want to go and look out to sea this time." Said Emma.

"Understood. I'll go and look though." So saying, Maira moved off towards the front. The clear view stretched in front of her. Taking care not to go too close to the slope, she gazed towards Dornoch and Embo. A cry from Emma made her turn back and run towards her.

"What's the matter?" she asked in concern.

"I've cut the palm of my hand. Look." Emma held out her palm to show Maria.

"How did. You manage that?"

"I was leaning against the base, and had my hands against it. When I went to move off, I noticed my hand had a cut."

"It's quite a clean cut. Something very sharp must have caused that. Show me where you were standing. Emma moved back to the base.

"About here." She smiled at Maria, who had taken a small pack of plasters from her running bag. "You are always prepared for any eventually aren't you?" Holding out her cut hand, she watched as her friend put a neat plaster across the wound then another crosswise to it.

"That will have to do for now. Let's see this base. Ah!" She pointed to a small rusty metal lock, set in the base and level with other stones, it would not have been visible to a casual observer. "Think that is what may have been the culprit." She bent down and looked closely at it. "Wonder what it opens?"

"We don't happen to have a key, so let's go back. We can go the longer route round the back of the hill and down past the old building." Said Emma with a hard smile. They set off, running side by side as the track was that much larger.

Lying flat amongst the ferns and heather a man with a rifle and telescope had watched all the proceedings. He waited till the two women had moved out of sight and then, standing up, he turned and went back down the hill. 'The Boss' would need to know this and quickly too.

Chapter 30

Golspie Police Station

Cooper replaced the receiver and looked at Bill and Jane who had returned a few minutes ago. The dead plant had been sown on top of ash belonging to a drug of some kind. Further investigations would be ongoing. Meanwhile, he had received an update of his own.

"The arm belongs to Tracy." Cooper told them.

"How do they know that for a fact?" Asked Bill.

"They have looked at the site where the demolition rubble was being taken. The rest of the body has been found there, well most of it. A few bits are missing, but the forensics are hopeful that some will be found on site."

"Work has stopped till they have finished, I assume?" said Jane.

"Quite. The demolition team are not thrilled about having to wait around for forensics to finish with the site. I can tell you. I have had their owners on the phone three or four times a day."

"Any news on Gray?" Asked Jane, changing the subject.

"Yes, not good either. He has had another heart attack, not as serious as the first one. Inverness want him to take early retirement. Can't see that happening somehow, can you?" Cooper looked at them both expectantly.

"It's his decision. Wait and see, it's early days at the moment." Jane said then noticed a look in Bill's eyes. "What is it Bill? You have that knowing look in your eyes."

"Well, I wonder if the demolition team might like to use their skills, to practice I mean, on the floor of the building? The one there was no money for?" He smiled at Jane and Cooper. Cooper looked back at him with a smile on his face.

"That might be worth pursuing. The main reason they said no money, was the high cost of getting the team up here to excavate. As you so rightly say, there is a team doing nothing in the neighbourhood. I'll ask and see what is allowed." He waved at them, to leave the office.

In Dornoch, Patrick sat looking at the rough sketches spread out on the table in front of him. The surveyor had done a few sketches, showing before and after. A five page report accompanied the sketches. He hadn't bothered to read that though. He was too occupied looking at the sketches. Rooms had been shown as knocked through, tunnels dug, secret passages and hiding places all had been shown as requested. He made one or two pencil notes on the paper pad. Rising he went and poured a glass of whisky without looking at the label. Then he took a cigar from the box and trimmed it before lighting it. Once he had it going, he returned to his chair armed with the whisky and cigar, he felt quite satisfied with the way things were moving. Had he been more alert, he would have spotted the flashing light on his answer phone. But under the influence of both the cigar and whisky, he drifted off to sleep. Papers dropped from his hands to the floor and spread out before him.

Cooper and Jane watched as the concrete floor of the building was finally removed. His request to use the demolition men to remove the floor had met with approval. Unable to trace the old couple again, it had been decided to demolish the whole building. From a safety point of view, it needed to either be fully restored or demolished. With the Police wanting the floor removed, demolition seemed the obvious answer.

"Wonderful how the drivers of those machines make it seem so easy." Remarked Jane as she watched another load of the floor being dropped into the waiting lorry.

"Suppose any job that someone is skilled at, looks easy to. Hello, what is that down there in the dirt?" He pointed to a piece of something bright yellow, half sticking out of the earth. Jane waved at the driver to stop. He swung the arm of the JCB around and jumped down from the cab.

"What is it?" he asked.

"Over there, that yellow coloured bit, see it? Sticking out of the earth." She pointed to it. He jumped down and made his way over to it. Giving it a hard pull, it barely moved.

"It's larger than it appears, heavy too. I couldn't budge it. Want me to try with the digger? See if I can scoop the earth back from it, whatever it is." He looked at both of them, and Cooper, after a moment's thought, nodded.

"But be careful." He added.

"Right you are."The driver swung himself back up to the cab and moved the rear of the JCB closer to clear the earth away.

Ten minutes later, the whole team had moved back. The digger had revealed, what appeared to be a WWII bomb. The yellow was a marker. Ten feet from it, now the earth had been moved, another one. Also marked with a yellow tag.

Cooper had phoned in the bomb disposal squad, it would be around four hours before their arrival. Meanwhile he had to tape off a large area and divert the traffic away from the A9. If they went off, however unlikely, the potential damage and radius wouldn't be small.

An hour later, the A9 was being closed both ways and yards of blue and white police tape had been wound around a wide perimeter, to stop anybody else getting too close.

'The Boss' awoke and decided to drive over to the hotel. Now armed with the sketches the surveyor had provided he would be able to visualise the changes planned. He pulled the car up and stopped at the police car straddling the A9.

"What's the matter officer?"

"Road closed. Unexploded bomb, found near to the A9. Will be closed till the defusing team arrive."

"Well how long is that likely to be?"

"Three, four hours. It's only just closed." Sighing, 'The Boss' turned the car and drove off back towards Dornoch.

Overlooking the taped off area, a man with a gun stood watching. Once the police had secured it, they had moved away. Checking the place was clear, he ran down and over to the edge of the tape and peered in. There were three yellow markers scattered across the floor area, He removed a piece of paper from his pocket and looked at it. It was a rough sketch of the floor, however this sketch showed five points on it. It had been quite a thing to get this from the old couple, before he had killed them. Before they died, they said they had been the last ones to know everything, but still refused to tell him what that was. Not even 'The Boss' knew what they did. If he had, then there would have been a lot more work going on here. Smiling, he pocketed the paper and turned back up the track where the 2CV sat waiting for him.

Once back in Golspie, he drove to the unit. Going round the back, he let himself in with the key and moved to the front of the unit. The smell was not good, but he didn't open the door. Two dead bodies might cause more than a bit of a stink if anybody was passing by and saw them. Swiftly he moved to the boxes. He picked one up and carried it out to the back door, then he returned and did the same with the remaining boxes. Leaving them where they were, he went and reversed the car as close to the rear door as he could, then moved the boxes into the car. It took him two trips to move all of them from Golspie to their new storage place. The last thing he did was to change the padlock from the fancy one to a plain one he had bought at Lindsay's in Golspie. Satisfied, he drove off heading to Dornoch to report what he had seen but failing to mention anything about the boxes he had.

'The Boss' listened.

"The police have closed off the main road, both ways. Looks as though there are three or more bombs up there. They aren't taking any chances by the look of things though."

"Yes, I found the A9 closed when I tried to get to the hotel."

"What are you going to do with it, the hotel I mean?"

"Run it as a hotel, what else did you think I would do with it?"

"Just wondered if it might be a base for you?"

"Why would I do that, when I have this flat?" Said 'The Boss'.

Jane nodded towards Cooper.

"He is managing to hold things together isn't he?" she said to Bill.

"At the moment. Let's wait till things start to move a bit faster. That will be a more testing time for him." He finished his coffee and looked at his watch. The phone on his desk rang. Jane reached across and picked it up.

"Jane Sutherland. Hang on, I'll get pen and paper." Flicking her fingers at Bill, as well as miming writing, he passed her a pad and pen. "Just repeat that for me, will you please?" Scribbling fast, she wrote down what was being said to her, then replaced the phone.

"Surprise me." Said Bill with a smile.

"The original owners of the land that *The Grand East Sutherland Hotel* was built on was, you'll never guess."

"Golspie Estates?"

"No. Ben Bhraggie Estates. They sold the land to the hotel developer. A man called," she peered at her notes. "Patrick Reily. Irish apparently. Had enough to pay cash for the land, then brought in his own team of builders to build it. Caused a lot of resentment in the locality."

"Could explain why it hasn't been bought yet then." Said Bill, looking at her.

"Also, there is a clause in the deeds saying that it cannot be built or extended further towards the road, and that the Broch must always stay where it is. Some sort of protection order on it."

"Wonder who has it now? There were signs of activity there a few days ago. Ask Cooper, see if he knows." Said Bill rising from his desk and going outside. Jane looked across at Cooper and walked over to him.

"We were wondering who has bought the hotel? Presumably the police know, as they were the last owners?"

"We weren't the owners, we had access to it. Hang on, there was a fax here somewhere about requesting permission to extend it, towards the A9." He fished around in the pile of paperwork on his desk." Ah, here it is." Jane reached over and took it from him. Reading it quickly, she saw the new owner was a Mr Patrick O'Conner. Had paid for it with a private mortgage supplied by a Mr, sorry, Count D R C Ulla."

"Don't suppose we have a name for this rich Count Ulla?" she asked as she tapped the paper. Cooper looked across and took the paper from her. Studying it, he burst out laughing. "What is so funny?" Jane asked.

"Read it quickly, the Count name I mean." Doing as she asked, she sighed.

"Not a real name then?"

"We can check it, but probably not." Cooper moved some papers. "Wait a minute, I have read that name somewhere else, recently too. I'll take a look, see if I can find if there is a mention anywhere else." Jane thanked him and followed Bill out of the office.

Outside Bill was stood looking up at the monument.

"It's something to do with that up there. At least I think it is. Any news on the bomb disposal people yet?"

"No. Nothing yet. They have to come from Edinburgh, it's

four hours to drive. That's assuming they are ready to go. If not, probably a lot longer. Have we had anything from that man we caught at the hotel?"

"He said nothing, we had to let him go. Nothing to hold him on. Frustrating, but there you are. The locals are keeping an eye open to see if he meets anybody on our radar.

'The Boss' took another look at the details of the hotel that lay spread out on the table in front of him. A few pencilled alterations had been made, he was itching to get to the hotel and see things for himself. The road stayed closed, frustrating for him and most of East Sutherland. Scratching the back of his head, he stood up and moved across to the windows. Overlooking Dornoch Cathedral, it had one of the best views of most of the properties in the area. A phone rang behind him. Sighing and turning around, he picked it up.

"Yes?"

"Our contact in London informs me that the police have put a name to the backer of the hotel."

"Yes, Count D R C Ulla. If they find out who is behind that name, I'd be very surprised."

"They have also found out that Patrick Reily bought it originally and that he used his own contractors. Now what do we do about that?"

"Nothing. Patrick moved away years ago. Nothing to connect him to me."

"Other than the tunnel job that is." The voice said softly in his ear.

"Well, a very select few know the background to that tale. I intend to keep it that way." He replaced the phone and paced down the flat and into the hall. His past was catching up with him. He would have to arrange a few 'meetings' with the men that still knew about his connection.

Chapter 31

A small suburb of Oxford

In Oxford, Patrick Reily sat in his small jewellery shop. Ever since playing his part in the IRA's attempt to disrupt the building of the channel tunnel, back in the 80s, he had kept a very low profile. Then an opportunity had arisen to buy a small jewellery business in a leafy suburb of Oxford. He had kept his prices fair and the business had slowly increased. Occasionally he was offered 'protection' but the sight of his shotgun soon put paid to any further discussions on that sort of thing. His name was over the door. Real Reily Jewellery. Modern and antique bought and sold. He went through to the back and picked up the ringing phone.

"Patrick Reily Jewellery. How can I help you?"

"You might want to keep alert. 'The Boss' knows where you are."

"I don't know what you are talking about. Goodbye." He replaced the phone before lifting it up again.

"You really should listen to friendly advice. I am still here Patrick."This time the caller replaced the phone and left Patrick holding the receiver in surprise.

+

The 2CV pulled up at the Golspie industrial estate. After a few minutes the roller door was raised and, if (as???) anybody had been watching, a man made two trips to the car. Each time carrying a decomposing body. Then the car was reversed into the unit and the roller door lowered. Inside a man got out and wiped down everywhere he could remember touching. He paused and looked at the car, should he dump it somewhere a bit more rural?

Then decided to leave it where it was, before leaving by the back door. He replaced the ornate one with a normal one purchased from the local ironmongers. Then he walked out through to the main road and on towards the railway station. A short while later he had got a ticket and was waiting for the next train going north. Happy to leave Golspie after his stay at the Police Station. He had said nothing, but was disappointed that 'The Boss' hadn't got him out any quicker. His own contact in Wick had a fast plane that would get him out of Scotland fairly quickly. With the pendant in his pocket, he thought that only the police had the remaining one.

In front of the hotel, a fleet of vehicles sat just waiting for 'The Boss' to arrive. Plans had been copied and materials purchased. Pallets of wood, bricks and cement were stacked all down one side of the long drive. Most had driven down from Wick and Thurso. A few had caravans behind the lorries. Staying on site was so much easier than finding somewhere to stay.

"How do I get on with the renovations, when the A9 is shut?" roared 'The Boss'. He was in a foul mood, had been for somewhile. He hadn't heard from his man who was keeping an eye on the Police in Golspie.

"Try walking?" replied his henchman.

"Walking!" From Dornoch, are you mad?"

"Not Dornoch. Drive to Golspie, park and then walk along the shore and up the side path to the hotel. Ok, you might take a bit longer than normally driving direct. You would be on site though to see the works being carried out." He pointed out to 'The Boss'.

"Not a bad idea. Not too bad at all. Well, what are you waiting for?" He walked out into the hall, grabbed his jacket and set off down the stairs. Sighing, the two men followed their boss.

An hour later, tired and weary from the climb up to hotel, 'The Boss' arrived, followed by his two men and looked at the string of vehicles spread out along the drive.

"I'm here now. Let's get going. I am not paying you for sitting around doing nothing." He turned and unlocked the large padlock. Inside the hotel it was still dark. Going back out, he walked towards the electricians van.

"First thing, get some emergency lighting and power. The whole place needs a..."

"...rewire. You told me that when you contacted me. I brought the small generator for now. I've arranged for a large one to be dropped off once the A9 has re-opened."

"It's quite dark inside."

"Get somebody to take the wooden panels down from the windows. That will make a significant difference I would think." He walked around to the rear of the van and opened the doors. "In the meantime, grab the other end of the generator and we'll get some electric going." Without thinking, 'The Boss' grabbed the other end and they carried it over to the main entrance. 'The Boss', now very happy that things were moving at last.

The bomb disposal team had been and made the bombs safe. Now they were moving the five bombs to a nearby field to blow them up.

The phone on Coopers desk rang.

"Hello, Cooper here."

"Bomb squad. You can re-open the road. We have moved them, the bombs, off site. It's all yours again." He hung up. Cooper looked at the phone in his hand and grinning turned to speak to Jane and Bill.

"Bombs have been moved. A9 open again and we can go back to the site." He clapped his hands together. "Let's move then." The three left the office and drove off in the direction of the now fully demolished building.

It was unfortunate for 'The Boss', that also stuck in the traffic was the local planning officer. He had been level with the former *Grand East Sutherland Hotel* for the past four hours. It had fascinated him that there was so many vehicles on the drive. Yet to the best of his knowledge, nobody had applied for planning or any other kind of warrant for the work. He had wondered if he should pull over and go and speak to the man in charge, but decided to return to the office, in case there had been a proper application that he had somehow overlooked.

In Brora at the remains of *The Double Headed Eagle,* the site had been cleared. No other bits of Tracy had been found. The Dutchman had been kept up to date with developments. Now back in Amsterdam once again, he was talking to the planning department based in Dornoch.

"So what I plan to do, is to totally rebuild the site, three floors. A basement, small entrance hall, lift and stairs, the main restaurant up on first floor, with large picture window overlooking the harbour."

"Why the small hall and stairs? The whole of the ground floor is a large site."

"Parking for guests."

"Well that would be helpful, as there is so little parking around that part of Brora anyway. I'd need to see detailed plans and what sort of material you are using. I presume timber framed and hard exterior?"

"No, block internal and stonework on the outside. If I can source a supply of the stone locally that is."

"That wouldn't be a problem. Send me the plans when you have them ready and I'll give them a look over. If they seem ok, you can submit them for formal approval."

"I'll get on to it." He hung up and swivelled in his chair. He looked across the water to the railway station. Maybe once the building was finished, he should move to Scotland. Sell up the illegal side. Do things legally and proper. Pay tax, employ people. Worth thinking about anyhow. He wasn't getting any younger. He got up and opened his office door.

"Get me an architect, anybody who has not had dealings with us in the past." Shutting the door, he moved across and took out a cigar from the humidifier and cut the end off. Lighting it and walking to his window, he stood there watching the students walk towards the railway station, smoking it contentedly.

At Schiphol Airport, the plane touched down on the runway and taxied to the end, before turning and parking by the refuelling depot. The pilot got out and walked over to the office to arrange a refuel. While he did so he was careful to block the officers' view of the parked plane. Inside the plane, the former henchman of the boss, stretched his legs and opened the door at the rear of the plane. He threw his small bag out first and then followed it by climbing down out of the plane. Keeping out of sight of the office, he made his way around the back of the large fuel tanks and onto the road that ran alongside the airport. A pair of wire cutters had made short work of the chain-link fence that surrounded the airfield. He soon was walking towards the terminal building. Easy enough to get a taxi or a bus from there to the centre of Amsterdam. Whichever was waiting there first, he thought to himself.

By that night, he had found a small hotel, just off one of the many canals near the centre. Close enough to walk, but not too big for there to be too many questions asked. He had signed in and taken the lift to the second floor. His room was directly above the main entrance to the hotel. If the window was open and he looked out, he could see below anybody approaching. Satisfied, he closed the window, put the 'Do Not Disturb' notice on the door handle and stretched out on the bed.

'The Boss' was pleased with how things were progressing. He had explained what he wanted, the plans, drawings really, had been put on display just inside the old kitchen and workmen were seen and heard all over the building. Tunnels being dug and walls ripped down and rebuilt in different ways. Pouring a drink and sitting down in his flat. He flicked through his address book on the side. A few of his old contacts were still in there. Seumas Kelly, Barry Ryan, Pat Doyle and Pat Reily. Maybe he should round them up for a talk about the old days. The three P's they had been when they all lived back in Ireland.

Chapter 32

Golspie

That evening PC Gray was doing his beat in Golspie. He had walked most of it. Only the Industrial Estate remaining, he thought to himself. As he turned into the Estate, he noticed one of the lights was out. He walked towards it and noted the number on the base. He'd report it when he got back. It made the place seem really dark. Flashing his torch around the units, he noticed that one had an upstairs light on. Gray walked around the back of the units where the entrance doors were. He could see that all of the units had padlocks on each door. Walking back around the front, he thought he had better report it, just in case somebody had locked up and left someone else inside, not knowing it.

PC Gray walked in through the office and saw Cooper sat working at his desk.

"Thought you should know that there is a light on in one of the units on the large Industrial Estate. The place is locked up though."

"So why bother telling me?"

"Wondered if somebody was locked in, by accident, I mean."

"Take a look at the log of keyholders, get somebody out to unlock and go and see. I have a load of paperwork to finish here." Cooper returned to the paperwork spread out in front of him. Gray turned and went to the front desk and looked for the log of keyholders. Opening it at the right page, he ran his finger down the list of names by each unit. When it came to unit two, he noted the name and number and went back through to Cooper.

"Sorry to bother you again Sir, but the owner of that unit was Tracy, lived in Nigg. Wasn't that the name of the person that owned the house where the drugs..."

"Yes. Thanks for spotting the connection. Come on." Cooper rose and grabbed his car keys off his desk.

Bill and Jane sat looking out at Ben Bhraggie from the rented apartment in the centre.

"Fancy a walk?" Asked Jane.

"Why not." Bill got up and they both set off to walk up the road opposite. Once at the fountain, they turned right, past the library and along to the large Industrial Estate. As they approached the gates the estate, a police car with flashing lights, turned in their direction. Both looked on as it slowed at the gates, a policeman got out and opened them to allow the police car in. Jane turned to Bill.

"Come on, let's see what is going on." She started to run along the pathway. Bill stood for a few minutes, then followed after her.

Cooper and Gray had parked in front of the unit and gone around the back to the rear entrance. This time armed with a large pair of bolt cutters they soon had removed the padlock. Cooper opened the door and reached for the light switch. Putting it on, he turned to the left and climbed the stairs. Gray, on entering, had sniffed the air and moved forward to the door leading to the main unit. A key hung on a nail to the left of the door. He took it down and found, not to his surprise, it fitted perfectly. Then he unlocked it and opened the door. The smell of death hit him at once. Coughing and retching, he dashed outside...

...upstairs Cooper turned his head at the sound of Gray running through the corridor downstairs. He retraced his steps back down to the rear of the unit.

Jane had got to the unit first and was now walking around

the back to be confronted by Cooper and a sick looking PC Gray.

"What are you doing here?" asked Cooper looking at Jane, then at Bill as he too appeared around the back of the unit.

"Pure chance, we were out for a walk. Saw you drive into the Industrial Estate and walked down to see what was going on."

"Don't go into the unit. There is a dead body in there somewhere." Said PC Gray quietly.

"What!" exclaimed Cooper.

"Someone is dead in the main unit. I smelt it as soon as I opened the door."

"Ok, let's call in forensics and take it from there." Said Cooper firmly. Then looked at Jane and Bill. "Until we know differently, I don't think that you need to involve yourself with this case. Do you?"

"No, you are right. Come on Jane, we carry on our walk." Bill took Jane's arm and led her away through the rear of the Industrial Estate and onto the main road.

Chapter 33

Golspie next day

The following morning Bill, Jane and Cooper all met at the Unit. Cooper had dropped by earlier and told them to meet him there around ten. Now the three of them stood at a respectful distance as the two body bags were brought out and placed in the van waiting to take them to Inverness. The van drove off, and the rest of the forensic team appeared from the unit.

"Ok, you can go in now. I'll write a report and send it to you. They have been dead for a while, not killed in there. We did find some evidence of an attempt to clean up the place. We found a small bit of amber on the floor. Looks as though it is a part of some larger item though. A chip, would be a better description for it." Cooper looked at Bill and Jane.

"Come on, let's go and see what has been found." Once inside, they saw the 2CV sitting with the doors open. Jane looked around the unit.

"It's quite small, I mean that with the car in here, there isn't much room for anything else."

"I agree, so does forensics. Appears there have been boxes stored on the floor before the car was parked there. Dust shows the outlines. The tyre marks run over some of the outlines, so obviously the car came after the unit was emptied." Said Cooper.

"Is It the same 2CV that the couple owned?" asked Bill.

"Yes. We ran the plates through the DVLA and it is. We are also assuming, until confirmed otherwise that the two bodies are of the same two people." Said Cooper. "However, we still need to confirm their names. Do you know their names at all?

"No idea. We only saw them once, at the building halfway

between the monuments, when they met us, unlocked the padlock, had a fancy key and then shortly afterwards, disappeared along with their 2CV."

"I doubt they drove it here themselves. So it appears that we are also looking for another person who knows about the padlocks and what is really going on." Said Jane with a shrug of her shoulders.

+

The Dutchman had arrived in London using the Channel Tunnel train. He stepped out into the busy morning traffic. He had received a phone call, last evening, from a contact of the Dutch Police. Somebody had tipped them off about him and his business. They, the police, planned a morning raid. Thanking his contact, he had quickly moved his paperwork to the bank vault, sold the boat to an unsuspecting person and taken the train to Paris. Once there, he had bought a ticket to go direct to London. Now he needed a new boat, one that would be good both inland on cannels and at sea. Picking up a free paper, along with the other passengers he scanned the classified adverts. Particularly of interest was a section titled 'Boats'. Stepping into a nearby doorway, he ran his finger down the small list. One firm stood out. James Boatbuilder (Graves End & Co. Apart from the obvious error, he thought it may be worth a visit. Looking at the large map near the entrance of the station, he worked out that he could get there in about an hour.

An hour and a half later he walked into the boatyard. He could see a light on in the office. The outlines of two people, arguing, were clear to see as well. Stepping up to the door, he listened before knocking loudly.

"Come in." Roared a voice from inside. "And you," a pause "can get out. I don't take threats easily." The door swung open and a tall dark haired man stormed out and down the steps. Turning towards the office he said. "I won't forget this in a hurry." Then got into a large black BMW and drove off. The owner stood at the top of the steps and looked at the Dutchman.

"Come in, how can I help you?"

"I need a sea going boat, that also will handle well on the canals. Needs to sleep four people. Adults not children. Do you have anything in the yard at present that would fit the bill?" Rubbing his chin thoughtfully, the owner nodded and opened his laptop. After a few keystrokes, he turned it around so his customer could see it.

"Something like this?"

"If that does what I mentioned, yes."

"Sleeps six, comfortably four, has twin outboard and a large inboard motor. Cost is…"

"Trust me, not important." Said the Dutchman interrupting him.

"We had one like this a few months ago. Removed some of the upper deck and gave it a new coat of paint. Sold it quickly to a man in London Dockland. Think though he might want to get rid of it. He phoned to say that he hadn't used it as much as he hoped. Do you want me to phone him and see if he would sell?" He looked hopefully at his new customer.

"Why not? I'd need you to give it full service and deep clean. Load it with fresh water etc and I'd collect it as soon as it was ready. The Dutchman smiled at the owner of the boatyard.

LICD office had been quiet, following the death of the DCI. The fact that both Bill and Jane were in Scotland didn't help matters. The team was a small close knit one and the death of one of them had hit the rest hard. Down in the carpark, repairs to the area that had been damaged by the fire continued. Bill's car had been undamaged by the fire and was now parked outside on a spare piece of wasteland. Two men drove up to the LICD office, parked their car on double yellow lines and walked down to the underground car park. Splitting up, they proceeded to check each of the car bays. Twenty minutes later, they met up and shook their heads before returning to their car which was in the process of being about to be lifted onto the back of the lorry. Saying nothing, the first man, removed his gun, shot the driver in the head. The second man moved forward, operated a few levers to lower their car back onto the road. A quick release of the straps, and they got in and drove off. It was much later that the dead man was discovered, by which time the two men were sitting in a private plane awaiting permission to take off and fly to Moscow.

Chapter 34

Golspie later same day

Later that morning found Cooper, Bill and Jane in the office in Golspie. On Cooper's desk was a long fax. He read it quickly before looking at Bill and Jane.

"In a nutshell it is the following:- They had been put in the car. Where they had been before that, she hadn't any idea. Had been dead for quite a while, more than two weeks. Death had been by being shot through the back of the head. Close range". He put the fax down and looked at both of them. "What did they know that we don't."

"Any sign of the pendant?" asked Jane. "They had one, it was used to get in the front of that building."

"And they went off after unlocking the padlock." Added Bill.

"Meaning that they must have had both the padlock and the key." Said Cooper thoughtfully.

"See if it is in the car, the forensic team might have found it somewhere on the floor of the car?" suggested Jane hopefully.

"Good idea." Cooper moved to the phone and dialled the number.

LICD had received an anonymous phone call. A boat that they had been looking for was going to be at James Boatbuilder (Graves End) & Co. If they hurried they might get the boat and another wanted criminal. A few phone calls later and a small team descended on the yard. They knocked on the office door, then went in.

"Yes? Can I help you Officer?"

"We have a warrant to search this place and the yard and your home."

"What for? I run an honest business."

"We are looking for a boat, a boat that a known criminal has used in the business of drug dealing."

"Look, I make and sell boats. What the customer does after I have sold them the boat, well, that is not my business." He shrugged his shoulders.

"Ok, this is how it's going to work. My colleagues are going to search the place. If we find nothing, we will leave you in peace. If on the other hand we find anything to connect you to the boat named Brora or Ben then we will arrest you."

"You don't know what he is like."

"Help us, we can help you."

"The owner of the boat, he sold it and didn't buy another. It was a cash purchase. I changed the style of the boat, had it repainted and it sold quickly."

"So where is it now, the new version?"

"Outside. A customer is coming today to buy it from me."

"Who exactly?"

"He didn't give his name, but is foreign."

"Foreign in what way? French, German, Far East, Middle East?"

"European." He glanced at his watch anxiously. "Look, he will be here soon, I have paperwork to prepare." He looked hopefully at them.

"Get on and do that. Then we will take over running the place till this new customer has been and gone." He looked at the owner who now realised that he had no choice in the matter. Sighing, he finished he paperwork and then rose and left the desk.

"You give him the keys once he has given you the bank transfer. Ok?"

"We give him the keys, he gives us the bank transfer. Got it." The owner got up and left the office to them.

In the boatyard, the Dutchman had returned. A phone call late last night had confirmed the boat was for sale. In his pocket he had a bank draft for the full amount made ready for the owner of the yard. He knocked on the door of the office and went in. Once inside, he realised that something had gone wrong. Two policemen were in the office, one sat behind the desk, the other just inside the door, who closed it after he had entered and now stood in front of it.

"Where is the owner? He has a boat that I am buying today."

"Do you have the bank draft?"

"Well, yes. He needs to be here to sign the paperwork and the boat over to me. Where is he?"

"If you have the bank draft, we have these." The officer held up a ring of keys. "Whereabouts are you from, exactly?"

"Europe."

"More specific please."

"Holland, The Netherlands. Rotterdam area." He smiled at the policeman.

"Address?"

"I don't have one. I plan to live on the boat, the one I am hoping to buy once you have finished asking all these pointless questions. Now can I give you this and you give me the keys please?"

"Yes, alright." He watched as the man pulled a piece of paper from his inside coat pocket and laid it on the desk. The policeman dropped the keys from his hand onto the desk. The Dutchman scooped the keys off the desk and left the office. Outside the boat was tied up to the wall of the boatyard. He made his way over and bent down to untie the rope at one end, then a sudden push sent him over and into the water below.

"I can't swim. Help me. Hel..." A man approached and looked over the edge, smiled and turned back and walked back to a car waiting outside the yard. 'The Boss' would be pleased how he handled that. He smiled and tapped the driver on the shoulder, indicating that he should drive on.

Half an hour later, a phone rang in Golspie Police Station. Bill picked it up.

"Highland Police. DI Sutherland."

"You might want to pass on the message that the Dutchman has died."The phone was replaced and Bill looked at the phone in puzzlement. Jane looked across at him.

"Who was that?"

"No idea, but he said the Dutchman has died."

"Did he say where or how?"

"No, nor did he identify who he was. Funny though, I thought I recognised the voice. Just can't place it." He replaced the phone and went back to his desk and sat down.

At the Dutch Police HQ a phone call informed them of the death of the Dutchman aka as Klaas Van Miere.

In Dornoch, a planning officer had spent a few days trying to get hold of the Dutchman who planned such a nice new restaurant in Brora Harbour. Having failed, he turned his attention to the building work that was being done on that hotel. Collecting his coat, he went out and drove off towards Golspie.

Inside the former hotel, it was almost impossible to see across the rooms for dust. The noise was loud as jackhammers and machines were all working in different areas of the hotel. 'The Boss' stood in the former kitchen looking at the plans. As work had been carried out, it was clearly marked on the plans posted on a large board. He didn't hear the Planning Officer enter. The first time he became aware he was there, was when he got a tap on the arm. Spinning round, he nearly sent the man flying.

"Who are you?"'The Boss' shouted above the noise. The man produced a business card and passed it to him. On it he had added in capital letters. STOP ALL WORK NOW AND COME

OUTSIDE. Curious, he followed the man outside and a few feet away from the building. "What's this all about, I have a tight schedule to run to."

"Whatever you may think, this stops now. No planning or warrants that I can find back in the office. Unless of course you can show me them now, in which case I will leave you to carry on."

"And you are going to stop me, how exactly?" Asked the Boss with a smile on his face.

"Like this." He walked to the generator and switched it off. Then took the key out of the ignition. Dangling it in front of 'The Boss'. "Now, stop the work, put in the plans, we approve them, you get to start again."

"No chance. It's my property, I do as I like." He jerked his hand in the direction of the hotel, where a lot of workmen had come outside to see why they had no electric. "I have these men to pay. They wouldn't stay while you process paperwork. Now get going." He took a step towards the man, who stood his ground. "I am warning you, don't make me do something I'll later regret." Still the officer stood in his way. 'The Boss' tried to grab the keys, but the officer moved them back out of his reach and put them in his pocket. Then he turned and walked back to his car and drove off towards Dornoch. His men crowded in on him.

"What are you going to do?"

"Is he right, can he stop you working?"

"Alright, get back to work. I have a spare set of keys in my car, I'll fetch them and start up the generator again. Look, the alterations you are all making are never going to get past planning, so just carry on and leave this to me." He waited and watched them return to the hotel, then went over to his car and retrieved the keys. Always best to keep a spare set handy, he thought to himself with a smile. Though how he would solve the problem of the Planning Department was going to be a bit more of a challenge.

In Golspie Bill had managed to trace the address of the lady who owned the 2CV. Since she was supposed to be living in Helmsdale, he went over to Cooper and waited while he finished signing paperwork.

"A minute of your time?" he asked.

"A minute it is. Make it quick I have loads of paperwork to clear."

"Owner of 2CV lives in Helmsdale. Thought a trip there might shed some light on the owner and why it was in Golspie."

"Not registered to the two bodies in the car then?"

"Don't know, but if there is nobody at home, then it is probably likely."

"Go on, take Jane as well. She might be better talking, woman to woman that is." Cooper bent back down and carried on signing.

Arriving in Helmsdale, Bill pulled up outside La Mirage and nodded at Jane.

"Go and see if they know where the address is." He handed the paper with the address on to her. Sighing, Jane got out and walked along to the Post Office. Going inside, she joined the small queue and shortly was being seen.

"How can I help you?"

"DI J Sutherland. Would like directions to this address please?" She passed the paper under the glass and watched the postmistress read it. As she did so, Jane noticed that her face fell, then she passed it back to her.

"Think she may have moved, or died. She hasn't been in for her pension for three weeks. Now how you get there is not that straightforward. First go to the end of the street, take a left over the bridge, follow the road around and up past the station. Turn first right, then right again. Drive for about two miles and you will see the green house on the left. It's about a hundred yards past that on the right. Got it? Next." Jane stepped to one side to allow the person behind her step up to the counter. She went out and back to Bill in the car.

"Well did you get directions?"

"Yes, here let me drive, I can remember them and drive."They switched places and she drove off in the right direction. Half an hour later she pulled up outside of a house. No lights on and a garage door was closed with a concrete block in front of it. "I think this is it. Come on." She got out of the car and walked up the small drive to the garage. Bending down, she lifted and moved the block to one side. A patch of dead grass showed where it must have stood. Bill pulled the door open. Apart from a pool of old oil on the floor, it was empty. Jane looked at the frame of the garage. Near to the door hinge was a row of keys. Attached to each one, a label showed what it was for. Moving over, she ran her eye over them, but no key to the house. Bill had left her and walked to the front door. He went to knock on it, but it swung open on his touch. Curious, he moved inside to the small hall and looked up the flight of stairs.

"Hello? It's the Police. DI Sutherland. Is there anybody there?" He stood listening. Not a sound. Then Jill spoke behind him.

"But no one descended to the Traveller.." Bill spun round.

"Don't do that. What do you mean, no one descended to the Traveller?"

"It's from a poem. Forgot who wrote it. I had to learn it at school. Are we going in then?" She pushed past him and went up the stairs two at a time. A few doors opened and shut and she returned back down. Bill had walked around the three rooms downstairs, kitchen, dining room and what appeared to be a study. Rows of books, mostly in either Russian or English filled the shelves. Jill re-appeared at his side. "Remarkable house. The three rooms are all empty. Not a stick of furniture in them. Bathroom looks as though it hasn't been used for a while. Yet this room." She pointed to the study. "Looks like a normal room in any house."

"I think, whoever uses it, only comes here to use this room. Let's leave it as we found it and go back. We can check who actually owns the house, might lead us somewhere, anywhere." Bill turned and went back outside. Jane paused as a book on the desk had caught her eye. She moved into the room and took a glance at the cover. *Pendant Keys and their locks in Europe and the UK. Book Two.* She quickly looked at the shelves to see if there was a gap, but there wasn't. Memorising the title, she left the room and went and joined Bill.

"Interesting book on the desk."

"Was there? I didn't notice it."

"*Pendant Keys and their locks in Europe and the UK. Book two.*"

"Book one not there then?" Bill said, looking at Jane with a puzzled gaze.

"Not that I could see. No gap on the shelves anyhow. Come on, we'll go back and see if we can trace a copy of it." She went back to the car and got in.

Chapter 35

A flat in Dornoch

'The Boss' was happy how things were progressing, but not too happy about the planning officer. Later, back in the flat, he gathered three of the men together.

"I need that Planning Officer frightened off, totally scared. I don't want or have the time to file paperwork. It wouldn't get passed anyhow. Now anybody got any ideas?"The men looked at one another, astonished that 'The Boss' was asking them for ideas. He was the ideas man, they just did as he wanted them to. One raised his hand.

"Maybe we shouldn't be the ones to do anything, get somebody else to do it, somebody unknown or connected to us or you." He glanced at the other two men, who were nodding their agreement.

"Ok, I do have somebody who might fit the bill. I'll give him a phone call and see if he will come up from London and do what is needed."

Jane was on the phone to Edinburgh. One of the six copyright libraries in the UK.

"No, I don't know the author, or the ISBN, the title was "*Pendant Keys and their locks in Europe and the UK. Book two.* Yes Book two, so I presume there is another book with the same title? Yes I'll wait." She made a face down the phone. "It was published privately? By whom? A firm in Oxford. Pen to Press Ltd. Do you have an address for them? You do? Good. 1 St Andrews Business Park, Headington, Oxford. Thank you." Jane replaced the receiver and looked at Bill. "You heard all of that I presume?" He nodded.

"A trip to Oxford?"

"Let's try phoning them first, shall we?" She smiled sweetly and went over to the coffee machine and switched it on.

The phone rang in Real Reily Jewellery. Patrick picked it up.

"Real Reily Jewellery, how can I help you?"

"I need you up here in Sutherland. You have forty eight hours."

"Be reasonable Patrick. I don't do that sort of thing anymore. I run an honest business. Have done for years now. Why should I go running of up to Sutherland?"

"One, because I know where your shop is, it would be a pity to see it go up in flames. Two, you owe me big time."

"Not a chance. I don't owe you anything." He hung up leaving 'The Boss' looking at his phone in amazement.

"He hung up on me. That is the first time he has ever hung up on me." His three men rose as one, they recognised the early signs of a potential temper from him. Nobody wanted to be anywhere near him when he lost it.

"Right, we'll be going on, it's getting a bit late." They made their way to the door and out of the flat. Leaving 'The Boss' looking at his phone.

The following day at the hotel, all work had ceased. Workmen were stood or in their vans waiting. At first light a team from the Council had arrived and issued a cease notice on the whole site. Not wanting to be on the wrong side of the Council, the workmen had all obeyed. Now everyone was waiting for the arrival of 'The Boss'. What would happen when he turned up they wondered.

Twenty minutes later, a large black car swept into the drive and up to the hotel. Two people got out, one they all recognised. The second wore a suit and carried a briefcase. He looked out of place compared to the rest of the workforce and 'The Boss'. The Planning Officer moved forward towards the two men.

"Mr Patrick O'Conner?" 'The Boss' moved quickly towards him.

"Listen, nobody calls me that anymore. I am 'The Boss'. Got it?"

"Right Mr O'Conner. I am here to serve an enforcement to stop work at once." He handed over the paperwork and turned to go.

"Not so fast." Patrick passed the paperwork to the man in the suit beside him. "This is my Solicitor. I'll let him take a look first." They waited while the paperwork was looked at, finally the Solicitor looked at Patrick.

"This is in order, however, they should have given you a pre-visit notice the first time." He turned towards the Council Officer. "Did you give such notice or did you just turn up unannounced?" For the first time, the official looked a bit worried. "Well, we are all waiting."

"I was stuck in traffic on the road down there. I saw all the vehicles on the drive. I drove on to the..."

..."Yes, yes, all very interesting I am sure. Did you serve a pre-visit notice? Yes or No?"

"No."

"Thank you." He turned to Patrick. "Then, until he does this doesn't apply. Having said that, I would go down the proper channels and apply retrospectively. You could ask the Council for a pre-planning meeting to ascertain the likelihood or otherwise of it passing planning." He took a look at the two men. "As a gesture of goodwill, the officer may like to have a look around while he is here and give you some guidance. Hmn?" Patrick looked at him in amazement.

"You want me to let this official, the same person who has shut down the works, look around the site and indicate what the likely outcome of any application might be? Is that it?"

"I would advise it. Yes, strongly advise it. I can be with the two of you if that helps?" He looked hopefully at Patrick.

"All right. But the first sign of."

"There will not be any trouble. Not from either of you. Now let's go in shall we?" The Solicitor led the two men into the hotel. "Perhaps you can explain what is planned?"

"Well, this used to be the kitchen, but that is going to be more central, the stairs remain going up either side of the dining area in between them. The Bar and Music Room will both go and be replaced by the kitchen. Diners will be able to see their food being cooked and prepared. The Bar had running water and it was easier to start with a clean area, than to have to walk through the kitchen while building work was progressing."

"All sounds good and reasonable to me. " Said the Officer. "What about the bedrooms?" He consulted his clipboard. "There were originally eight, I believe?"

"That was the original hotel. The last owners reduced it in size, had installed en-suites in all the rooms. We are planning on just re-decorating and putting in new en-suites. We are strengthening the floors, as well. The Jacuzzi baths will weigh a lot, don't want the guests to be soaked do we?" Patrick laughed nervously

"No. The Reception Area and Games Room?"

"No change, other than replacing the floor, rotten under the reception area it was." Patrick remarked.

"Outside?"

"Tarmac the drive and new coat of paint."

"No extensions then?"

"Not at this stage. Later, maybe."

"Well, Mr O'Conner, if that is all, and put in correctly on the right forms, I don't see any problems arising. I'll look forward to receiving the right paperwork. Good day." He turned and had almost left the old kitchen area, when he turned back. "This floor, it needs to be replaced, trip hazards and so forth. I would suggest that you apply to have a ramp to the door outside for ease of access to anybody in a wheelchair. Not mandatory, but it would probably ease the load. Bye." He turned and left the hotel. Patrick looked at the Solicitor and sighed.

"Paperwork, I hate it. Can you deal with that side of things?"

"Easily. I noticed you didn't mention some of the work you are doing?"

"I mentioned all the bits that the public will be using. Behind the scenes, well that between me and my building contractors." He smiled and then moved outside where he goaded his workforce back to work.

"Pen to Press Ltd. How can we help you?"

"DI Sutherland. I am enquiring about a couple of books I think you published."

"Do you know the title or the ISBN?"

"Title only. *Pendant Keys and their Locks in Europe and the UK*."

"Can I take your phone number, I'll phone you back when I have checked for you."

"Certainly. Its 0408 6342" Bill replaced the receiver and looked at Jane. "They are going to check and phone me back. Coffee?" He rose and went over to the machine.

In Amsterdam, a man had walked to the usual mooring spot where he thought he would find Klaas. It was empty and a Dutch policewoman stood on the edge of the canal.

"Yes? Can I be of assistance?"

"I was looking for the boat that is usually moored here."

"That boat has been impounded. The man you are looking for, sold it to another person. We have traced the boat and are examining the contents very carefully. What is your connection to the man?" She took out a notebook and pen and looked at him expectantly.

"I had heard he might be in the market for buying some old items."

"That is so different to what we knew he dealt in. I think you had better find another person to buy your items." She closed her notebook and put away the pen. Taking the hint, he walked away towards the railway station. This was going to change his plans. Once inside the station, he went and ordered a coffee and sat down to have a think of what to do next.

The phone rang on Bill's desk. Grabbing it quickly he answered.

"Bill Sutherland."

"Pen to Paper Ltd here, I have looked up the books you mentioned. It was a special favour to the author. We had a very small print run. Five hundred copies. The author had thought it would be a good seller. Sadly the market was not that great. We sold ten copies, or sets and the rest are still in the warehouse. Do you want to see a set? I can get them couriered up to you."

"Is it just the two volumes then?"

"Good heavens no. It ran to five volumes. Book one was *Pendant Keys and their Locks in USSR*. Book two you already know about. Book three was *Pendant Keys of India,* Book four *Australia and New Zealand the first Pendant Keys.* Book five *The Index to Pendant Keys.*"

"Hold off sending them just yet, I appreciate your finding out this for me. One more question. Is the author still alive?"

"There were three co-authors. Two have sadly died, one was killed in a motor accident, when in working in Russia. The second one was killed in a motor accident when driving in Norway, near the Russian border, both were researching material for an additional volume. Sad really. The third person is a lady who lives, hang on I'll find out for you." He heard the sound of papers being shuffled. "Oh, she lives in Russia too. I'll fax you her details. She might be able to help you, if you can get hold of her that is."

"That would be great. I'll give you the fax number. 0408 6344

You have been most helpful." He replaced the phone and walked over to Cooper and Jane to tell them what he had learned.

"So only one author remains alive?" Said Cooper.

"It would seem so." Replied Bill. Though I wouldn't want to be her, two others die in motor accidents, while carrying out research for another book. One might be a coincidence. Two, well I am a bit more suspicious. I think we need to return to the Helmsdale, what do you think Jane?"

"If Cooper agrees it. Yes, a return there might reveal something worthwhile." Cooper looked up on hearing his name being mentioned.

"Go where you please, anything that might help solve this would be appreciated." He picked up a file and passed it over to Jane. "Take a read of this, the factory that used to make locks and keys in Dingwall. I went and spent a day finding the old business files. The file contains a rough draft of a report I was drawing up to give to Gray."Then he waved them away from his desk.

Bill read the file to Jane while she drove them back to Helmsdale.

"Set up in the early 30s, they produced one off padlocks for firms which needed high security. When the Second World War broke out, the premises were enlarged to supply locks to the Armed forces. In 1939 a Russian locksmith came to the factory and worked alongside the staff. He had his own method of working as well and used to produce one off pieces of work for clients who needed such items. In 1940, the factory was approached to produce twelve sets of three padlocks each one to look alike but to only open with an individual key. The sets were to be kept together for securing large items that needed to be safely stored from the Germans. The parcel of locks and keys were sent to Russia and never seen again. A set, similar to the ones asked for were made as a trial and he used a nearby village as the original artwork." Jane glanced across at Bill.

"So basically, the Russians have thirty six padlocks in sets, securing something valuable, and a set of similar items, using a nearby village are in this area."

"Doesn't tell us what they were for though does it?" said Bill thoughtfully.

"No, now look we are nearly here." Jane slowed down and turned off the road into Helmsdale.

Once inside the house in Helmsdale, Bill and Jane carefully scanned the bookshelves. Now that they knew the titles of the other books it became a bit easier. The hundreds of books that lined the room had been arranged in no particular order.

"It's like looking for a needle in a haystack." Said Jane. She was frustrated that there seemed to be no order to any of the books. Unlike her own book collection, sorted by author and then alphabetically by title, this was a muddle.

"Found volume three." Cried Bill in delight. He took the book over to Jane and then spread it out on the desk.

Pendant Keys and their locks in India. Book Three.

"The cover matches the book two. Just need to find books one, four and five." She gazed at the wall of books and sighed.

About two hours later, they had found all of them, except volume one. Bill looked the pile of books on the desk.

"Do you think it is significant that there is an author still alive in Russia, the first book was about Russia and the back of the pendant that the police have, is in Russian?" He said to Jane.

"It is stretching coincidence a bit far, I would say. Let's take the books we have found back to Golspie. We'll leave a note to say who has been here and taken them." She went around the desk and pulled the chair out to get to the drawers.

"Don't do that. We don't know who else might want to find the same five books."

"Ok." She stepped around the books on the floor and in doing so, knocked a big pile of paper across the floor. "Bother!" Bending down, she picked up the first page. Reading it, she stood up excited. "Bill, it's the first volume. Look." She pointed to the piece of paper in her hand. *Pendant Keys and their locks in the USSR Book One. 1st DRAFT. NOT FOR PUBLICATION.* Was stamped lightly across the page. Excited now, she picked up another piece of paper, it also had lightly stamped 1st DRAFT stamped across the page. Jane gathered the remining paper together and tapped it into two bundles. Then clutching the paper bundles to her chest, followed Bill out to their car.

Unseen by them, an old man was watching the house through binoculars and smiled to himself. He walked through and dialled an international telephone number.

"They have the whole set. Yes, including the first volume. It must have been missed before, it looks like it is in loose paper."

"Thank you. The usual amount will be in the post to you in the next day or so." The man hung up and walked back to his window, the police car had now gone.

Patrick, aka 'The Boss', had got things moving again, workmen had been told to carry on working on the side of things that the planning didn't need to know about. Patrick decided to step outside for a moment. His phone was ringing, with the noise inside, he hadn't heard it go off.

"Hello."

"Thought you might like to know that our friend the Dutchman is no more. A totally vacant restaurant site is available if you want it? Say in exchange for the London and Oxford side of your business?"

"Well that is very interesting, presently I have my hands full with other things. Lots of balls to juggle, you know how it is?"

"Only too well. One thing I would appreciate from you, find out how much the local police know about the Pendants." The phone went dead and Patrick looked at it with a worried look on his face.

Chapter 36

Golspie Police Station

Late that evening, Cooper sat at his desk. The Pendant lay on a white piece of paper in front of him. Key in shape, but not your usual key, outline of the Ben on one side and Russian text on the other. He turned and looked for the fax that had been sent to him from Invergordon. When compared to the picture, he noticed that there was a slight second outline just visible. Holding the pendant up to the light, he could just make out the outline. Satisfied he put it down and looked up as Jane and Bill came in clutching books and piles of paper.

"We have found the five books." Said Bill.

"Four books and a first draft to be more exact Bill." Jane remarked as they put the two piles down on an empty desk. Bill scanned the pile to get volume two out and quickly started to flick through it. Jane looked at him puzzled. "What are you doing?"

"Looking to see if there is a match to the pendant we have here. If so, it might tell us a bit more about it." Sighing, Jane put the other books on the floor and took the bundle of paper of Volume 1 and stacked it on her desk. Methodically starting at page one, she slowly started to turn the pages one by one. Cooper looked at both of them, then got up and picked volume three off the pile. Then returning to his own desk he started looking as well.

Three hours later, the three of them looked at one another, the pendant did not match any of the pictures in the books. A photocopy lay in front of each of them. A piece of text from the first volume had been photocopied and enlarged:-

The Pendant, unlike most of the sets found in Russia was first made in a small workshop near Inverness. Sold on a one padlock one key basis, was unusual in that the key could be worn around the neck as jewellery. Early examples can be found in Amber and Bronze.

"And this is the only reference, a tenuous one at best, linking our Pendant and Russia?" Asked Cooper.

"Be fair, we were looking for pictures not reading all the text. That would have taken a lot longer than," Bill looked at the clock. "Three hours that we have been here."

"True." Sighed Cooper. "Let's all go and have some sleep. We'll meet up again in the morning."

In Russia, in his office, the Russian listened to his man in silence.

"Did you remove the illustration from the first draft?"

"Yes. The pages were numbered, but not the illustrated plates."

"And you learnt nothing from the woman?"

"She never would have told me what we needed to know Sir."

"Thank you, you did what you could. Do you think we will ever find what's at the bottom of this, or are we wasting our time?"The man looked at the Russian. Say the wrong thing and he would be dead.

"I wouldn't like to hazard a guess Sir. I do feel that there is still some connection to the North of Scotland. The Convoys sailed from that part of the world. Scotland is not that big."The Russian waved his hand indicating the meeting was over and to leave the office. Pleased to be leaving alive, he backed out of the office and set off down the ornate stairs to his car.

Once he was back in his office the Russian picked up his phone.

"Did you do as I asked?"

"Yes."

"Good. How long?"

"Ten minutes."

"Good. Arrange for a clear up to be done as soon as it happens." He hung up and smiled. Too many people knowing the full picture, that would not be good. Standing up, he moved to his desk and looked down the line of trees. A single car was driving away. A large explosion and the sound of car alarms going off. He turned back and picked up the phone again.

"Get me some bodies on the ground in Scotland. We are going hunting."

"Including yourself?"

"No, not this time." He replaced the phone and looked at the book open on his desk. *Pendant Keys and their Locks in USSR. Book one.* A colour plate showed a picture of a pendant, not too far in likeness to the one sitting on the police desk. Under the picture the text was most unhelpful.

Though not usually found in Scotland, the exception was a set of three of the pendant's being made in the 1930s A proof set they are believed to have been the first cut before a design being engraved in the mid 1940s At least two examples are known of today.

A design, he mused to himself. The time fitted, but what would be the connection to Scotland? He picked the book up off the desk and took it to his safe. Once inside, he spun the lock and set off for his Dacha he needed a break to think things over.

In Golspie, the landlord of the industrial units was getting cross. All the tenants, bar one, had paid their monthly rent. He had tried to phone her, but had got no answer. Now he had driven to the units and was prepared to break in. At the back, the padlock he had supplied with the unit was lying, rusting, on the ground. A new large combination padlock was in place.

Along with a police notice saying not to enter. He grunted and went to his car, he had come prepared for this. A few passes with a hacksaw and the padlock dropped to the ground. He pulled the door open and went in. Switching on the lights he saw the empty unit in front of him. Moving forward, in the dust, he could make out that cartons had been stacked on the floor. There had been some red paint spilled but that was not of concern to him. He went up the stairs and into the first of three offices. All were now empty. Now very puzzled, he returned downstairs and using a new padlock, locked the unit. He would re-advertise it. He made his way to the car and looked up. One of the lights wasn't working, he made a mental note to get it fixed and drove out of the yard.

A small plane touched down at Wick Airport and taxied to the end of the runway. At that time of night, nobody was about. A couple of people got out of the aircraft and watched it take off again. They had two small cases and made their way to the edge of the field. A pre-arranged car sat there. Keys in the ignition and a tank full of fuel. Both of them got in and looked at one another.

"South to Golspie or West to Loch Ewe?"

"Loch Ewe is west, but the best way is South and across. We can deal with the Golspie problem on the way." He fished in the back and produced a battered AA guide. His companion started the engine and drove out and south.

Two hours later, the two Russians had parked at the car park in the centre of Golspie and were on the track to Ben Bhraggie. Their torches flashed on the path in front of them. The two rucksacks had more than enough material for what they planned.

At the top, they kept their lights pointed downwards on the base, looking for the lock that was set into the base. Once found they moved together to shine more light on it. Painted the same colour as the stonework, it would have been difficult to see unless you knew where it was located. Unfortunately for them, the flashing of the lights had been seen by the local villagers.

At the police counter three villagers were trying to tell the police what they had seen.

"It's flashing, the Mannie is flashing."

"No, there are spotlights that are faulty."

"I think it is torches and nobody should be up there at this time of night."

"I've said it before, the Mannie is flashing. Go and take a look if you don't believe us." Sighing the policeman lifted the flap of the counter and followed the three men outside. He looked up and could see flashes of light now and then near the base. Sighing, he went back inside and told Cooper what he had both had reported and just seen.

"Up on the top. Looks as though it is near the base. What do you want me to do Sir?"

"Leave it till morning, it is too dark to go chasing up in the hills. First light we can see a lot more clearly." He turned and went back to his desk. He knew how Gray must have felt, the paperwork was never ending.

At the top of Ben Bhraggie, the two men, both now freezing, were attempting to open the small door.

"It's stuck fast. The key that he supplied doesn't fit it."

"Option two then." Sighing, the first man went over to his rucksack and produced the explosive needed to get inside the safe. First they packed a very small amount in and around the keyhole. Then the second man produced the detonator and set it going. Both men scrambled back, well away from the safe door. The explosion was not too large, but a couple of villagers saw the flash. Bending low, the two men ran back and fished inside the blackened hole. Smiling with relief, he withdrew his arm, holding a rusty metal box about one foot square. The second man took it from him and put it safely into his rucksack. Then he looked at the huge monument and grinned at his associate.

"Put a bit more around the base, blow that away and any evidence of us being here will be obliterated." The other man nodded and they set to with gusto.

Chapter 37

LICD Headquarters London

At LICD, the team in charge overall, had received some troubling news. It appeared that somebody had been feeding information to the Russians. It also appeared that Harvey, Bill's Superior, was one of them. With the death of both him and his wife, the PM and the European Parliament were both demanding immediate answers and quickly too. The best solution that anybody could propose at such short notice was to get Bill back and give him a promotion to take over the situation. The four officers sat in an office glaring at one another. Two of them wanted their own men to be in charge, while the remaining two wanted Bill to take over.

"Look, were exactly is he at the moment?"

"North Scotland. At least that was the case last time we heard from him."

"It's a long way to travel down to London." The man put his fingers together as though in prayer. "What is he doing up there anyhow?"

"Helping link two cases, one down here and one in East Sutherland. It could be also linked to the recent events in Oxford."

"The warehouse fire at Eynsham?"

"Amongst other things. We think a person known as 'The Boss' is in charge. However, the Russian angle is not looking as likely as it was."

"Why don't we put this on the back burner for now. When is Bill due back from Scotland?"

"When the case is wrapped up. Why?"

"They wrapped up that case a couple of years ago pretty quickly. Let's see if they can do the same now with this one. Then if they do, we can talk about promotions and other things then. What do you all say?" A murmur of agreement went around the room and the four officers rose and left the room.

Chapter 38

Golspie

In a house in Golspie, Maria was talking to Emma.

"Please say you will."

"I don't know, the last time we went up the Ben I cut my hand on that lock. I still think we should have told somebody. Anyhow it will be dark."

"But this time we will be prepared. Think of the sunrise that we will see."

"I'm not sure." Emma sat thinking. "If we go, the first sign of any trouble we turn back. Agreed?"

"Trouble? What sort of trouble do you think will be at the Ben at this time of year?" Maria laughed out loud.

"Ok, what time should we set off?" Maria looked at the clock.

"Say about six o'clock. Dawn is about eight in the morning at this time of year. Two hours for a comfortable hike up the long way round would be about right."

"Right, wake me about five then. I am off to bed." Replied Emma yawning.

Very early the following morning, both of them were out of their house and on their way up Ben Bhraggie, their head torches flashing along the ground in front of them.

The two men on Ben Bhraggie had managed to place the explosive all around the base, the detonator was all that was needed and a timer to delay the explosion until they were well clear.

"Look over there." Pointing across to where two lights kept flashing on and off. "Looks like somebody signalling. Do we go back the same way we came up or?"

"Stay here, we can see what this is all about then."

"They'll see us as soon as they get level with the top of the hill."

"So? We are just two walkers out for a nightime walk. Probably like them." They both sat down on the grass and watched as the lights disappeared.

"Where have they gone now?"

"Probably too close for us to see them. Just be patient."

An hour later he nudged his partner to wake him up.

"They are just getting level with the slope, let's move around the side of the base. Come on." The two men moved away, leaving their two rucksacks on the ground. Maria and Emma approached the base and leaned against it.

"Be careful, you don't want to hurt yourself. That lock is here somewhere." Emma flashed her headlight at the base and gasped.

"Look here." She pointed at the small opening in the base. "It wasn't like that before. Wonder what is inside?" She reached forward and removing her head torch, she used it to lighten up the inside. "It's very small. Thought it would be so much bigger with the size of the monument. Here you have a look." She pulled her head back up and gave a gasp. Two men stood there, one of whom was holding Maria, her arm behind her back. The other stood a few feet away with a gun pointing at her.

"Why did you have to come up here tonight? You have seen too much."

"I haven't seen anything." Said Maria in a fearful voice. "We just came for a hike and to see the sunrise."

"Ok, you will see your last sunrise. We all will. Now just sit down with your backs to the base." Emma and Maria did as they were told. The two men now both had guns trained on them.

"What is this plastic stuff around the base?" asked Emma.

"No talking, just wait for the sunrise." They were under no illusions that they were to be killed.

'The Boss' emerged from the hotel into the night. He was satisfied, the workmen were just finishing up his special improvements. Only the work needing the approval of the planning remained to be finished. He glanced up at the outline of the monument. A flash of light seemed to be at the base. Blinking, he moved to his car and took out a pair of binoculars. Adjusting the focus, he peered through them at the dark base. The light flashed again, he saw the outline of two people. Now what would anybody be doing up there at this time of night? He wondered. He walked back into the hotel and got two of his workmen to go with him. Once in the car, he drove off towards the road up to the monument. He had put some heavy tools in the boot, just in case..

An hour later, the two men prodded Emma and Maria awake.

"Time for your last sunrise. Take a good look." The two women struggled to their feet. The men had tied their hands behind their backs while they had slept. Glaring at the men, they turned and looked towards the sea. A flash of orange was starting to appear on the sea horizon. The four were so intent on looking at the sunrise, they didn't see Patrick and two others get out of their car and walk up to them. Patrick stood back from the Russians and indicated for his two men to move and stand behind each of them.

"And a fine sunrise it is too. Who are you and don't make any sudden movements my two men are right behind you." The two Russians looked slowly towards Patrick and then at one another.

"We are just here for the sunrise. A nice gathering. Just us and our wives."

"Tell me, do Russians always tie their wives hands behind their backs to look at sunrises? And just why is the base of the monument packed with explosive? A nice present to the village

I am sure." Patrick moved closer and produced a gun, which he put near the face of the nearest man. "Do tell me the truth, as if people lie, I tend to get trigger happy. Understand?" He stepped back a bit and aimed the gun at the side of the man's head.

"We have been sent to recover a small object. One that has been up here for years. We have it, so we can leave. And you can leave as well." He nodded at Emma and Maria. "Everyone goes down unharmed and uninjured. Agree?" He looked at Patrick hopefully.

"Give me the object first." Patrick held out his hand. The two men looked at one another and nodded.

"We need our rucksacks."

" I don't see any. Where are they? No tricks mind."

"At the base. We were standing there till the two women arrived." Patrick looked sceptical, but waved his gun at one of the women "You go and find it." He moved across to her and untied the ropes that tied her hands. Then he returned and tied one of the Russian's hands behind his back. "Take him with you. If he is lying, push him down the side."

"I'm not lying." Said the man as he was led away. Shortly they both returned clutching two rucksacks.

"Over here." Patrick waved his gun at a spot in front of him. The Russian, glaring, put the two bags down where indicated.

"It will do you no good at all. You wouldn't understand at all." Sighed one of the Russians. They watched as Patrick opened the two rucksacks and tipped them out on the damp ground. He pushed his toe amongst the contents and spread them out before him. Bending down, he picked up the small tin.

"This is what you came for?" he asked.

"Yes, but how did you know that?"

"It's the only old thing in there." He pointed the gun at the two women and then at his two men. "Untie the other one." They did so and then looking scared, approached Patrick.

"I don't know who you are, but thank you." Patrick smiled at them

"Get down from up here and don't look back. Forget about this or any of the people you have seen. Don't think of going to the police."

"And why wouldn't they do that?" Asked Cooper in a loud voice. "DS Copper. Nobody is to move. Not until I know just what is going on up here. You," Pointing at Patrick. "Tell me what is going on."

"Ah DS Cooper, you have arrived just in time. I was going to bring these two men down to your office. They have been tying up and threatening these two ladies. Now you are here, you can take over." He smiled at the Russians, who frowned back.

"And you two ladies. What are you doing up here?"

"We came to see the sunrise. Having seen it, we plan to go back down again into the village. Unless you need us for anything officer?"

"No, not at the moment. You can go, but leave your details at the Police Station." He watched as they set off at a pace down among the trees.

Cooper looked at the two Russians. "Why were you up here? I want the real answer." One looked at the other and smiled.

"Officer Cooper, you wouldn't understand the half of it. Even we don't know the whole picture. We came to collect a small item, an item that has been here for some time. This man, with his gun, made us give it to him." He pointed at Patrick. Patrick looked at his hand and took the tin over to Cooper.

"Don't open it, until you get a witness or two. I haven't seen inside it yet, but it is something very important for a Russian to send two people to retrieve it from Scotland." He turned and walked back to his car, indicating to his men to follow him. They drove off, leaving Cooper and another officer looking at the two Russians.

"How did you get here?"

"Walked up the hill. Why?"

"I'll ask the questions. Who put the explosive around the base?" He pointed to where it was pushed into the brickwork."

"Haven't got any idea Officer. It was like it when we arrived. We just assumed that..."

"A likely tale... However, I don't want to waste hours of my time and paperwork on you. Go back and tell whoever sent you, that you couldn't find what they wanted. Got it?" He glared at them both. They nodded and he turned and got back into the police vehicle along with his young colleague and drove off down to Golspie.

Patrick said nothing on the way back to the hotel. He knew that what had occurred up there probably had a link with the Russian somehow, but was too tired and scared to try and sort it out. He had a hotel to finish and now had to arrange for somebody new to take over Oxford and London.

Bill and Jane had fallen asleep at their desks. Cooper looked across at them both and smiled. From the book he had looked at, he thought he now knew most of the pieces of the puzzle. Not waking them, he turned back out of the office and switched out the light.

The Russians had found a phone box and put a lot of change into it. Now connected to himself, they paused before speaking.

"It isn't there. We blew the lock, it was empty except for a small tin. That was rusted and empty. Sorry."They replaced the phone and looked at one another.

"We can't go back can we?"

"No, not if we want to live, we can't. I have a relative near Oxford. We could go and stay there. Till things quieten down a bit, I mean." His partner nodded his agreement and they set off, heading towards the railway station.

In Russia, the man sat at his desk. He wasn't sure he believed all the call, but it was impossible to prove they were lying. Frustrated, he pressed the button on his desk and his secretary walked through.

"Yes?"

"Destroy the file. I don't want any trace of me having been in or near Scotland. Understand?"

"Yes. Destroy the file. No copy to be kept?" But he didn't hear him. He turned and left the room. A few minutes later the shredder could be heard shredding a lot of sheets paper. The Russian walked out of his office and smiled at his secretary.

"Good job done. Never want to hear of it again." Once he had left the building, his secretary picked up the bundle of papers on his desk and placed them into his own briefcase. He looked at the shredder, before deciding to shred the paper wrapper that had belonged to a new ream of paper and smiled to himself happily before letting himself out of the building. On his desk sat an envelope addressed to his former boss.

Chapter 39

Golspie Police Station next day

Jane and Bill awoke with stiffly. Both stretched and looked at one another.

"Falling asleep at work. That will never do. Coffee?" Said Cooper holding out two cups at them. "Go and freshen up, come back in an hour and I'll explain most of it to you. Lot's of things have been happening overnight. You might want to pack, LICD want Bill back in London."

"Is the case closed then?" asked Bill.

"As much as we can do, yes. Now go home and come back fresh and ready.

Bill led Jane through the door of the Police Station and over to where Cooper was sat at his desk. He looked up and smiled as they approached him.

"Let's go into one of the offices, I've got tea and coffee ready, this may take a while." Rising, he led the way. Once they were all seated and had their preferred drink in front of them, he leaned back in his chair.

"Do you know all of the details?" Asked Bill. Cooper nodded in reply.

"So this quiet part of East Sutherland had attracted the attention of four people with an interest in drugs and other things. We now know that the man we have kept refering to as 'The Boss' is actually Patrick O'Conner. It appears he may have had some connection to a plot to blow up the Channel Tunnel when it was being constructed."

"By himself?" asked Jane.

"No, he had help, but it's thought that he was in the IRA at the time. Anyhow, as I was saying, four people," he ticked them off on his fingers one by one. "Patrick, a Dutchman called Klaas, a Russian and a lady known as Tracy all had an interest in setting up and distributing drugs."

"But hang on a minute, surely the population of East Sutherland is too small to sustain a constant supply of drugs." Said Bill.

"Which is why some of them thought of other businesses to run alongside the drugs. The Russian for example, set up a new restaurant, *The Double Headed Eagle,* in Brora Harbour. Ideal, boats can land, unload and be away before anybody notices. He opened the restaurant, put a man in to manage it and it started to thieve on both sides of his business. Klaas, had tried to get into this area two years ago. He saw a new opportunity, when, we think Tracy decided to start selling drugs, but in a new way. It is thought she planned to use logs, some with drugs packed inside the hollowed out middles and those would be sold in a different colour net to the ordinary normal logs. We found some remains of both a blue and red netting at the house in Nigg. It seems that she had contacts and some money behind her. Enough anyhow to be able to let the neighbours go away each time a supply was dropped off.

"Where does Patrick fit in though? LICD thought that he was running up to Oxford and back. East Sutherland is miles from there." Asked Jane.

"You need to remember that he had been up here two years ago, we think that he was going to own the flat in Dornoch, then the Police got involved and he moved back to Oxford. He did buy the flat when it came up for auction. Paid a huge amount for it, well outside the amount that a local would pay. We think that there was another reason why he moved up here. The Pendant that was found in the body at Fyrish, it appears may be one of three. Made in Dingwall years ago. Other than the wording being Russian, we really don't know what they are for. It appears they are a key of some kind. For what purpose we probably shall never know. The Russian was after the Pendant as well, as we have found a bit of paper at the bottom of a box of drugs mentioning Ben Bhraggie's pendant. Apart from Tracy, all the others had men on the ground doing a lot of the work for them." Cooper leaned back in his chair.

"So what happens now? Who have we arrested?" asked Jane. Bill looked across at Cooper and raised his eyebrows as if to say, well?

"Right, The Dutchman, Klaas, has met with an unfortunate demise in a boatyard in Graves End. Tracy, has died, how we don't know, but we think that some of her remains were, at the very least, placed in the Double Headed Eagle before it was blown up. Paperwork shows that Klass had bought the place a few days before. It would seem that the Russian has pulled out of this part of the world for now at least. That leaves Patrick. He seems to be renovating the old *Grand East Sutherland Hotel*. More interestingly is that he appears to be doing it all above board and proper. Your superiors at LICD have said that we are to just keep a watching eye on him. We have no proof of anything to connect him to anything up here. He has bought a flat, and it appears, a disused hotel. From what HMRC say, he is paying the staff and workforce correctly and they are happy to leave him alone. Personally, I am not so happy to have somebody of that nature up here, but there is nothing I can do about it. Talking of LICD, they want both of you back as soon as you can. Bill is to fly down, while Jane can drive more leisurely back down, via Oxford. From LICD arranging a phone tap on Patrick, it appears that there is a group of four in Oxford who are trying to restart supplying drugs to the students again. LICD want you, Jane, to help in any way you can. A file has been faxed up, here take it and read it." Cooper passed a thin file over to her.

"So we don't have anybody to arrest then? Said Bill.

"Nobody, not this time." Agreed Cooper with a smile. "It's been one of those cases where there appears to be nobody to arrest."

"So, what name is going on the file for this case then?" asked Jane.

"No Body at Ben Bhraggie." Said Cooper with a smile as he rose to indicate the meeting was over.

Chapter 40

Six Months later, rural western Russia.

The five Oligarchs first had meet with the ex-secretary six months ago. All six had agreed to form a pact. Each of the five Oligarchs, would put up five million and take a year off to look for it. If after one year they hadn't found what they wanted, they would split whatever money was left evenly between the remaining members.

Now one of them had tracked down a report that there may be another pendant in existence.

It had taken a lot of time and money, now he stood on the threshold of finding a lot more than just another pendant. He moved into the house and pushed open the door of the downstairs room. Pointing his gun before him he entered.

"Don't move. I've got a gun."

The old lady sat looking at the man in front of her. He held a gun in one hand and it was pointing at her head.

"How many pendant's are there and how many does it need to unlock the real reason for them?"

[1] "Я хранила секрет подвесного сейфа от таких, как ты. Убийство меня ничего не даст тебе ничего, кроме подвесного. Он не скажет вам причину для них, или сколько было произведено. " She fingered the pendant that hung round her neck then took

---

[1] I have kept the secret of the pendant safe from the likes of you. Killing me will not gain you anything, other than the pendant. It will not tell you the reason for them, or how many there were produced.

it off and held it in her hand. "[2]Мне сказали, когда я впервые получил его много лет назад, люди будут воровать, убивать и грабить, чтобы добраться до того, что он показывает. У меня была хорошая жизнь. Здесь вы берете его." She offered it to the man. "But I will never reveal the reason or its purpose. Do you understand that?" He nodded sadly at her. "Then I will leave without it. I do know that others, who are more ruthless ,will be coming to get the same information." He turned and left the room and the lady looked down at the pendant and smiled and replaced it around her neck. It was all so long ago, she thought to herself as she closed her eyes..

[2] I was told when I was first given it many years ago, men would steal, kill and rob to get to what it reveals. I have had a good life. Here you take it

EPILOGUE

On his return to LICD, Bill was offered his late bosses job. He has taken it for a six month trial. Jane is still working at LICD, but would now prefer to move to Scotland.

In Oxford, the drug scene has been reduced for now. The River Police, LICD and Oxford and County Police are co-operating to try and control any dealing of drugs.

Patrick Reily is still running his shop in a suburb of Oxford.

Patrick, aka 'The Boss' got his planning for his 'public' side of the hotel. It has started trading and he is still living in the flat in Dornoch. Currently he is not dealing with drugs or anything else of a criminal nature. Golspie police now know of his background and are keeping a close eye on him.

DI Gray has returned to work, but is talking of taking early retirement. His son, PC Gray, might look to take his next set of exams to rise up through the ranks of the police.

Both Tracy's flat and house are still empty and unsold.

Emma and Maria both are running again, but have not been up the Ben since the last time.

The remaining shareholders of Ben Bhraggie Estates have had the damage to the monument repaired before formally winding up the company.

In Oxford two Russians are working unpaid for a small antique business for their keep. Since doing so, the amount of credit previously given, has dropped and people seem happy to pay quickly for some reason.

Authors Notes

While the story is set in East Sutherland, Oxford and London. Readers are reminded that this is a work of fiction and any similarity to any Business's or person, living or dead is not intentional. Lindsay's and Co Ltd in Golspie and La Mirage in Helmsdale both have allowed their names to be used. Most of the villages mentioned in East Sutherland all do exist, however do not go looking for Great Ferry, as this is only in the imagination of the author.

You can walk up to the monument on Ben Bhraggie if you wish. Climbing boots and waterproofs are strongly advised as is letting somebody know that is where you are going.

TUNNEL UNDER THREAT

A DI Sutherland Case

Prologue

LICD Headquarters 1992

The New Head of the London and International Crime Department looked around the room. Most of her senior staff sat at the oval desk, she observed that they were all men. Well, that would have to change in the near future. Ruth had risen to the current post the hard way and knew that a lot was expected of her recent appointment. A large file sat opened in front of her. It contained a review of two cases that had been solved by Bill and Jane Sutherland. She glanced at her notes, not really needing to, as she already had rehearsed what she was about to say.

"Gentlemen, if I can have your attention please?" The low conversation that had been going on, stopped at once. "Thank you. I know that some of you will be shaken and disappointed by my appointment. I want to work with all of you, however, there will have to be some changes." A hand went up. "Yes Simon?"

"Are these changes to be limited to London or to the whole network?" She smiled inwardly to herself, trust it to be Simon to raise the International question. He had been considered to take charge of the International side of things, but that decision had been delayed following the deaths of Harvey Brown and his wife.

"For the time being, they are limited to London. I have ordered a full investigation around the deaths of both Harvey and his wife, until that is concluded, things will probably stay as they are." Ruth paused and took a sip of water from the glass in front of her. "Having said that, there is a matter that needs to be addressed fairly quickly. I am talking about a replacement, on a temporary basis, to cover Harvey's workload. I have a couple of names in mind, but am open to suggestions as well. Anybody at all?" She looked around the room, as she had thought, nobody would put their hand into the air. Ruth was too new for them to know anything about her yet. "Well then, I would like to consider either Bill or Jane Sutherland, does anybody have any objections?" A silence greeted her, then a hand was raised. "Yes?"

"Either of them would be good, on a temporary basis. They usually work as a team though and that might cause a bit of friction if one was promoted over the other one. Just saying, that's all."

"You raise a good point. I'll bear that in mind." Simon raised his hand somewhat hesitantly.

"How long will the post be temporary?"

"Probably till the investigation into Harvey and his wife has concluded. I take it that there are no objections to them being considered then?"

"Not from me." Said a lone voice at the other end of the table. "We need to have young blood at the top and they have helped solve two very large cases. I would propose that you get a small team of two others and yourself to look into the background of both of them and then take the decision." Ruth smiled and nodded her approval.

"Let's have a show of hands to that proposal shall we?" All the hands except Simon went up. "Then the meeting for today is finished. Simon, a word please." Ruth rose and picking up her file and water walked out of the meeting room towards her office. Simon reluctantly followed her out.

Chapter 1

London

Unaware of what was being discussed, Bill and Jane sat in sunshine overlooking the Thames sipping hot drinks that they had just bought from the van that parked outside LICD each day. The sun sparkled on the water as small boats made their way up and down the mighty river. Jane tapped Bill on the arm.

"Take a look at the boat over there, the red one moored near to *HMS Belfast*. It looks like the boat…"

"…Bragging Rights. Here, let me go and get a set of binoculars from the office." Bill handed his cup to Jane and walked quickly back to the office. A short while later he returned with a set of each of them. He put his to his eyes and scanned the boats side. The name *Bragging Rights* stood out clearly. He put them down and took the two cups off Jane to let her see for herself.

"Well, of all the places." Said Jane with a smile.

"Not really that surprising, the boat was converted at Graves End and the boatyard had to sell it to somebody else. Wonder who bought it."

"Probably some Yuppie or other. They would have loved that name." Laughed Jane, putting down her glasses and reaching for her drink. "Peaceful after the last case isn't it?"

"Well, isn't that is what we both said just before the last case started?" said Bill with a smile. He finished his drink and crumpled the cup in his hand. Jane did the same and they both stood and went back into the office.

+

On the outskirts of Golspie a hotel was on the last stages of a major refurbishment. Most of the main contractors had packed up and driven off, the only ones still on site were busy moving the furniture from five large vans into the various rooms. In the kitchen a chef was giving orders to his small team as to where to put the various utensils. Stood just inside the main door a tall man looked on with a clipboard in his hand, ticking off the items as they came into the hotel. Two men, holding a large oak cupboard, came slowly up the stairs and entered the hall.

"Where do you want this?"The man consulted his clipboard.

"Ground floor, room opposite this one." He pointed with his hand, then moved across and held the door open for them to take it in.

"Thanks Guv" came the comment as they manoeuvred it into place. They went out to the van to bring in the desk that was due to go into the same place. The phone rang on the reception desk. The man with the clipboard looked at it with a surprised look on his face. The phone hadn't been connected yet, at least that was what he had been told. Putting down his clipboard, he picked up the phone and spoke.

"Hello."

"Hello Patrick. Now there is a voice I have heard for ages. How is the new hotel coming on? I understand you have gone into the accommodation business these days. I wonder if you might like to put one or two of the lads up for a few nights?"

"Now you look here Pat Doyle, I want nothing more to do with you or your type. I have moved on, things are different now. How did you get this number anyhow?"

" Now, now, don't go losing your temper Patrick. You know, there are supporters of the cause all over the place, if only the UK Government knew of it they would have kittens. I'll come up and see you sometime, don't know when exactly, but it wouldn't hurt for you to be civil now would it?" Patrick took a deep breath.

"Look Pat, things are different now. I want to move on and run a business. A hotel business in Scotland."

"Yes, I know that, but why Scotland of all the places you could go to?"

"Business and it is a nice place to see."

"I'll take your word for that, until I see it for myself that is." The phone was put down and Patrick stood holding his phone, then he replaced it and returned to telling the removal men where to put the large desk they had just brought in.

+

In Belfast, Pat Doyle replaced the phone and looked at his group of men that had gathered in the warehouse he used.

"Well?" Said Seamus "Did he agree to what you proposed? We need to fly out tonight if he did."

"No Seamus, he did not. He said he wants nothing more to do with us. We can't have that now can we?" The men growled their disappointment at the news.

"Look Pat, that is well and good, but we need to get out of the province and tonight, the police are prowling around, next thing we know, we will all be arrested." Said Barry with a look that could kill, if the long crowbar in his hand hadn't already that is.

"Ok, I would come with you, but have a boat shipment to collect. Now I'll let you have some ready money for now. Lie low and when you have found somewhere suitable, get a message to me somehow. Meanwhile I am going to look into Patrick O'Shane or whatever he is calling himself these days. Stay in touch." Pat moved over to the office safe and opened it and removed a bundle of money. Quickly he divided it up into seven even bundles and put three back into the safe. The remaining bundles he put into separate brown envelopes and stuck them down. Then he walked out to the group of men and placed the envelopes on the table nearby before returning to the small office. The men had seen this many times, the amounts would probably be the same in each envelope, it was just luck as to who had which one. Silently they picked up the envelopes and left the warehouse one at a time. The last one to leave turned and looked across at the office, where Pat now stood outside with his arms folded.

"He came through in 1988 and 1989, why not now I wonder?"

"Who knows? I'll try and find out. Good luck." Then he turned back into the office and closed the door behind him.

In Sutherland, late that night Patrick looked tired but satisfied. The furniture had all been placed where he wanted it, Now he was in the new bar helping himself to a soda water. Normally he would have a whisky, but tonight he wanted a clear head. He had moved on from the days that Pat Doyle had talked about. He was also concerned that the police or some Government agency would have arranged for his phone to be tapped. He finished his drink, locked up the hotel and drove off down the drive to his flat in Dornoch. Had he known it, he would have stayed at the hotel.

On a Broch within the grounds of the hotel a lone man stood, he held a shotgun, broken for carrying, loosely in his hands. He had seen Patrick lock up and leave the hotel. He wasn't too concerned he had already found out where Patrick lived. Smiling he left the Broch and made his way towards his car parked by the track that led to the beach.

+

In his flat in Dornoch that night, Patrick made a few discrete phone calls and found out what Pat Doyle had really wanted. Satisfied that he would be able to deal with things if they turned up, he retired to bed.

The car swept into the square and parked in one of the parking spaces that lined the square. The driver switched off the engine and waited as the engine cooled. Bending down, he felt under the seat for the small box that contained the gun he sometimes needed. Not being able to see the flat from the car, he got out and locked the car doors. You couldn't be too careful he thought to himself. He crossed the road and walked through the cathedral churchyard, silent and quiet, though that may change in the near future he thought to himself. Turning to the left, he could see the flat and the lights had just been switched off. Good, he had the element of surprise then. He moved to the metal gate and lifted the latch and pushed it open. Unlike earlier this morning, when it had squeaked loudly, it now moved silently. He stepped inside and reached down to the ground and picked up the small can of oil he had left earlier in the day. Quickly he stepped up the small path and up the staircase to the front door. Reaching into his pocket, he removed the copy of the front door key that he had arranged to be cut the day before. He had already tried it earlier when Patrick had been at his hotel. Inserting the key, he took the oil can and as the door opened, put a small amount on each hinge. Quickly he stepped inside and closed the door behind him and went slowly along the corridor, he could see a light coming from under the door at the end of the corridor. He felt in his pocket for the gun, took it out and smiling, walked slowly towards it. It was times like this, that he really enjoyed his job. Should he knock or just open it he wondered to himself? The light under the door went off, that decided it, he thought. He would wait for ten minutes, then surprise the sleeping Patrick.

Ten minutes later, he heard snoring coming from the room. He reached out and turned the handle and flung open the door. Taking in the form in the bed, he fired in quick succession three shots and then closed the room and left the flat, he had done what he had been asked to do. What happened next was up to others.